I0537006

James McDonald

Bound and Hagged

Book One of Home Summonings

Infinity Limited Group Publications

Copyright

Copyright © 2014, 2015, 2016 by James McDonald. This book is a work of fiction. Names, characters, places, and incidents are either products of the author's imagination or used fictitiously. Any resemblance to actual events, locales, or persons, living or dead, is entirely coincidental. All rights reserved. No part of this publication can be reproduced or transmitted in any form or by any means, electronic or mechanical, without permission in writing from James McDonald.

James McDonald. Bound and Hagged, Book One of Home Summonings.

Infinity Limited Publications, Charlotte, NC

Fifth Edition, V1.8

Print ISBN: 978-0-9960504-6-3

eBook ISBN: 978-0-9960504-0-1

Cover Art by: Aleksandra Shiga www.gorillaconcept.com

Edited by: Neila Forssberg, Red Adept Editing

Other Works

For Adrianne, who talked me into publishing this little tome.

And many thanks to Ruth and Julie for all of the editing and editorial comments.

Prologue

Nora crossed her arms and stomped her foot, even if no one was around for the show. She had better things to do on her thirteenth birthday than go to some dusty old house to meet an unknown relative. She stood on the crumbling walkway of what had once been a graceful stone mansion in its prime. After so many years, the house looked weary from a lack of maintenance. Even so, it was still intimidating. Up until the moment she arrived at the doorstep, Nora had convinced herself she wouldn't have to do this.

"Well," she said, "I guess I'll get this over with."

The twisted black ring of the iron doorknocker looked like flames dripping from the mouth of a dragon's head. She grabbed the knocker in her small hand and jumped when it thundered with one swing. The mahogany door opened to an empty hallway.

"Hello?" she called.

A melodious voice responded. "In here, child."

Nora steeled herself and looked around as she stepped through the door, then swallowed when the door closed on its own behind her. Her hollow footsteps echoed as she made her way down the hallway in the direction the voice had originated. Sketches and paintings of people from various ages covered the walls of the hall. An ancient tile mural of Greece occupied the entirety of the floor in a small room she passed.

The hall ended in a large study. Dust and mites swam in the daylight that streamed in through tall windows. Books, real books, were stacked from floor-to-ceiling. They sat on every table, chair, and shelf. The room smelled musty, but she wasn't sure if it came from the books or the old woman who sat behind more books at an old wooden desk.

Nora used her most polite voice and said, "Hello, ma'am. I'm—"

"Yes, child." The thin and wrinkled face of an old woman appeared over the stacks of books that formed a fortress around her. "I'm pleased you have come to meet me, Nora. I get so few visitors."

The woman was small and frail. A few strands of her long white hair had escaped from the rest that was pulled back into a severe bun. Her face was thin and kind, but hardness hid under the surface. Nora knew well what could hide under a friendly face.

She wondered if this was another of her mother's tests and studied her surroundings as she had been taught. One doorway. Multiple windows. She selected one of the windows as an alternate exit if necessary and noted which alcoves could hide an assailant. She began to stretch her Senses but detected only the old woman. Soon enough, Nora would be able to determine what sort of being the woman was. "My mother sends her well wishes."

The old woman gave a kind smile. Nora had grown to expect that such a smile was usually followed by a spell or flying monkeys the size of gerbils. Instead, the woman said, "You may call me Miss Tee. Do you know why you're here, Nora?"

Because my mother is insane? "No, ma'am, um, Miss Tee."

"I assume you know the story of Grey Forrester?"

Nora rolled her eyes. "Of course. Everyone knows him. He's why things are the way they are now."

Miss Tee smiled again. "No, child, you know the rumors and legends. Your mother and I think you should know the truth."

A feeling of unease welled in Nora's chest. "Why? What's done is done."

"You, Nora, will be one of the people to lead us from these dark times. You should know how we got here so that we can find a new path."

Nora wanted to scream and storm out, but she knew it would do no good. If her mother had gone to so much trouble, she would learn the truth eventually. She was there, so she may as well get it over with. "What is this great truth?" Nora expected her question would lead to an afternoon of being regaled with more useless stories and legends. She had suffered through those many times before.

Instead, Miss Tee held out a book. "You can start with this one."

She wants me to read a book? Nora hefted the book from her hands and was surprised at the weight of the tome. A leather cover surrounded parchment pages. Cracked gold leaf script on the front read, "Chronicle of Greyson Forrester: Volume I." Nora had never seen an official chronicle. Chronicles were supposedly scribed from the memories of select people through the ages. She'd thought all of them had been lost or destroyed.

Nora looked up at the old woman. "You want me to read all of this?"

Miss Tee nodded. "It's a start."

Bound and Hagged, Chronicle I of Greyson Forrester

I CRUISED OUT of Las Vegas, heading toward Boulder City to see a client I'd picked up by referral. My gut had told me to turn down the client, but the job would be a quick cash infusion and not much of a trip since I had just wrapped up a gig outside of Scottsdale. Well-paying jobs were hard to find for outcast wizards, or so they told me, and the last couple of years had been nothing but side jobs.

The referral sounded like an easy search-and-retrieve job. Plus I would get the opportunity to tour the house of Henri Clouse, a.k.a. Henri the Magnificent, a.k.a. the best comedic illusionist in history. Unfortunately, he was dead. I was also looking forward to meeting Katerina, Henri's assistant, a.k.a. Katie Ashe, the jazz diva, a.k.a. Katherine Clouse, pain-in-the-Ashe widow. That last one had been the headline in the magazine racks when her Vegas show got cancelled.

I'd assisted Henri a few times myself. His stage act had been helped by the fact that he'd been a pretty good practitioner of the magical arts—the real stuff. Even with my abilities bound, I had more raw power as a third-rate hack wizard than he did, but he'd had the flair to make it work beautifully.

I pulled up in front of the nice-sized adobe house. From the lack of neighbors, either the Clouses had a lot of land, or it was a hell of a neighborhood being this isolated out in the middle of the baked desert. I parked my classic motorcycle—an Indian that was older than I was—in the drive and made my way up the gravel walkway to ring the front doorbell.

A bottle-blonde wearing a white skirt and red top opened the door. Even though she was pushing fifty and a raging alcoholic, Mrs. Clouse still looked pretty good. She managed to slur, "Are you Obi's fixer?" It was nearly noon, and she already looked as though she was a couple of martinis in.

I offered my hand. "Grey Forrester."

She waved for me to come in and stumbled down the few stairs that led into the living room from the foyer. "I'm Katie Ashe Clouse." With an air of derision, she added, "Welcome to the great Clouse estate."

She motioned to a chair in a large open room and walked behind a well-stocked bar. Memorabilia from both her and her husband's careers lined the walls. An outfit Henri had worn in a short-lived television variety show from the seventies was in a glass case next to the wall.

Mrs. Clouse slurred slightly and topped off her glass with a slightly cloudy liquid from a silver shaker. "Care for a drink?"

"Water will be fine," I said.

She handed me a chilled bottle of water from the mini fridge under the bar. "So what are you? What's your trick?"

I took a sip from the bottle to wash down some of the dust from the road. "I find people, objects, information. I have a few talents."

She gave a dismissive wave. "Yeah, sure. Obi referred you to me. Said you were legit or something."

I was really starting to understand why her career had crashed. She was well on her way to being drunk before noon, her voice holding that raspy quality that came from decades of the party life, and her not-so-charming personality topped it off. I thought about

Obi Ramla, my friend from Los Angeles. I was trying to figure out why he was so pissed at me that he'd sent me to deal with this woman. "I do a little work for him now and again. Why don't you tell me why I'm here?"

"I've had a number of scammers come through since my Henri died," she rambled. "All of the money is in the safe in his office, and I don't have the combination. I miss my Henri, but a girl's gotta live. I have enough to get by, but barely. Honest locksmiths and expert safecrackers have all taken their shot. I need the combination. The jackass hid it around here somewhere."

It looked as though I might get lucky, and this would be a quick job. I could get back to Vegas by nightfall. "Let's take a look."

She opened the doors to a nice office off the den. More memorabilia lined the walls, including props and pictures from Henri's lifetime in entertainment. He had loved the crowds, big and small. Mrs. Clouse seemed to love herself and her husband's cash.

She waved. "I haven't cleared any of his crap out in case it has the combination, or is worth something." I felt lucky that I'd never met this adoring wife of his when I'd worked with Henri.

She led me to a large, old-fashioned floor safe that looked to be at least a hundred years old. The name on the front was J. Baum Safe & Lock Company. Cracking it should have been an easy job. I couldn't understand why even a hack hadn't been able to get it open.

Then I opened up my Sight and looked around the room. One of the few abilities not taken from me was my capacity to open the world in a flood of color from the energy stored in everything. At the least, objects and people showed a fine aura. Stretched to my limits, the universe around me looked like a Technicolor cartoon. Enchanted or magically charged objects shone with a distinctive shimmer, and the safe was lit up like the strip in Vegas. Many of the props, books, and memorabilia were charged as well.

I realized that Henri himself sat in the chair behind his old desk. His ghost looked at me. "Hiya, kid. How'd you get roped into this?"

I turned to his widow. "Ms. Clouse, any chance I could be in here alone for a while?"

"Sure. And call me Katie. I'll be back in a few." She walked out and closed the door.

"Hi, Henri. You look good." I could see some spirits when I tuned in just right.

Henri looked as if he was putting some effort into being seen. His ghostly projection appeared just as he had in his forties, his heyday. He was thin, and his wavy dark hair had just a little frost at the temples. He was dressed in what had once been his favorite polo-and-khakis look. The tassels on his loafers were worn, but the shoes were polished.

"How'd you tick off Obi so badly that he sent you to deal with the old lady?" he asked.

I laughed. "I think he's trying to get his jabs in before I go back for the Inquest and they execute me. So keep me a seat at the bar."

Henri smiled. "Ah, kid, I wouldn't worry about that. If you can survive the next few weeks, the Inquest will be a snap. I have it from good inside sources."

The Inquest. My reason for being banished from home. I wasn't any closer to finding out what had happened in my former home, but all of the people who'd died were always on the edges of my mind, especially my parents. If I didn't have an answer soon, Henri could perform for the family reunion. "So, what's the deal with the safe?"

Henri stood and bowed, ever the showman. He walked over and ran his fingers across the top of the safe. "You like this one, do you? The alchemist who did it for me was a real craftsman. The wife's brought in all sorts of hacks to take a shot. Then when they fail, she bangs them all over the house so the trip isn't a waste. And so she doesn't have to shell out any cash. Young stud like you, I bet she tries to bed you before you even get a crack."

Well, that was uncomfortable. "I'm not going to sleep with your wife, Henri."

"Widow. She's fair game. But thanks for that, kid. You're still better than most, even if you have sent more than a few of your friends and family to this side of the Veil prematurely."

More uncomfortable feelings caused me to shuffle from one foot to the other. "So... speaking of that, where did you wind up?"

"I can't tell you that, kid, but they don't let spirits out of Hell on field trips."

That made me feel a little better.

The door opened behind me. Mrs. Clouse, um, Katie had made herself more comfortable by changing into a short kimono and matching thong. "Talking to the safe? How's that working for you?"

I really was starting to not like the snippy harpy. She plopped herself on Henri's desk, showing a little leg. I understood how she was getting "free" services from the safecrackers. "Well, Katie, I'm not talking to the safe. I'm talking to Henri. Catching up, in fact."

She rolled her eyes. "Okay, the psychic friends network scam. And what did dear Henri say?"

I fumbled for a response that wouldn't get me slapped but couldn't think of one. "That you've been banging everyone that came through to get freebies from the safecrackers."

Katie flushed a bright red. "I…"

Henri piped in. "Tell her not to do it on my desk again. Or if she does, to at least wipe off the ass prints. The plumber got grease all over the wood."

"I'm not telling her that," I said.

"What?" Katie snapped.

I sighed. "He said don't bang the plumber on his desk again. Or if you do, have the decency to wipe it down. He left grease everywhere."

Katie's jaw hung open, and she paled. Henri broke into hysterics. I was trying to figure out how a ghost could snort when it laughed. Ghosts don't need to breathe, right?

MRS. CLOUSE SAT on the loveseat, obviously shaken. "Get the hell out of my house. I don't know how you think you know something, but get out."

I was happy to leave even if the trip was a waste. I needed to hit Vegas and see an old friend. "Later, Henri! Keep the bar stool warm for me."

I was almost out the door when Henri popped up in front of me. "Okay, kid, tell her this. The security is a time lock. The safe is only really there during the same window every day, from the time she poisoned me to the time I died. The rest of the time, it's just an etheric shell."

I was close to getting out the door. My better judgment told me to wish Henri luck and leave. Instead, I shook my head and turned around. "Okay, Katie, here's what he said…"

Her voice was barely a whisper. "Mrs. Clouse." Anger and shame crossed her face for a moment.

I couldn't understand how Henri had married this shrew. "Okay, Mrs. Clouse. Henri told me that the safe is on a time lock. It's only here on a daily basis during the window between when you poisoned him and when he died."

I expected a lot of things. Yelling. Cursing. Throwing stuff. Instead, she started to cry. "I'm sorry, Henri. I miss you. I'm so sorry."

I started back out the door, but Mrs. Clouse stopped me. "Please, wait," she cried. *So close.* "I didn't mean to do it. I was just… angry."

Henri stood over his wife, trying to console her, even though she couldn't tell he was standing right there. "Henri, do I care that she killed you?" I asked. "You know, enough to do something?"

Mrs. Clouse turned pale and trembled. Her eyes darted around the room as if she was searching for something before leaning against the arm of the couch for support. If I'd thought it through, I might have been worried she would do something rash.

Henri smiled. "No, kid, it's fine. I was dying anyway. She saved me from a lot of pain. Besides, if you pull this off, she'll be here by her own volition soon enough."

"Henri, in that case, should I be doing this? If what you say is true…"

The specter of my mentor cast a look at his wife. "Either way, her fate is set. At most, you might speed it up a little."

I looked closely at Henri's black widow. I should have been more disturbed by the fact that she had killed Henri, but if he was fine with it, who was I to argue? It wasn't my job to keep her from doing something stupid. And she had killed my friend. "He says it's fine. So what time did you kill Henri?"

She shuddered. "I don't know."

I pleaded on her behalf. "Henri, help me out here."

Even Henri must have been getting a little bored with his game because he got right to the point. "12:47 to 1:05 p.m."

Okay, an improvement. It was 12:40. "What's the combination, Henri?"

He waved his hands. "How easy am I supposed to make this one for you? All right, seeing how it's almost time, and you've had to put up with my dear wife, I'll toss you a bone. Twelve left, thirty-one right, nineteen left, eight right, four left."

"Twelve, thirty-one, nineteen, eight, four," I replied.

Mrs. Clouse started to cry again. "Our wedding day."

After a few minutes, I saw the energy field dissipate that had been projecting the safe, and the physical safe materialized in the etheric footprint. "Henri, you're going to need to teach me that trick."

I used the combination and unlocked the safe. I turned to Mrs. Clouse. "Would you care to do the honors and open the safe?" I made it look chivalrous, but really, I wasn't sure if it was booby-trapped. Henri had said she would join him soon.

She grasped the handle and closed her eyes as if she couldn't believe it was finally happening. She gave a slow turn of the handle and pulled on the heavy door with all of her strength. I caught a glimpse of the contents just before she opened her eyes and saw that the safe was almost empty. A lone envelope sat on the shelf.

She turned a lighter shade of pale. "Where is it? Where's the money?" She removed the envelope and opened it, taking out what looked to be a handwritten letter. As she read it, her face went from pale to ruby red, and she shrieked like a banshee swinging a chain saw. "Is this a joke, Henri? Are you trying to torture me more?" Apparently, she finally believed Henri was around.

Henri kicked his feet up on the desk and leaned back in the chair, tenting his hands. A self-satisfied grin crossed his face.

I grabbed the note out of Mrs. Clouse's hands.

My dearest Katydid,

If you are reading this note, then you finally sobered up or found one of the few talented people in the world able to get the safe open.

My remaining fortune is hidden on the property. IT IS CURSED. Don't mess with it. Live a long life on your monthly stipend.

I love you and will see you soon enough. Don't hurry it along. If you insist on chasing it, then whoever got in the safe should be able to find it for you.

Yours in eternity,

Pookie Bear

I cut my eyes to Henri. "Pookie Bear?"

Henri shrugged. "Better get your witching stone and a shovel. Your day isn't over."

I shook a finger at Henri. "With a message like that, I'm not messing with it."

I heard a guttural growl from Mrs. Clouse. "I want what's coming to me, Henri."

Henri looked at Katie quite sadly. "I'm afraid you will get it, *ma cheri*. It will come quite quickly."

"You owe me, Henri," I said.

THE NEVADA DESERT was hot, a good 114 degrees in the shade. Standing out back of the house and surveying the Clouse estate, shade was hard to find.

I was seething. Mrs. Clouse was as repugnant a person as one could find in Vegas, but I had really liked Henri. I was ready to get out of there, but I hated to admit that I was also curious.

Henri rolled a coin between his fingers. Knowing him, it was probably two-headed. "It'll be a good game. You should be able to knock this one out in no time flat. It will be a good test of your skills." His little grin reminded me of why I had been so fond of him.

"So, Henri, I don't guess you'd give me a hint?" I asked.

He shook his head. He was having way too much fun with his game. Then again, he must have been working on this for years when he was still alive. "You've used your allotment for the day. Maybe you can try to phone a friend."

I scowled. "Mrs. Clouse, there are a few things I'll need." I wrote out the few items I didn't have in my pack. I didn't expect I'd need cotton balls and creosote blossoms. "I'll start my preparations while you're gone."

"How do I know this isn't just a scam so you can find the money while I'm out of the house?" she snapped.

I'd hit my limit. If I really wanted to run off with whatever treasure Henri had hidden, I could do it while she stood there. A few choice words said over her drink, and she'd carry it out and load it on my bike. "Look, if I get back on my bike, I'm going to Vegas, and you're on your own. I need that stuff, and I need to prepare myself, and it needs to be ready at dusk. The spell works best when the day gives itself over to night, and it'll be a lot easier to see what's going on when the sun isn't blazing overhead. You choose. You can trust me, or you can figure it out yourself. Or take my suggestion and leave it alone."

Somewhere in her martini-addled brain, she opted for plan D. We went inside the cool house, and she called a delivery service to bring my supplies. It spoiled my hopes for a little quiet, but at least she put on some clothes.

I meditated for an hour and began making my preparations. By the time the delivery guy arrived, I was mentally ready to start the process. I'd managed to find a couple of glass bowls in the kitchen and grain alcohol in the liquor cabinet. I pulled sea salt, bloodhound musk, and a couple other vials from my pack. Now I just needed the last few items.

Mrs. Clouse looked even more irked when the delivery guy showed up, if that were possible.

Henri looked wistful. "She bangs him twice a week when she gets deliveries. You just deprived her of an afternoon roll. And she had to pay with a tip."

I let out a small, sad laugh. I felt sorry for Henri.

She dropped the bags on the counter. "You really are talking to Henri?"

I started poking through the bags. "Yep."

"And you knew him? Before?"

I decided to cut it off before she wanted to talk. I was not about to become a medium for this woman, much less a marriage counselor. "Henri mentored me. He used to come to my village a couple of times a year. After I left, I worked with him a few times on the road. He was very good to me. I cared for him a lot. I'm sad he's gone, but it happens to the best of us."

She looked as though the light bulb in her head had been dimly lit. "So you're that kid. He used to talk about you. Some kind of prodigy. And everything went to hell. You vaporized a bunch of people or something."

I smiled with the most condescending look I could muster. "Something like that."

Dusk approached, and the temperature lessened to a broil.

As the sun set, I dumped a bag of cotton balls into the mixture I had concocted. Based on Henri's lack of information, I threw in a drop of essence of gold to help the potion do its job.

All magic was based on the energy of the being using it and the environment around them, but it still took intent to make it work. I touched the bucket and Pushed with a little Will to charge and bring the enchantment to life. As the sun crested the horizon, I tossed the bucket of elixir-soaked cotton balls into the air. Instead of falling to the ground, the tufts took on the glow of the setting sun and hung in the air.

I waved my hand. "Seek." I was using more theatrics than were necessary, but I did it for Henri as an homage to his time in show business. And Mrs. Clouse was all about a little glitz.

Glowing cotton balls scattered off in every direction. They looked like fireflies on speed as they jetted around the property. Gradually, they started to fall in spots around the yard. Some spots held one or two balls, and others collected a small pile. Under the spell I had cast, the cotton balls would seek out anything of value. The bigger the pile, the bigger the payoff—it worked great for consulting with prospectors.

Henri's face lit up. "I didn't know all of that was out there."

The nearest spot had only a couple of balls. They glowed a bright golden color, which meant they had found precious metals. Mrs. Clouse handed me a shovel.

I should have expected she wouldn't have planned to do any physical labor. I started to dig, and six inches down, we hit pay dirt, literally. We found a small bag of gold dust.

Henri looked at the bag. "I've found dozens of treasures over the years—those bags, silver and gold coins, jewelry and gems. Best I figured based on the history, this is where one of the confederate treasure wagons wound up."

Mrs. Clouse's eyes glowed with gold fever. She was mumbling something about Henri hiding all of this from her, but I tuned out her rambling. We dug in a few more spots and found a cache of gold and silver coins, another bag of gold dust, and a beautiful jeweled necklace. She immediately put it on. She ran spot to spot in the yard, studying the cotton balls until she found a big pile that looked a little different. The balls glowed green and blue, meaning cash and indeterminate materials.

Henri gave a little sigh. "The devil's treasure box."

Mrs. Clouse's eyes danced with greed. "Dig here."

I threw the shovel to the ground. "I won't dig that up, and you shouldn't either. You have enough in your cache over there for a lifetime."

Mrs. Clouse sneered at me. "Fool. I will have what's mine." I watched as she sweated out the martinis and changed over to a different high. I had been wrong. She was willing to get dirty to get what she wanted. After digging down three feet in the sun-baked earth, she hit an aluminum case, wrapped in oilcloth. She dragged it out onto the desert sands. I could almost hear her thinking *My Precious*. Maybe I was just imagining it.

She unlatched the case and opened it. Stacks of large bills filled it to the brim. Another note was gently folded on top. It fell to the side as she clutched the stacks of bills. I picked up the note.

My dearest Katydid,

Please heed me for once. Or whomever finds this case.

This money is cursed. When the last dime is spent, so are you.

22

Bury it, destroy it if you can. Just don't spend it.

I implore you.

An odd energy interweaved between the money and Mrs. Clouse as she dragged the case into the house. I turned down my Sight. I just didn't want to see any more.

"What can I do?" I asked Henri.

He shook his head. "It's done, and so is she. I buried the curse in the middle of more than she could spend in ten lifetimes. But that money has a history. It creates an addiction. Once it has you…"

My curiosity was piqued. "How did you get it?"

Henri stroked his stubbly chin. "When I first came to Vegas, I had plenty of money, we were newly married, and my life was wonderful. I did a couple of special performances for a mob boss, and that's what I was paid with. I saw it for what it was, blood money that had been passed around so many times, it took on a life of its own. I found this place, and I buried it where it should have been hidden forever. But when I took it, everything changed. Katie's career tanked. She couldn't handle the pressure. It never seemed to affect me until I saw it from this side. It just took longer to kill me through her."

"What about the rest of your fortune?"

Henri shrugged. "She gets a big stipend monthly from the estate. We never had any kids, so it's all there to take care of her. I was never rich like some of the performers, but we were better off than most. She's set for life. That payoff never hit me with the greed bug, but it latched onto her like a leech. Now it has her. Let her be."

"I'm sorry, Henri." I was starting to understand why he had continued to work and travel. He hadn't been able to bear watching

23

his wife deteriorate, yet he'd wanted to make sure she was taken care of after he was gone. And he'd loved the work. That much I knew.

Henri nodded. "You've done more for me than you know. I look at you like the son we never had."

"Thanks, Henri, for everything you did for me. I know it was hard… after I had to leave home."

Henri shrugged. "You're a good kid, no matter what anyone else says." He had told me that for as long as I could remember. "Before you go, two things. First, go to my office."

I sneaked into the house. Mrs. Clouse was in the den on the floor, rolling around on the stacks of bills, the bags of coins and gold dust set aside. I could see she was totally enveloped in the energy from the power embodied in the cash. The shadow of a malignant spirit was taking form and feeding off of her. I tossed a small tracer into the nearly empty case. If I couldn't get it out of her hands, I wanted to make sure it didn't taint anyone else. The agency on the other end were experts in cleaning up this kind of mess, and were used to keeping people away from magic and monsters. I'd done a little work for them in the past.

Her eyes were glazed over in ecstasy. "Care to join me?" she asked offhandedly. I walked past her without answering. She didn't seem to notice or care.

Henri pointed to an old hearing aid on one of the shelves on the wall. It looked like a giant brass horn. I remembered it from the séance routine in his act. "Take this. It's a vintage spirit trumpet." I grabbed the horn and placed it in a case I'd found underneath the bookshelf. "And now to the next bit," Henri said.

Mrs. Clouse rolled her head toward me in what I assumed she thought was a seductive pose as we walked toward the door. She had managed to lose most of her clothes while rolling around. Seeing her lying in the middle of all that tainted cash reminded me of someone stoned falling through a coffee table. "Last chance," she said.

I smiled back. "You're right."

I reached into my pocket for a couple of, what I called, Holy Hand Grenades. They were basically water balloons filled with a mixture of holy oil, holy water, and a few herbs. I flung one at the empty case and the other at Mrs. Clouse. I gave them a small Push of Will, and they burst.

As they exploded and coated the room, I couldn't tell if Mrs. Clouse or the demon snarled. From my Sight, they were both displeased.

"You bastard," she sputtered.

"Good-bye, Mrs. Clouse." The effects would be short-lived, but I felt a little cleaner.

HENRI FOLLOWED ME out of the house. I turned to him once we were outside. "Why did you have me do *that* to her? Help her find that case? Your treasure? Even she doesn't deserve that kind of curse."

Henri grimaced slightly. "You did nothing wrong. Okay, the holy water was a pretty good gag and probably stung a little, but she'll be over that by now. It's hard to explain. That case is no treasure. She was obsessed with it before I died. The entity in the money hooked her, not me. Once it has you, death is the only way out. The reason I first came to your home back in the day, in Phoenix Grove, was because I was looking for an answer, a cure. I had hoped to destroy the cycle. She got twenty more years of life, such as it's been. And now I will be with her until it happens. I still love my wife, and I'll be with her until the end. After that, who knows?" Guilt was written all over Henri's face.

I was numb. "How will it happen?"

Henri shrugged. "That's the bitch of free will. She'll make that choice."

"So you said there were two things. I got the horn. What's number two?" I really felt the urge to get away as quickly as possible and take a long shower.

Henri smiled again. "Your fee, of course."

"Henri…" I felt dirty enough. "It's really not necessary."

"I won't hear of it. Follow me." We stopped close to a pile of rocks. A lone dying cotton ball lay on the ground. "Dig."

I went back to the pit behind the house for the shovel. I dug down two feet and hit a small cache of gold dust and coins. "Henri, I can't. This is blood money."

Henri smiled at me, more fatherly this time. "No. This little cache is far enough away to not be tainted, but I'd cleanse it anyway. Consider it your inheritance."

After a brief hesitation, I grabbed the cache. We walked back to my bike, and I put the haul into the saddlebag. "Thanks, Henri. I miss you. And I miss your sometimes questionable advice."

Henri laughed. "Good news. With the trumpet, you can call me up any time. Thanks for helping me out, kid. And for helping her.

You don't see it now, but it will release her from years of torment. I thought I'd handled it when I buried it, but I wanted to make sure no one else… but it was still too close to the house. To us. I didn't see that I was making her suffer, but once I found out about the power of the cursed box… just don't let it get anyone else."

"I'm still not convinced *that* was helping, letting her actually get a hold of it." I knew my part in this job with the soon-to-be late Mrs. Clouse would haunt me. I would have to add it to the list. Unfortunately for me, it had a lot of contenders for my nightmares.

Henri nodded. "Sometimes the hard choice is the only one you can make. Take care of yourself, kid." He turned and walked back into the house.

I hopped onto the Indian and drove toward Vegas. Early the next morning, I reached the outskirts of town. I did not feel like partying it up anymore. Instead, I opted for a quick bite and an old casino motel room. The casino consisted of six slot machines in the lobby. The registrar was also the house blackjack dealer, and the lobby counter doubled as the blackjack table. Two guys were losing to the house when I checked in. The cost was sixty bucks a night for a clean enough room, so I checked in for a week. I figured that would be long enough for the inevitable.

I SLEPT IN late and rolled out of bed just before noon. An inventory of my rucksack showed I was running low on ammo and supplies, but for the first time in a while, I was high on assets. My better judgment told me to do the smart thing before I wandered out for the day and made sure my cache was safe. The bathroom seemed to be the best option for the trip I needed to take.

My reflection in the bathroom mirror caught me off guard. I could have looked worse, all things considered, but the view was marred by the chips and blisters in the reflective surface. It had been a rough night, but just one of many.

I hadn't looked at myself in a while. My sandy hair had grown a little long and shaggy. My ice-blue eyes looked cold and half-dead, but at least the bags under my eyes weren't too deep. My cheeks were hollow, but my time in the sun had given them a little color.

The bathroom had a big enough tile floor for my needs, so I grabbed a hotel cup and got started. A little water, lemon juice, and a few miscellaneous items from my bag combined into a yellowish mixture that I used to draw a circle and a familiar set of sigils on the floor. The few designs probably would have looked like scribbles to anyone else but me.

The sigil dried within a few moments, then it was time to take a short trip between realms. Traveling between dimensions was a lot easier than most people believed for those who had the right talents. All someone really needed was focus. It wasn't as much about what someone did or said as it was the sigils, which had the ability to act like a lock and key.

"There's no place like home," I mumbled.

Traveling through a portal felt like an instantaneous lifetime. An infinite number of disconnected images, sensations, and emotions surged through me quickly and left me chilled and tingly. A millisecond later, when my senses were again my own, my surroundings changed to the familiar large stone room. Ancient wooden shelves lined the walls, and they were filled with books, scrolls, herbs, chemicals, minerals, and assorted knickknacks. The worktables were covered in dusty lab equipment and the remains of a sandwich. I really needed to spend a lifetime or two down there to clean up.

I stepped out of the lone entrance. The permanent portal was surrounded by intertwined threads of precious metals and glowing veins of energy, which were tightly woven into a knot-work circle and surrounded by crystals and gemstones. An ancestor of mine, lost to history, had embedded the ring into the granite floor, and it had become the foundation for the lab. These days, it was as close to a home as I had.

The trumpet found a home on a shelf with my other few prized possessions.

After a quick cleansing of the haul from Henri's, I pocketed a few of the gold coins.

I put the rest in an old safe that occupied one entire corner of the room. Plenty of cash and valuables filled the safe, but gold was getting hard to come by and was a handy element. No need to lock the safe, because no one knew where this place was, including me. And if someone could get in the stone room, an old tumbler lock would probably do little good. Mom had always told me that only one person could ever control access to the room at a time, and for as long as I was alive, it was me.

She hadn't seemed to know what or where this place was either. It had been passed through our family as a hideaway. There were no other doors besides the portal. I didn't know who had built it or how, but some of the artifacts in the room went back to a time before Gobekli Tepe was an idea.

I quickly restocked my rucksack with a few boxes of ammunition, some holy water, and a few extra knives. Then I mixed a few of my standard potions and concoctions. Some quick work with a torch sealed the glass amperes.

I sat down in the old leather recliner and thought of how tempting it was to hole up away from the world. But if I had only a few months to live, I figured I may as well have some fun. I held out little hope the Inquest would turn me loose once I returned home. I wondered who would inherit this place after I was gone. If I didn't tell anyone about it, who would know? But I had a suspicion it would find a new caretaker no matter what.

I hopped on the portal. "Viva Las Vegas."

I REAPPEARED IN the hotel bathroom. The nearly invisible circle disappeared with the swipe of a towel. With a glance in the mirror, I surveyed my old *Star Wars* T-shirt and jeans. I decided I looked about as good as I was going to get and walked out the door.

A couple of old ladies were sitting at the slots in the lobby as I passed through to the front door. My near-mythical garnet 1955 Indian Warrior got a lot of looks as I climbed on it in the parking lot. A lot of people argued the classic motorcycle had never existed. But most people argued that magic and all that went with it didn't exist either. Both became very real when the bike roared to life even if most of my abilities had been taken away. *No bitterness at all.*

My first stop was to cash in a few of the gold coins, which gave me a little traveling money. After a quick round of haggling and coming out on the short end of the deal at one of the off-strip coin shops, I decided to go see Father Mike O'Brien. The Mission of St. Cayetano was a small house and mission chapel located a few miles from the strip. Fr. Mike lived there and held a variety of meetings and services to help the poor souls devastated by the charms of Vegas.

The front door was unlocked as usual. "Padre, are you home?"

Fr. Mike appeared from his office, a twinkle in his eye. His brogue from the old country was still strong. "Greyson, my son, it's been a while. Come in. Have a seat. What brings you to my den of iniquity?" He patted my back and pointed me toward the small den and a well-worn couch.

"Been in town on a job for an old friend." I looked around for Mike's partner in crime and deacon. "And how's Brother Jake?"

Before he became a priest, Fr. Mike had been a professional gambler. He had been so good that he had wiped out a lot of people. He'd run into one of them on the Vegas strip one night, homeless and begging. Mike had barely recognized Jake Higgins, a former heavyweight in the world of poker and an old adversary.

Mike had bought this house in Vegas to serve as a retreat when he was in town and to host private parties and off-strip invitation poker games. Thirty years ago, he took Jake in and set him up to start helping the lost people of Vegas. Mike had joined a Jesuit order to help make reparations and was eventually ordained.

"He is out catering to the lost souls on the strip. He'll be here later." That meant he was looking for the ones on the brink, ones that could still be saved.

I gave Fr. Mike a handful of the gold coins. "A few shekels for the poor."

"Bless you, my son." Fr. Mike gave me a big hug. "Might I ask the provenance?"

Mike sat me down, and I told him about the events at Henri's. Fr. Mike and Henri had been great friends. "I pray for Katie every night," he said. "Henri brought that box here. We couldn't pull it across to sanctified ground. It was like it hit a wall. I'd wondered where he hid it. I even tried to go see her, but she would have none of it."

"Based on what I saw, she's been checked out since Henri died."

"Aye," Fr. Mike agreed. "So, to better things. For what does a practitioner of the forbidden arts such as yourself come to darken my door?"

I rolled my eyes and put on my best bad Irish accent. "I come a-casting and need a spot of holy water to boil the eye of newt for soup. And can you bless a bit of ammo?" We had a routine. Both of us were trying to make up for our past in our own ways.

I stacked my weapons and ammunition on the kitchen table. Fr. Mike added several bottles of holy water and holy oil to the pile. He shook his head and set to his work. Within a few minutes, the whole pile was blessed and anointed. Mike was good enough to keep me well stocked even when I was on the road.

The old priest breathed deeply. "What are you out hunting? That's more in one pile than I've seen you bring in collectively." He was fishing for an update on my progress. He was probably a little worried for me. I had been trying to find out what had happened to me years earlier that had caused me to be bound and exiled from my home. Time was running short before I would be called back to face the consequences.

I shrugged. "You know, hellhounds on my trail, werewolves in the closet, bloodsuckers in the clubs. The whole Inquest wants to hang me. Good times."

Fr. Mike placed a hand on my shoulder. "Son, you can't fight your way out of the Inquest. You still haven't told me what it's for? What do they say you did?"

We sat down in the small kitchen, and I stared at the worn wooden table. I really had not told anyone, at least from my point of view. A lot of stories, more myth and legend than truth, were circulating, but I didn't know much more than the people making up the tales. "You know we moved to Phoenix Grove when I was three. Mom and Dad had grown up there, and Mom's father Josiah runs the Librarium Occultus, the library for lost and rare texts. The whole village is only a few thousand total."

"I'd still like a visit to that town and a trip through the history of the world," Fr. Mike said.

"I'll see what I can do." I knew the only possibility of that was if he joined me on the trip for the trial.

Fr. Mike prodded. "So what happened in the 'incident' that has everyone in an uproar?" I knew Mike had gone digging after we'd met. He'd wanted to know if he had let a monster back into the world. Unfortunately, even I was not sure.

I hesitated. "I don't remember much. And at this point, I don't remember much of my life growing up, but I'm not sure if that's because of the trauma or from when they bound my abilities. I was almost sixteen. I was kidnapped along with a dozen kids from my village. Because of how the village is protected, someone on the inside had to coordinate the attack and let them in. There's no way they could have gotten past the field and through the wards otherwise."

Fr. Mike interjected. "And they don't know who?"

"Not as far as I know, and it's not like I can get much from the village these days. I'd hope if they found something, they would let me know, and I could go home."

Fr. Mike pulled the story from me like water from a well. It started to come easier, and it felt good to talk about it. "I think we were only missing for a few days. A group from the village managed to trace where we were. I have snippets of memories from the time we were held, but nothing I can hold onto. Our village has a lot of people experienced in fighting the creatures of the dark. Many of them have taken refuge in the village because of fighting the dark. They assembled a rescue party of two groups, mostly family of those taken.

"From what I was told, the second rescue party arrived to find a disaster. I was passed out on a sacrificial altar. Everything within thirty feet was scorched. Three of the village children and several other adults were dead, including my parents, who had been in the first group that came scouting for us. They also found a few outsiders dead, also apparently taken from elsewhere. Some of the missing were never found, presumed vaporized in the apparent blast. The bodies of five acolytes were left behind. They wore the sigil of Erebus, an old god of darkness."

Fr. Mike shuddered. "Erebus? I thought their order was destroyed during the inquisition."

I sighed. "I tried to find something out about them, but the best info I have access to is in the village. There were also a few dead Fomorian and Unseelie mercenaries."

Fr. Mike still looked puzzled. "So why you?"

I shook my head. "The ritual was happening in an old ceremonial site in a dimensional pocket controlled by my family, and I was on the altar. The blast looked to originate from me, but I have no idea what happened."

Fr. Mike sympathetically looked past me. "Too much of a burden for one as young as you to bear."

I felt resigned as I stoically waved my hands. "So they held the start of an Inquest. Not even the survivors could say what happened. The rest of my family was dead. A strong suggestion was made that there be a hiatus to investigate. They used the law of seven and determined the Inquest would restart no later than six years, three hundred sixty days after the date of the kidnapping. The kidnapping happened three days before Samhain."

Fr. Mike puzzled out the date. "Your birthday."

"Yep. Sweet sixteen massacre. So, for the good of the village, they decided I would have most of my abilities bound except those needed to defend myself. And I got to keep a few abilities like my tracking. I guess they left me with some skills to find things, people, to give me the chance to figure out what happened… or at least pretend they were. My grandfather set me up with some of his contacts in the outside world to continue my studies and hopefully find some answers."

Fr. Mike smiled and nodded. "And seven years comes up…"

I finished the sentence. "Soon. The trial will resume in late October of this year. In four months. And I have no answers."

Fr. Mike gave me a stern look. "You are a good man. You have a good heart. There's no way you are responsible; I don't see it on your soul. If you had committed so grievous a sin, you wouldn't sit before me now."

I thought back to the first time I'd met Fr. Mike. I had wandered into his church when I'd stopped in Vegas on the way to Los Angeles six years ago, not long after I'd been ostracized and banished. Part of the reason Mike was so good at poker was that he possessed some abilities himself. And I learned that with the Jesuits, he'd honed his skills to see the sins of man and of those not so human. "I remember."

Fr. Mike poked me in the chest over my heart. "I'd have dropped you right there if you had been one of the soulless beasts or one who had sold yourself over." He had been carrying substantial firepower when we'd first met. Instead of fighting, though, we'd gone for breakfast. "Even now, your actions weigh much more to the good."

I looked Fr. Mike in the eye. "You know, I've never told anyone that story outside of the original Inquest."

Fr. Mike nodded. "Confession is good for the soul and the mind." Fr. Mike stood. "It's time for a late lunch." He rubbed his small paunch with a big grin. "You're buying."

THE LATE AFTERNOON SUN beat down on us. We wound up at Fr. Mike's favorite greasy spoon, which overlooked the strip, and sat in a booth to watch the people walking by. Fr. Mike studied the sea of humanity, pointing out the foibles in the passersby and the occasional bright spot. With my Sight turned on low, I saw that at least ten percent of the people had some sort of nasty attachment. I pointed them out to Fr. Mike.

"Yeah, those are the demonic bottom feeders. They hop on for a snack of depression and then go on to a main course of despair. There's plenty of it around here. Of course, there's a lot of good stuff as well. Newlyweds. Vacationers who brought the whole family and are doing the shows."

"Well, the sin in the city is a little better obfuscated these days."

"So how long are you going to be in town?" Fr. Mike asked.

I shrugged. "A few days. Maybe a week. I'll soon start heading back east. Make a few stops on the way. I can't really stop anywhere for too long. I've got a lot to do, and not a lot of time if I'm going to have any chance at the Inquest."

Fr. Mike nodded. "So what's your plan?" I'd told him what I knew of the disaster in my home, but he held out a lot more hope for a fair trial than I did. How does one defend themselves when even you don't really know what happened?

Several options had presented themselves, but none seemed more promising than any other. "With the time I have left, I've got a stop to make in Laredo. One of the gangs down there has enslaved a werewolf pack to do their hits. There's a witches' coven in Detroit stirring up some trouble. I'm hoping to have a sit-down with them before the law comes and sets them on a better path than my own. I'd still like to find the Erebites for some answers."

Fr. Mike waved a finger in my face. "If you whiz in the Wheaties of the powers that be, don't be surprised they're pissed because breakfast got soggy."

I was a little taken aback. "What?"

Fr. Mike gave me a stern look. "There's an old saying: 'The nail that stands up gets pounded down.' As best I can tell, you were sent out to find yourself and keep a low profile. Instead, you have gone head-to-head with some powerful players, even if for small affairs. You're taunting Erebites and demons. No wonder the dark side is hunting you. If you're doing this much damage without your powers, what can you do at full strength?"

I hadn't really thought of it that way.

"And if you get to full strength, what will that do to you? That's a lot of power for a mortal."

"Mike, I'm still a wizard of sorts, like it or not. If I'm going to die, I'd rather do it for a reason. I am what I am." I did my worst Popeye imitation.

Fr. Mike shook his head and smiled. "That you are, and may God help us all."

I PROMISED FR. MIKE I would stop by before leaving town. I really didn't have any reason to stay or any other errands to run, so I decided to wander the strip and do a bit more people watching. Fr. Mike always got me in that mood. Before it got late and trouble found me, I opted for an early evening. I sensed the storm on the horizon and figured I could use the rest while I could get it.

My cell phone awoke me early the next morning. It was Fr. Mike. "Grey, can you stop by this morning?"

I had a bad feeling. An hour later, I parked in front of the mission.

Fr. Mike looked solemn as he greeted me at the door.

"Okay, what is it?"

I could tell Fr. Mike was conflicted. "Katerina Ashe Clouse was killed last night in a one-vehicle accident. She and another gentleman were in her new Italian sports car. She had just closed the deal on the car, and the dealership owner went with her for a test drive."

"What happened?" She must have moved quickly and spent the last dime on the car. Of course, pent up for that many years, whatever force was in that box would have been ready to wreak havoc. What better town than Vegas to cause mayhem?

Fr. Mike looked uncomfortable. "Apparently, they had stopped at a cliff overlook and began to engage in relations. It looks like one of them hit the brake release, and they rolled over."

"The devil got his due," I said. Henri had said it would come quickly, but I'd expected to be able to get out of town first. "So, where's the cash?"

Fr. Mike shook his head. "I know what you said about the money. Maybe it's still at the dealership. It's a small, exclusive one outside of town." He gave me the address, and I saw that it was only a short drive away.

I'd promised Henri that I would keep the money from doing any further damage. I had to give it a try. "I'll check on it."

"I'm to do her funeral," Fr. Mike said. "Arrangements had already been made. But with what you say about her being possessed..."

I put a hand on Fr. Mike's shoulder. "When she spent the cash, the curse had done its work, and it killed her. It would have passed to the guy she bought the car from. If they were both killed, and the cash hasn't moved, I may be able to end the curse."

"Mr. Haight, the dealer, and his family are members of my parish," Fr. Mike said. "I'll be asked to do his funeral as well."

It couldn't be easy for him, knowing what I'd told him. "It was a curse. I believe it has done what it was meant to do. The cash is what is possessed, not the people. Last rites and consecrated ground for both of them."

He clasped his hands and nodded.

"Let me go check on the cash," I said. "I'll stay in town for the funeral."

Fr. Mike smiled slightly. "Thanks, lad. Be careful."

Yeah, that's me, Mr. Cautious. I would need to figure out a way to deal with the tainted cash.

Haight's location was on Las Vegas Boulevard, seven miles from downtown. The dealership was definitely not your average car lot, but more of a giant glass temple for finely crafted, high-dollar personal transportation. And despite the loss of the high priest, those with enough cash could still come and pay homage. The door to the building was open, and a young, tall man who looked like a GQ model greeted me with a look that said he hated when tourists stopped in to leer. Obviously, I was not well-dressed enough to breathe the same air, but from their view, you never know when an Internet geek might come in to drop some spare change.

He quickly figured out that I wasn't there to give him a shot at a last sale before they figured out the future of the dealership. When I asked about his old boss, he expressed genuine grief, but he didn't know anything about a big box of cash. He said no one had been by since LVPD officers came by to check on the location and make sure there was no incident to be investigated on this end. They closed out the case as an accident.

Haight had been there alone the entire previous day until he closed up to take Mrs. Clouse for the test drive. The service department was a block away, and no one had seen Haight since the previous morning.

A total dead-end. The cash and the box were gone.

I hung around Las Vegas a few more days and stayed for the funeral. A handful of Henri's old friends came out. Best I could tell, Mrs. Clouse had run off any friends she'd had years before. When the service was almost over, I saw Henri and Katie in the church for the Mass. They both looked happy and waved. They held hands as they faded away.

After the funeral, Fr. Mike and I grabbed a bite and said our good-byes. He promised to come for the Inquest for moral support. It had nothing to do with him trying to sneak into the Librarium, an archive and repository of lost and hidden knowledge in the Grove. After a bit of prodding, he promised to handle my funeral if it came to that.

MY LAST NIGHT in Vegas was restless. I'd decided to follow up on a rumor that the Erebites had a temple in Iowa. It seemed unlikely the rumor was anything more than a few kids that found something on the Internet. But I never knew if some group would make a corn maze to the underworld in the shape of Lord Erebus.

I strapped my rucksack onto the Indian, threw a few things into the saddlebag, and found an unwelcome surprise. A FaeMail scroll stared me in the face. FaeMail was the secure mail delivery system for the people of the Veiled world. Nothing good came of receiving a scroll, at least not for me. I wondered if I was being called home early.

Instead, the message was cryptic:

Please help us.

A lock of hair was tied to the parchment.

I debated ignoring it. Obviously, it was someone that knew who I was but was not willing to broadcast his identity. And they clearly had access to the magical realms and tools. A little voice murmured in my head, *it's a trap.* But if Fr. Mike was right, I had drawn some dangerous attention to myself, and I couldn't risk an innocent on the other end pulled in at my expense.

The tracking formula I whipped up was simple, just a few words and a surge of energy. A tuft of hair landed in the concoction, telling me it was ready. A few drops of the mix sent a ball bearing rolling around a map of the US that I had spread on the bed. It stopped on San Diego.

I could be there in six hours or so. I supposed the cornfield tour could wait.

I RODE HARD for most of the day, stopping only twice. When the skyline came up over the horizon, I poured a bit of the tracking spell onto a cotton ball and followed its lead to a bench overlooking Sunset Cliffs on the outskirts of San Diego.

I hadn't seen this view or heard the crash of the waves on the rocks below in years. It made me wonder why I had come back and why I was following the breadcrumbs. As the sun neared the horizon to set over the Pacific, my senses screamed a warning. The presence of hellhounds knocked me out of my trance.

I opened my Senses. While tuned in, I was able to perceive everything around me well beyond the ordinary. Paired with the Sight, every movement or fluctuation in energy pulsed as a form within my mind's eye. The distraction faded just as the first hound dove for my throat.

My reflexive protections kicked in. I spun around from the bench and used the hound's momentum to fling it over the cliffs into the ocean below. Two other hounds appeared at my flanks, twenty feet away. In the last rays of the sun, I took a good look at the hellhounds. Their two-hundred-plus-pound muscled frames, short, jet-black fur, and flaming eyes would have terrified any sane being. I had faced this pack before, and I let my instincts take over.

My Colt 1911 flew into my hand, and I put three blessed silver rounds into the head of the hound on my right as I was run down by the hound from my left. It knocked me over and leapt past me. I rolled to my right as the hound landed where I had been.

As I scrambled to my feet, I felt a strong presence and looked behind me. Oh joy, the rest of the pack was watching and waiting for their turn. Their leader, whom I had nicknamed Scar, looked as if he was the size of a small buffalo, covered in the beauty marks of his trade. I could see a couple of gashes I had given him, including the one from a few months back. I had gotten a good slash down his neck but had missed taking his head.

From the look of the pack, most were new and unwilling recruits. I had made a pretty good dent in Scar's entourage. On this side of the Veil, some hellhounds had the ability to forcibly recruit new members to the pack if they survived the process. Their method involved the pack attacking and taunting the prospect until the demon of the pack took over or the poor creature died. From the looks of it, Scar must have been desperate. I could've sworn one of the hounds must have been a Chihuahua in its former life.

A fresh magazine of ammo found its way home in the Colt and was quickly emptied to drop four more of the new recruits. The rest of the pack charged. Scar motivated his band of malevolent mongrels, using flaming eyes and guttural snarls to give commands.

With the pack closing in, I chose my option of last resort. I ran. Fast. I wouldn't be able to stay ahead of them for long. I counted three Holy Hand Grenades remaining in my satchel as I scrambled away. I cut to my right, down a path that ran along the ledge of the cliff. As I ran, I tossed one of the grenades into the air toward the nearest hound. "Fetch," I yelled.

Apparently, the former German Shepherd had played a lot of catch before being turned. He caught the fragile vessel in his maw, and it burst on contact. The hound dropped in an uncoordinated roll and started to dissolve.

A curve ahead led into the edge of a scattered neighborhood across the street from the cliffs. The faint sounds of people echoed nearby. I needed a new plan and jumped back up onto the cliff face from the trail. The hounds had to run around the end of the trail to get back behind me, which bought me a few valuable seconds. The last two grenades arced through the air in a panicked toss. With a little Push, they exploded into the pack as a fine mist. As the half-dozen or so hounds plowed through the mist, they all began to howl as their skin sizzled and smoked. One of them made it far enough to jump and grab my left arm. He turned loose when my silver dagger spiked him in the head.

Most of the remaining pack scattered, finally more afraid of me than Scar.

Scar rushed in low and attacked. He alone remained dedicated, and the hound dove high for my neck. I countered with a silver blade and sliced through its throat. Scar got a good bite into my thigh then rolled in midair, knocking me down. He released me and began to circle. Blood trickled down my leg, and I hoped the scent wouldn't attract the rest of the pack back to the action. The hound I had sliced open was still twitching but was out for the count. As Scar came around for another pass, my hand found my last blade.

I pushed myself onto one leg as he latched onto my left arm and landed all his weight on my chest, knocking me back to the ground. I held him back with my arm, which was conveniently in his mouth, and plunged the silver blade into his chest. With the fight going out of Scar, I rolled him over and crawled to the bench as the night lights on the beach started to replace the sunlight.

Once out from under Scar's control, the rest of the pack scattered into the twilight. Hopefully, a few of them were lucky enough to revert to normal. I suspected the rest would come for me again out of instinct if they lived that long.

When I was able to stop gasping for air, I realized I needed to check out the damage. I could feel a couple of cracked ribs and a few spots with broken skin. Luckily, my leather and Kevlar motorcycle gear had gotten the worst of it. A little patching and a few days' rest, and I would be as good as used. I dug for a potion that would speed up healing and kill some of the pain.

A couple of cars passed by as I cleaned up the evidence, but no one seemed to pay any attention. I stood over the nearest of the dead hellhounds. I quickly yanked my knife out of the mongrel and wiped it on the hound's fur. My silver blade was clean, and I slipped it back into place. I dragged hound number two closer to the edge of the cliff and rolled it off into the ocean. It landed with a splash, and the sea began to bubble as the hound dissolved. Water didn't mix well with most demonic critters, but salt water seemed to do an even nicer job.

It was time to dispose of my old friend Scar. His pack of hounds had been on me for years. A dozen old hellhounds had been in the original pack. Scar was the last of that pack. My leg ached as I half-dragged and half-shoved his body toward the ocean. He let out a snarl and growled as I yanked my blade from his chest and rolled him over the edge. He thrashed violently as he landed in the Pacific.

I couldn't help myself. I looked over and yelled, "Stay. Play dead."

I sensed I was not alone even though no one else was within sight. I threw the last few dead hounds over the cliffs into the ocean and limped back to the bench. Walking wasn't nearly as comfortable with my new injuries. It hurt like hell where the hound had bitten me, but that was the least of my troubles.

A voice I had not heard in several years sang out to me. "Well, look what the hellhounds dragged in. Grey Forrester graces my neighborhood, and I don't even get a FaeMail."

After cutting a quick glance to the side, I had no doubt the silhouette was Andrea. I tried to work up a quick quip, but the best I had at that moment was a pained, "So, Drea, miss me?" Without giving her time to answer, I followed up with, "Did you send a few pets out to find me?"

She stepped in closer, and the streetlight framed her silhouette. After a few seconds, I got a curt reply. "Actually, in watching them, I thought they might be your watchdogs and that the rumors were true, that you really had gone to the dark side."

"And now?"

She sighed and relaxed slightly before snapping her hip holster shut. "I see you're the same jackass who ran off four years ago and hasn't written since. Did you find what you went out looking for?" She slid onto the other end of the bench, staring out at the Pacific. The stars looked especially bright, and the crash of the ocean was pulling the remaining fight out of me.

46

We sat on the bench for a few moments in silence. I poked a few tender spots and poured a mixture onto the open bites. They stung as they bubbled.

After a few moments, Andrea stood and walked back to the road. "Get your bike and load it on the trailer. You can ride in the truck with me. Priscilla wants to see you."

Several profane thoughts flitted through my head. I had hoped to avoid this. "Priscilla knows I'm here?"

Drea rolled her eyes. "Who do you think sent your care package?"

Sonofabitch.

I FOLLOWED HER the short distance up the hill and sat on my Indian, which was old before I was born. But it ran like a tank and was old enough that neither magic nor cheap gas seemed to hurt it. I debated heading anywhere but where Drea wanted me to go, especially if Priscilla had sent me the invitation. Underneath it all, I wasn't surprised she was involved. Four years had passed since I'd continued my little walkabout, four years since I'd seen Drea or Priscilla. At times like that, the reality of my situation hit home.

Priscilla was a powerful creature, even though I had not figured out what kind. She'd taken up residence on the West Coast in the days of the California Republic and brought the Amazons to support the short-lived rebellion. Eighty years later, she moved her operation to Los Angeles. When I was first banished from my home after the Samhain incident, my grandfather and only surviving family member sent me to study with Priscilla and "The Daughters." Most of The Daughters were adopted, but best I could figure, Drea and Priscilla were blood relatives.

I had lived and traveled with Priscilla, Drea, and a few others for eighteen months, working on my espionage, tracking, and obfuscation skills. I'd learned everything I knew about glamour in those days. I cared for Drea and Priscilla greatly, but I may not have left on the best of terms.

Against my better judgment, I drove up onto the small trailer then climbed into the cab of her green F150 and took a good look at her. At a little over five feet tall with light olive skin, raven hair, and intoxicating gray eyes, Drea was breathtaking. She could pass for anywhere between eighteen and thirty. Slipping her Beretta, knife, and holster in a slot under the driver's seat, she looked at me and smiled. "Don't get any ideas."

At least that meant she was not going to kill me outright. "So where are we headed?"

Priscilla and her daughters could be found anywhere up and down the West Coast, depending on the winds. Priscilla had a number of operations and floated with her whims.

With a sly smile, Drea looked over at me. "Long Beach. Priscilla decided to settle down for a while. I think you'll like it."

All I could think of in Long Beach was the Queen Mary. "She didn't happen to acquire a little boat, did she?" One never knew. Word had it that she'd sold London Bridge at least twenty times after it was moved to Lake Havasu in the desert. Her company had managed a lot of the process behind the scenes when it was brought in through her backyard in Long Beach.

With her throaty laugh, she said, "No. But close. She negotiated for a bit of beachfront property and has a couple of small shops." I felt her Push her Will and saw a faint shimmer around the truck. "They won't be able to track us."

I debated which "they" she meant. We drove up Mission Boulevard and headed for I-5. "So where the hell have you been since you ran off on me without so much as a 'kiss my ass'?"

Yeah, this is going to be one long ride. I settled back in the seat and tried to fake sleep. Instead, I got poked in a hellhound bite.

Drea's eyes were hardened with anger and hurt. "That was not a rhetorical question. I need to know where you've been. There are a lot of… rumors."

Living with Priscilla's tribe should have taught me a few lessons about women, but I was a bit dense. I had little doubt Drea was still mad at me, but she was most likely trying to determine if I really had gone over and if I was a risk. If she even questioned my allegiances, she would kill me, or at least give it a good try. The worst part was that I really didn't know if she would be able to go through with it. We'd had some feelings for each other all those years ago, as much as someone like Drea would allow herself to show. But we'd been kids, or at least, I had been.

I slapped her hand away when I sensed she was readying to poke the bite again, and a sharp pain shot through me. Apparently swatting at her didn't count as self-defense. The best I could do was to channel my inner child. "Stop poking me," I snapped. I was quickly remembering how much of a nuisance it was to be around other people. One of the more aggravating parts of my powers being bound was that if I acted aggressively without cause, I was hit with a charge that caused me greater pain than that resulting from my action. I could only imagine the pain if I were to kill someone.

Drea gave me a saccharine smile. "If you can't play nice, I'll turn this car around. Now would you like to have a little share time and tell me where you've been?"

There was the condescending witch I knew and loved. This was her shot across my bow. At one time, I would have surrendered anything to her for a little attention. The current game was one in which the prize was my ability to keep breathing for a few more moments. "You remember when Dorian showed up in Sonoma?" I asked in a tone just as nice as hers.

Her face turned sour. "Yes, and his odd friend Nicomedes."

"Dorian and Priscilla decided it was time for me to move on to my next round of studies." What I did not tell her, but I felt sure she knew, was that I had been shipped off before I became too close with The Daughters, especially Drea. "We took a ship and cruised over to the UK and then to Paris. We spent a few weeks plodding through a few of the old libraries, and then they dropped me off in a little town in Spain overlooking the Mediterranean. I spent the next year with an alchemist as his lab assistant. From there, it was to a village in Brazil with a shaman and healer for six months or so." I'd never been very good at fixing living things, only breaking them.

Even though I knew this was what Drea was looking for, it was hard for me to open up. When I'd left, it had been the first time in my life I had been totally on my own, and I'd had to do it without warning and without a plan. I swore that would never happen again.

"Eighteen months ago, Dorian was asked to look into a series of attacks in the Vancouver area, possibly done by some sort of Were. Dorian thought there might be something pertinent to my situation, so I came back to join him. We spent a couple of months working our way across Canada on the trail, and we were attacked outside of Calgary. I saw Nicky go down under a couple of hellhounds, and

50

Dorian shoved me into a portal. I came out in the middle of nowhere Montana, and I haven't heard from them since.

"I've worked my way here and there with some of the old family friends, doing odd jobs, but I haven't stopped anywhere for long. I've been playing guerrilla tactics with the hellhounds from the beach ever since. I figured at some point, they would get me and save me the trouble of going back for the Inquest, but until then, I'll get as many as I can."

Her look softened, if only slightly. "I'm sorry," she said with a hint of empathy.

I felt the energy in the truck lessen. She had lifted a protection ward. Had I had done anything she didn't like, I would never have known. I would have just ceased to exist.

We continued the drive for a while, chatting about nothing. "So what is the deal with Dorian?" She slipped in the question.

The question had few answers. Anytime I'd asked, Dorian would skirt around the question. Nicomedes had done the same. "You know, some called Dorian the Wanderer. In the time I was with him, he met with a lot of people. If I had to guess, he is part Divine. The relationship he has with Nicky is odd. Nicky comes and goes a lot. I really can't tell you what either one of them is. All I know is they seem to be on tap when the odd things start to happen."

Drea looked over at me with greater concern. "Do you think they survived?"

I knew Dorian had a special relationship with Priscilla. How special was up for debate. I shook my head. "I don't know. Dorian and Nicky seem like they would be hard to kill. The rest of the people we were with... who knows? They worked with some advanced tech and tactics. When the hellhounds hit us, we were working with a tactical team led by Homeland Security under something called the Longbow Initiative."

She nodded. "I think they've visited with Priscilla a few times. I've only met their guy in charge… Wynn, I think? Dorian came with him a few times. A couple of times, he came alone. Last time was six months ago. Self-righteous bastards, but they seem okay as long as we aren't in their way."

Interesting. Girard Wynn had been the agent in charge for the Were hunt and had apparently survived. Maybe some of the others had as well. He was tough, but good to work with and had let me work with his team. We had traveled with them for months.

"So, what have you been up to?" I asked.

A slim grin greeted me in return. "Not yet. You have a lot of making up to do." About that time, we passed the city limits sign for Long Beach. She smiled. "Home, sweet home."

WE CRUISED UP Ocean Boulevard until we came to a block of houses that had been converted into storefronts. Drea pulled into a garage large enough for a fleet of trucks. After we parked, she closed the bay door behind us with a remote. She climbed out of the truck and slipped the Beretta back into place in her holster. "Come on, we'll go to my place and clean you up first. You look and smell like hellhounds used you for a chew toy. Let's see if there's any chance I can make you presentable."

I climbed out of the truck and onto the trailer and took my travel pack off my bike. "If you're nice, I'll let you hose me off."

52

"You wouldn't be so lucky," she said with an amused wave. I followed her out of the garage and up the block, and we stopped in front of a two-story house. A crack ran through the painted name on the glass door advertising "Pac-O-Tees."

A handful of customers ignored us as we entered. Drea was leading me through the store when a squeal rang out. "Hey, Drea—picking up strays again?" Then, one hundred twenty pounds of teenager tackled me with a hug.

I returned the squeeze and set the girl on her feet. I was a foot taller than she was. She looked a lot like Drea except she had a blue streak in her blond hair, a multicolored miniskirt, and a T-shirt emblazoned with a wooden stake and "Vampires don't sparkle" across the front.

I laughed. "Hi, Onyx. God, you've grown."

Drea grabbed my jacket and pulled me along with a grunt. "You aren't cleared for fraternizing yet. Hands off until Priscilla says so."

"You two have a good time," Onyx yelled.

It was quite clear I was not going to be in good graces until—or if—Priscilla gave approval. It appeared as though I'd passed the first test with Drea, but likely not the last. I had no doubts about my fate if I was found unworthy. She had little patience for anyone she felt had betrayed her.

Drea led me up the stairs into a living room on the second floor. The décor was West Coast beach house, decorated in blues and greens with a few pictures on the walls. A mural of ancient Greece and the Mediterranean covered one wall. The large picture window at the front of the house had a great view of the dunes and the ocean.

"How long until the store closes?" I asked.

Drea stretched out on the loveseat in the corner. "Another hour or so to let the party crowd wrap up." I glanced at the clock and saw the time was eleven. "The shower is in there, and you can sleep in the spare room. We'll go see Priscilla in the morning."

I wanted to believe this was a positive sign, but it was just as likely that this was quarantine and observation. Or maybe I would be swept out and banished to the netherworld. I was too tired and sore to care, and I needed a hot shower.

The layers of my clothing stuck to me as I peeled them away from my body in the spacious bathroom. Between the heat, a drive through the desert, and my evening workout, I was sticky, ripe, and more than a little bloody. At least not all of it was mine. The fact that Drea had only cracked the window with the two of us in her truck was a sure sign of fortitude. I looked at my arm where the hound had bitten me. The skin wasn't broken, but a nice black-and-blue collar wrapped around my arm. One of the first things we'd learned as kids was how to protect ourselves until it had become a reflex. In the last few years, that ability had gotten a lot of live workouts. It wouldn't stop a bullet, but it certainly made a difference.

My leg was another matter. Scar had managed to get through the leather and Kevlar of the pants. Black tendrils ran along my blood vessels from a piece of tooth buried in my leg. I opened my kit and used a pair of forceps to pull out the tooth. It hurt, but nowhere near as badly as when I poured on holy water to rinse it out and packed it with healing herbs. A sharp cry escaped me as the malevolent infection was burned out of my system.

Drea kicked in the door with her gun drawn then looked at me. "Oh." She bent over and examined the wound. The tendrils were evaporating, emitting a stench of sulfur. She dabbed on another round of holy water and shoved me toward the shower. "I'll bandage it up when you get out."

The scalding water pulled the ache from my muscles and scrubbed off the coagulated gore and residual energies from the day. My last really good hot shower had been weeks ago. Even the hotel in Vegas had been just lukewarm. I relaxed as stress and pain washed from me and down the drain. Standing under running water was one of the purest forms of meditation and cleansing for me. When I got out, I dressed in a pair of shorts and a T-shirt.

When I emerged from the bathroom, I saw that Onyx was sitting with her sister on the couch. They both laughed at me as I staggered out of the bathroom. Drea critiqued my ensemble. "I would change shirts before tomorrow."

I had grabbed a T-shirt off the top of my bag. I looked down to see what I wore. It was Cookie Monster wearing a Darth Vader helmet. Underneath, it read, "Come to the dark side. We have cookies."

"Nice to see you're still on the dork side," Onyx piped up. I had to love family even if they weren't blood-related.

Having grown up in the Librarium Occultus, I had read and seen items most people believed were mythological in addition to those people hadn't even known existed. I had a penchant for places where I sometimes got to see how mythologies changed. Sci-fi was packed with lore, both good and bad, but all of it was fun. I had to take the small pleasures where I could get them. I loved seeing how my world retold and interpreted the oldest of myths. How could a wizard not be a little bit of a nerd?

Drea pushed me into a chair. "Let me see the leg." She had mixed up some goop and began to spread it liberally on my arm and leg wounds. She stitched up my leg then wrapped both in bandages. "You'll live, or at least *this* won't be what kills you." She didn't seem to have a lot of remorse for having poked me in a hellhound bite.

Onyx handed me a sandwich and a beer. I loved that girl. Sadly enough, this was working out to be the best day I'd had in months. After I demolished the sandwich and beer, Drea pointed me to a sparse bedroom. "Sleep well. You need to be rested for our trip in the morning."

Just as I fell asleep, I sensed the field she had raised around the room and the house. I wasn't planning on going anywhere anyway.

I FELL INTO a familiar dream.

I was eight or nine, going through the exercises of all young students. I laboriously drew a circle on the ground around me and Pushed my Will into it. A small cyclone formed around me inside the field, lifting me off the ground, and I slowly began to twist in the wind. With another Push of Will, a small energy ball manifested, and I used all of my focus to levitate it between my hands. For wizards, that exercise had been the equivalent of stretching before starting a workout. Since I had been several years old when we had moved to the village, I'd gotten a late start compared to most of the kids, so I was always trying to practice.

A fireball flew from the woods and evaporated against my circle. Two shadows flew from the woods and began to stalk me. I tried to focus on them when a boulder flew from the woods straight at me. My concentration broke, and I fell to the ground from the whirlwind, breaking the field. My shield fell, and the rock flew over my head. I jumped up and ran, hurling energy balls behind me. Then I saw what threw the boulder: a six-foot troll.

I picked the shortest trail home through the woods and ran as fast as my small legs would carry me. It was at least another mile to the village, and I knew I wasn't going to make it. An energy ball flew past my shoulder, and I tripped over a log on the trail.

The two shadows stopped in front of me, and the troll stomped up behind them with a grin.

"Tag," bellowed the troll.

The two shadows materialized into the Watson twins. "Ms. Romero thought you needed a little spice in your workout," Elwyn gleefully declared.

The troll shifted back into her human form of Emma Wright.

Brighid Sinclair, my first crush, tousled my hair as she strolled by, coming up from behind. "Better luck next time." With a kiss on my cheek, she ran off into the woods with the rest of my childhood friends.

I climbed to my feet and brushed myself off. Looking around, I realized I was alone in the Great Hall. I stood there naked. A short sword lay nearby on the floor. My small hand grasped and swung it in time to swat away the dagger thrown at my head. Reflexively, I jumped to the right, toward the nearest wall. A huge Viking Berserker dropped from the rafters, covered in furs and armor. All I could focus on was the huge broadsword and shield he held. My slaps at the shield with my sword bounced off harmlessly, and I rolled to the left, ducking under his whistling blade. I dove forward into a roll and jumped to my feet. With a thought, I manifested a small shield.

The Viking was big and slow to turn and face me. His lack of speed gave me an opening to slice at his calf. My reward was a grunt and a backhand from his shield that sent me flying across the floor. With a shimmer, Sven Jürgen shrugged out of the heavy gear, setting the sword and shield onto a table. Walking over, he reached out his huge hand to help me up. His face was stern. "You have improved, but you can do much better. I know you can. You have all of the tools you need, yet you sit there in your skin. We will try again tomorrow." I watched his hulking figure walk out of the doors of the Great Hall into the sunlight.

The sunlight grew into a glow, and when it faded, I stood in the middle of the annual May Day festival. Brighid stood before me; it must have been the year we were thirteen. Her flaming red hair blew in the breeze. With a look of impatience only a teenage girl could muster, she looked at me and said, "Well." It wasn't a question.

"Well?" I asked.

She melodramatically rolled her eyes. "Are we going to dance or what?"

Her hand was warm in mine, and we dove in with the rest of the group, spinning, turning, and laughing in time with the music. That is, until a meaty hand grabbed the back of my shirt and hurled me outside the ring. I jumped up into the face of Brun. Okay, I came to his belt buckle until he lifted me to his face. "Me brother wishes to dance with your date."

Brighid had sadness in her eyes as she looked back at me while Hans led her to the dance circle. She shrugged and blew me a kiss. I kicked Brun in the shin, causing him to drop me. Expecting to be hit, I rolled to the left and stood again, this time in the forest.

Cries of panic echoed through the woods. Loud crashes were approaching me rapidly. Four people from my village ran through the field and passed me, crying, "Run! Run!"

Before I could move, a huge boar burst onto the trail and ran at me. Without thought, I pelted the boar with energy balls to get its attention and keep it from chasing after the others. It worked too well. The angry and injured boar charged at me. I unleashed a fireball with all my strength and flash-fried the boar where it stood. Behind me, Sven walked out of the woods. He roared with laughter. "So much for slow-roasting. Nice fireball, though." He leaned over to check the boar, and when he stood up, night had fallen.

When he turned around, it was Dorian, not Sven. And where the boar had been, a member from the hunting party lay. He had been split from head to waist down the middle. Little detail was visible in the moonlight. Snippets of the conversation floated back to me. "We need to take the boy back. It's too risky having him here."

Another voice piped in. "Breaking up the party? We're too few already. The boy comes with us."

"No, he needs to be in the protection of the village," Dorian commanded. "Have Cedric take a few men to escort him back, and then bring reinforcements. We know where they have them all. There isn't much time."

I felt myself being whisked along through the forest. Cedric led the way, but I wasn't sure who the other three around me were. We hadn't gotten far when Cedric fell to the ground, an arrow through his side. The guard to my right lost his head in the flash of an axe. Darkness wrapped itself around me like a blanket. When the darkness lifted, I was bound to an altar by energies I couldn't see with normal eyes. My Sight revealed black cords circulating around my body. Others waited in the shadows, chained to walls with the same black cords.

Gray stone walls circled the chamber, which felt familiar. The door at the end of the room dissolved into a white light. My father rushed through the doorway with Dorian at his side and others streaming in behind. "Right on time," the voice behind me whispered.

"No. Go back!" I heard myself scream. An energy burst from around me in a brilliant flash of golden light.

When the flash cleared, I stood naked in a small stone chamber. A wooden drawbridge was open behind me, and a larger pair of doors was closed in front of me. The doors were held fast by a giant padlock. Looking out of the open drawbridge, I saw rolling hills spread to the horizon into the low-hanging light of the sun. I couldn't tell if it was dawn or dusk. With a Push of Will, I clothed myself in a pair of jeans and a tunic.

Semi-lucidly, I realized this part of the dream was new. Until now, the dream had had different elements of my time growing up, but it had always ended the same—with a blinding flash, and I would wake up in a cold sweat.

With a Push of Will, my Sight exposed a room bathed in a myriad of colors. A large pair of solid wooden doors, reinforced with black iron bars, dominated the far end of the chamber. The large lock was fortified with buttresses that glowed a deep blue. I could sense something was pushing against the doors to escape. I moved closer to study the tendrils of energy running around the edges of the door past me and flowed out of the drawbridge to the outside. A woman's gentle but commanding voice called to me from the doorway outside. "Greetings, Greyson."

I spun around, and even with my Sight, little was revealed to me beyond a gray cloak and veil. "Hello."

The figure stepped closer. "We have little time now, but we will chat again soon. Your time is coming. Trials within trials. Choices to be made."

"And you are who? What?" It was becoming clear that this was much more than a dream.

The figure glided closer to stand beside me. "There is not time for that now. I do apologize as this may hurt a bit, but I have a gift for you."

Before I could ask any questions or say anything in protest, the figure drew a small sigil on the double doors then placed her hand on my chest. As the figure faded, a stream of light shot from the door and landed where she had touched me.

My chest was on fire, and I bolted upright in bed, screaming. Drea had been holding a washcloth to my forehead. She leapt back and stood a safe distance away, calmly palming a silver blade behind her. "Grey, what the hell?" she panted.

The pain in my chest gradually faded. A gaunt reflection stared back at me from the mirror at the end of the bed, and the sigil on my chest was fading from a bright yellow glow to a faded red patch. The symbol was unfamiliar to me.

Drea sheathed the knife and sat me up on the bed. She traced the sigil with her fingers. "You were thrashing and moaning. I came in, and you were burning up. I couldn't wake you. Are you okay?"

"She said it was a gift," I croaked.

She looked at me with concern. "She who? What gift?"

No explanations came to mind. I was as lost as Drea, if not more so. Once we had both calmed down, she asked, "Can you return it? That's really not your look." The edges of a smile formed as she decided the potential crisis had ended. She handed me a glass of water.

I gulped down the whole glass. Drea listened intently as I went through the details of the dream.

The concern returned to her face. "So, a woman dressed in a gray cloak and veils. And she didn't ask you for anything. She just made statements. Did you eat anything, drink anything, agree to anything?"

"No," I said. "Any idea what's going on?"

Drea stood. "Get dressed. It will soon be time to see Priscilla." With a nervous smile, she walked out of the room and closed the door behind her.

I DRESSED QUICKLY after inspecting my assorted injuries. The bruise on my arm was fading rapidly. I changed the bandage on my leg and was surprised to see a small scab around the stitches and a fading bruise. Even for me, this was healing quickly. I downed another of the healing potions. They tasted horrific, but if a person got hurt often enough, he learned to accept certain tradeoffs. I expected to be fully healed by the end of the day.

Since I was to see Priscilla, I opted to dress in something a little more formal. I pulled on a white button-down shirt and wrapped my kilt around me. Most of my community was originally from the old Celtic lands, and Priscilla stood a lot on tradition. Steel-toed boots slipped snugly over the kilt hose. I strapped three daggers to my left leg, just above the bite—one silver, one cold steel, and one ceramic. To my right leg, I strapped my silver-plated combat knife. The kilt covered both quite effectively. I fastened my dress sporran and belt. The shoulder holster for my Colt 1911 hit a sore spot. I felt a twinge of pain when I checked to make sure the Colt was fully loaded and examined the two spare magazines. A light jacket covered my firearm and gave me a spare pocket for my other implements.

Onyx greeted me as I opened the bedroom door and handed me breakfast. I greedily grabbed the juice and breakfast sandwich she offered.

She rolled her eyes as she appraised my selected wardrobe. "Nice legs. It's a good thing you won't stand out at all on the beach. Eat up. I'm taking you to Priscilla. Drea has already headed up there."

The time had come to find out what game was being played, and it could go either way. Drea had left me in the care of Onyx. My Sight showed that Onyx was happier than the night before, and no major power brewed around the house. The wards were still in place. With my Senses stretched as far as I dared, I found that everything was quiet.

Onyx had a short lead on me. Almost as if reading my mind, she chirped, "No ambush down here, so get a move on. I need to be back to open up the shop shortly."

Every storefront along the block displayed a sticker with a stylized winking owl—Priscilla's logo. Onyx noticed my interest. "Priscilla owns almost everything for five square blocks."

"What?" Just the value of the real estate alone was more than a fortune. The extent of her empire was becoming evident. "How did she pull that off?"

Onyx gave me a kiss on the cheek. "Ask her yourself. We're here. See you later." She pushed me toward the door and sauntered back up the street to the shop.

An elegant sign painted on the door read, "Calypso Enterprises." The door opened into a small receiving parlor. The décor was straight from a bordello in the Victorian era. Red velvet wallpaper covered the walls, and delicate porcelain lamps sat on end tables. An uncomfortable-looking settee was pushed against the wall.

A young woman I did not recognize greeted me and led me into a larger version of the receiving room. An ornate desk sat in one corner, and chairs circled a round office table in the other. She motioned for me to sit in one of the seats across from the desk then passed through a doorway to a back room.

Left to my own devices, I snooped around for a few minutes. My Sight showed a number of sigils glowing in the walls, protection and privacy mostly. The presence of the entourage filled the room long before their arrival. Tendrils of power swept in, feeling every corner of the room and frisking me like an expert bouncer would. Priscilla strode through the door with Drea and three others behind her. My judge, jury, and possible executioner flowed through the door with the presence of a coiled snake, ready to strike.

Priscilla had not changed in the four years since I'd seen her. To my knowledge, she was at least two hundred years old. Even so, she looked to be in her mid-thirties. She was tall and thin with raven hair and penetrating gray eyes. Her emerald executive suit and matching high heels exuded a presence of being in absolute command.

Priscilla looked me over, front and back, as I stood for inspection. She grabbed my hands and looked into my eyes. Her penetrating gray gaze dove deep into my soul. I couldn't move and could barely breathe. I felt her pull back. I had been through it all before, but it never got any less disturbing.

Finally, she stepped back from me and smiled widely, winking at Drea. "Welcome home, Greyson," she said in her unique, obscure accent.

Drea and the other ladies visibly breathed a sigh of relief as Priscilla used my name. Given names held power for those who knew how to use them. I had seen hints of what she could do to people just by speaking their names.

"Come, let us be comfortable." Priscilla led the way through the door. The décor progressed centuries as we moved into the next room. Although the front of the house had been an 1800s motif, this room was a bleeding-edge, open, modern office.

An assistant directed me to an overstuffed leather chair. Drea crossed her legs on a loveseat by the window, and the rest of the women disappeared. One of the Daughters entered, placed a tea set on the table, then left. Priscilla flowed through a side room and returned, dressed in a green silk blouse, skin-tight white riding pants, and black thigh-high boots, with a golden sash around her waist. She sat in the overstuffed chair to my left and began to pour tea.

I greeted Priscilla with as much of a smile as I could muster. "I see you're well and settling into the retired life?"

Drea snickered.

Priscilla handed me a cup of hot tea. "Yes, if you can consider this little enterprise 'retirement.' It provides for the family, and we are safe within these borders. It's not quite as protected as your home village, but few places are. It was time to integrate with the modern world. I provide my services for corporations, executives, and politicians now, and I needed a bit more of a legitimate front. Gone are the old days." A small note of nostalgia crept into her voice.

My time with her 'family' had left me few questions as to what those services included. Even if she had gone mostly legitimate, the Daughters of Priscilla could still walk a fine line with the law and deliver where most others could only dream.

"So, I'm assuming this came from you?" I held up the FaeMail and unrolled the scroll, laying it next to the tea set before taking my cup.

Priscilla wore a patient face. "You were always quick to the point. Yes, I sent you the package to see if you still had it in you. You are one of the best trackers I've ever seen. And with your other skills, none of my daughters can do what needs to be done as well as you."

"And what is it that needs to be done, exactly?"

"I believe our client will be better able to tell you directly," she said.

Drea opened a side door. A middle-aged executive type walked in with his blond trophy wife, two teenage daughters, and young son. They all found seats.

Priscilla and I stood as she introduced me. "Grey, this is Mr. Evan Underhill, his wife Anya, daughters Emma and Fawn, and little Evan. Their daughter Claire and niece Abbie are missing. Mr. Underhill is one of my dearest associates and clients and has asked me for help, as law enforcement has been unable to do anything. Drea took a team and found few leads. I'm hoping that you can help them, Greyson."

Missing kids. If Priscilla had gone this far to get my assistance, then she had to be desperate. Plus, if her own people were not making headway, finding the girls wouldn't be simple.

A quick appraisal of Underhill told me he was accustomed to getting his way—quickly. He was a tall, strong man, slightly graying at the temples, and very fit. Being powerless was something he did not handle well, and it showed in his slumped shoulders and the deep bags under his eyes.

"Mr. Underhill, what can you tell me?" I asked.

Underhill robotically launched into a narrative he'd obviously given several times before. "Claire is just short of turning sixteen. Her birthday is a few days away. She and her cousin, Abbie, were shopping. Robert, their driver and bodyguard, dropped them at some store in Santa Monica to buy decorations for her party."

One of the girls—Emma, I thought—added, "Bella's," as if the store were the most important place on the planet. I figured it was one of the teen temples of the arts district.

Underhill cleared his throat. "Yes, Bella's." From the tone in his voice, he did not hold the place in high regard. "After the girls had been in the store a while, Robert walked in to check on them. A clerk told him they had left a few minutes earlier. Robert rounded the corner to find a pile of packages, and the girls were gone. Police got video of a van and a couple of masked men grabbing the girls and speeding off. Robert couldn't have missed them but by a minute or so. Police said they found the van a couple of miles away. It had been stolen and was thoroughly engulfed in flames when they found it an hour or so after the abduction. We haven't seen or heard anything since. No ransom, nothing. A homeland agent visited us that night, and he's had a command post running from our house since."

A sinking feeling quickly became a mental free-fall. I braced myself and turned my Sight to the family. With a little work, my Sight could tell if family members or close associates were near or far, dead or alive, by the tendrils of energy that ran between them. Living things built bonds as they interacted. Most were tenuous and only lasted a few minutes after parting. With close family and friends, and sometimes enemies, those bonds were almost always permanent, unless cut by extreme emotion or some divine or magical act. On first look at the Underhill family, my perceptions were fuzzy. It took me a little time, but the tendrils between the family and Claire came into focus.

A strong and unusual energy permeated each of them individually and flowed between them. Anya appeared to be in a heavy stupor, and it occurred to me she may have been sedated. It took thirty seconds before I finally recognized it as a weird shield or glamour over the family. Wading through the glamour was almost like swimming in molasses. I had never encountered one so strong or detailed. The smallest of flaws drew my attention and then, ugh, I realized what they were. Fairies.

I SIGNED ON to help them. They didn't seem to know much more, and I made a promise to visit their home shortly to continue the investigation. Underhill and his cavalcade of mayhem headed home. It wasn't that I disliked the Fae, fairy folk, Sidhe, Cacophony of Chaos, or whatever you wanted to call them. Most of my childhood was spent with the Fae. A large part of the reason my home in Phoenix Grove existed was as a sanctuary for peoples of the Veiled world. The problem was just that dealing with fairies was never as straightforward as it seemed.

To make the job more interesting, what I had seen with Underhill and his family was confusing to me. Usually, the Fae and other shape-shifters presented themselves in a human physical form. With my Sight, I could see their true forms, like an aura or shadow or overlay on top of the taken form. Others could not, or would not, physically change their forms and used an elaborate glamour instead to make people see them a certain way. Regardless, the Fae and other beings of the Veil masked themselves in some way and did as they liked. Underhill looked as though his form had been shoved rather uncomfortably into a shell or a meat suit. I was also unclear as to which clan they belonged to or even what type of Fae they were.

It was apparent enough, though, that they weren't Unseelie, the more malevolent and destructive side of the Fae. The Underhill clan felt more like Seelie, who are more impish and manic. I felt as if they might have belonged to the Summer or Woodland Fae, but too much was hidden to be certain. But no matter what, when I played with Fae, I got burned.

Priscilla sat across from me and watched me process the encounter. "So what do you think?" she asked.

Thoughts and questions flooded forward. "Who are they? Do they even know?"

Priscilla leaned back in her seat. "Evan owns Underhill Productions and a few other interests. Anya owns a modeling and talent agency in Los Angeles. They represent some of the finest talent in town."

Of course they were from LA. A louder-than-planned sigh escaped my lips. "You know that's not what I meant. I got a look under some of the packaging."

Priscilla gave the thin smile of a proud parent, not wanting to look too enthusiastic. Drea appeared confused. "What are you talking about?"

Priscilla smiled slyly. "They are Fae. And no, they consciously don't know who or what they are. They are all from the House of Samhradh and are in hiding."

Drea's eyes grew wide, and bile bubbled in my throat. This had to be a violation of the Accords.

Priscilla continued, "Evan and Anya brought Claire here when they came through. Abbie is a cousin. The others are Evan and Anya's children, born here. They're on a hit list after the change in power from the Summer Court years back. I owed them a favor, and

I returned it in such a way that they would be hidden. In essence, they're asleep."

She paused. "Be sure, for their own safety, they cannot find out what they are. They cannot be exposed or awakened. You must find those girls and get them home safe."

"And what if we can't?" My hands clenched as I asked.

Priscilla appeared shaken at the thought. "We cannot allow that to transpire."

Anger and frustration won out over my better judgment. "You know the trials I'm facing soon. And now you want me tied up in a fairy war? You know how the Accords are written. The two don't mix. Divines and Veiled. I'm a low-grade wizard with a hell's bounty on my head, and I don't know why. The Inquest—"

Priscilla lost all of her humor and grew stone-faced. "I know all about the Inquest and how this may play out. I know the Accords much better than you. But you're a member of this family, and you have a debt to me. I'm collecting. And if you remember, you just agreed and are bound to help them. Besides, it seems to me that having a debt to you from the Fae world would be to your benefit."

Her look told me that the conversation was closed. She knew more, but wouldn't be sharing. "Okay, Priscilla, I'll play for now."

Her smile chilled me. "Two things. Andrea, please take him by the locker. He's still carrying that old 1911."

I supposed Priscilla's aural pat-down had revealed that. Drea looked downright giddy with anticipation.

Priscilla studied me intently. "Secondly, I hear you had a rough night, and you woke up with a mark. Tell me of the encounter."

Suppressing the irritation building in me, I threw myself into a chair. The short version would probably get me out of there faster and on the hunt. "I was in a dream, in what looked like the entryway of a stone castle. The drawbridge to the outside opened to rolling green fields. A large set of wooden double doors were heavily locked, reinforced, and buttressed. I could see something shimmering around the doors. It looked like energy ribbons. A woman in a gray cloak and veil said she was giving me a gift, touched my chest, and it began to burn intensely. I woke up screaming with a glowing mark on my chest."

Priscilla tilted her head slightly and narrowed her eyes. "I wish to see it."

I removed my jacket and opened my shirt. Priscilla moved forward to touch the mark. Tendrils from her aura reached my chest first, tracing and probing. Her fingers traced the outline of the mark on my chest, and her touch sent shivers through my entire body. My Sight trembled when it flared up to her touch.

Priscilla backed off and sat down behind her desk. "Interesting. It seems somewhat familiar but not exactly like any sigil I've seen before. It's powerful. You have been marked, my one and only son." She bowed her head and made a few notes. "I will look into this for you. Now, please go find those children. And quickly."

Priscilla's voice carried the weight of the situation. It told me two things. First, there was much more at stake than she had not-so-subtly hinted. Second, somehow my fate was tied to how this played out.

Drea touched my hand. "Let's go."

WE JOGGED BACK to the garage. I was surprised to see the Blue Bomb, the little travel trailer I pulled behind my bike. Really, it was just a long cylinder on wheels. "How did you find the Bomb?"

One of the Daughters stood up from under the hood of a blue Chevy. She was tall and strong. Her long auburn hair was pulled back into a ponytail, and she filled out the dirty coveralls nicely. "Bomb? I towed in a bomb?" She looked as though I'd just told her she'd invited the starving wolf into the henhouse.

Drea motioned at her. "It's fine. That's the nickname for the piece of junk he likes to haul around." Drea turned to me. "Isn't that right?" Her tone told me I was an idiot.

Priscilla's personal grease monkey trotted over and extended a hand. "Hi. I'm Kizzy. Nice knees."

I took Kizzy's outstretched hand. "Grey. I'm pleased to meet another Daughter."

Kizzy asked, "How do I get into your toy box over there for an inspection? It hums like Las Vegas at night."

Okay, now I had to laugh. "Are you saying you couldn't open a simple lock?" I walked over and flipped the two latches that held it closed.

"Wizards and their enchantments," Drea told Kizzy. I could feel them both roll their eyes behind me.

Kizzy rifled through the weapons, clothes, and miscellaneous gear. "Okay, it can stay. I'm tuning your bike while I have it here. You must be hard on the poor thing. But it's a beautiful machine. I've always wanted to work on one."

I took out a small, beaten leather satchel containing the tools of my trade and locked the Bomb back up. I handed Kizzy a charm that would allow her to unlock it again. The thought of leaving my Indian with her was daunting, but looking at the dozens of high-performance machines in her care, I figured it was all right if she gave me a tune-up.

I looped the pack over my shoulder. "Okay, let's go."

Drea slid behind the wheel of a black BMW. She directed me to the passenger side, and we rolled out onto Ocean Boulevard toward LA. *Oh, joy.* After some time, she finally took my hand. "It's good to have you back with us. We missed you."

"I've missed you, too." That statement was truer than I'd thought. I had been gone longer than I had lived with them, but I'd felt as though I had a home. Being the only male of the bunch meant I'd received a lot of attention from big sisters, doting aunts, and the occasional wicked stepmother. More than a few had been torn between chasing me and their fear of Priscilla. Fear had always won out.

"So, Fae?" Drea asked. "I thought they were small and flitted around, causing trouble. And Divines? I'm lost."

My internal debated churned as I thought of how to describe it all. "Supernatural world, 101. There are what have long been referred to as Divines—Angels, Demons, some demigods, and some of the creatures made of their realms. They're technically in our natural order but supposedly have some direct connection to the energy of the creator, the ultimate energy of the universe. They're usually immortal but can die. They tend to make their homes in the dimensions but at the far ends of the spectrum. Some have taken up residence in the middle realms."

Drea nodded for me to continue.

"Then we have the Veiled, or supernatural beings. The Fae folks, Wizards, Magicians, Vamps and Weres. They're part of the created, natural world, but they have some abilities beyond what the human world considers normal because they can open to and use the energy of the universe. Usually mortal, they can have very long life spans and tend to reside in the middle realms.

"In between is the narrow view that humanity sees as the real world. Mortal humans basically stay in a thin realm, one dimension in the middle of all these layers. And everyone passes through this plane at some point in time. Mortal humans are sometimes referred to as the 'Asleep' because of the Accords. Most of humanity voluntarily elected to ignore what goes on around them, at least consciously, and in return, they're mostly protected."

Drea stopped me with an evil grin. "So, vamps really don't sparkle, do they? I've never seen one."

I shook my head. I had expected her to know better. "Number one, in LA, you have definitely seen a vamp. And the only way they sparkle is to roll them in phosphorous before you throw them into the sunlight… I recommend at noon."

I continued. "For the most part, the Divine run along traditional lines—Angels, Fallen; Heaven, Hell. They operate in realms that are extremely dangerous and difficult, if not impossible, to reach and survive as a mortal.

"The Veiled realms are a bit different. A few of them are right here next to us, just tuned a little differently. For those of us who learn it, the Sight and the Sense allow us to tap in, at least to some extent. Most of their realms are different. Some of them seem like other planets. Others operate on their own different physics, as if it were another dimension or universe. My home in Phoenix Grove sits in a dimensional pocket and is Veiled if you don't have access and know how to get there.

"Among the Divine and Veiled, they're like anyone else. Some are really good, some really bad, and most are just looking to be entertained throughout the day. For the most part, the idea of the supernatural is mislabeling. It's more like the block of the universe that humans blindly insist can't exist," I said.

"And how about you?" she asked. "I know you're some sort of magician, but—"

I interrupted. "Wizard. Magicians do stage stuff. And as for me, I'm mostly a locator. I think I had other... skills. Now I can only do some basic defense when I'm under threat, but I can find almost anything or anyone." *Anyone except someone who can tell me what really happened all those years ago.*

Drea seemed to be processing it all as we drove. "How do you know all of this?"

"Mostly from old texts, teachers. A lot of it is postulation from evidence gathered over the years. Some things I've seen for myself. The pieces seem to make sense. But I would have thought you would have known most of this, if not more." The feeling that I had been played became stronger when Drea gave me a thin smile.

She gave me a non-answer. "Just a different perspective, that's all."

I debated whether or not to bring up Priscilla, to try to determine what she might be, but decided it was not the time when Drea pointed out our destination coming up. We passed Exposition Park and pulled up to a small office building. As we entered the building, Drea flashed her ID badge at the guard booth. A medium-sized but fit woman in a nondescript guard's uniform slipped a badge to me. "Mr. Forrester, your ID." The picture had been discreetly taken from Priscilla's office.

"Thanks." I clipped the badge on.

Drea swiped her badge in a reader in the elevator, and we started down instead of up. The doors opened into a small, bright-white reception area. Drea swiped her badge again and slid through the clear glass turnstile. She waved me on, and as I entered the gate, I realized there was plenty of room to seal the entryway in the event of a security breach. Another guard in a booth to the left nodded as we walked through. She sat behind thick panes of bullet-resistant glass.

We continued into a long, bright corridor and passed several doors until we finally turned left into a locker room. Twenty lockers lined the walls, each about three feet wide and secured with a code lock and ID reader. Locker one was Priscilla's. Locker two was Lala's, Drea's mother. I wondered where she was. Locker three was Drea's, and locker four was labeled as mine.

She opened her locker. "Your code is 0328," she said from behind the locker door.

Her birthday. Cute. My locker held seven identical, charcoal-gray tactical suits and matching boots. Four helmets hung in the back. Two pre-packed bug-out bags of the same material were racked in the bottom.

She closed her locker door. She'd changed into a skin-tight tactical suit, similar to the ones in my locker. "Get changed," she said.

"Um, are we going out in public like that? Are we raiding the Underhill home? I like my kilt. I'm good."

Drea rolled her eyes at me then waved a hand. Suddenly, she was wearing a schoolgirl outfit, including a way-too-short kilt of my tartan. I was pretty sure my eyes bounced out of my head, and my jaw hit the floor. Yes, I had all of the suave machismo of James Bond.

She laughed, waved her hand again with a curtsy, and shifted into in a charcoal-gray business suit, cream blouse, and high heels. "Better?"

"Uh, for what?" I stammered. I was still visualizing schoolgirl Drea.

She stepped into a drill instructor pose. "My turn for class. These are enchanted tactical Leviskin skinsuits. They're stealth, provide full mobility, and are high-quality body armor. They also take on the energy of any glamour you want to throw and take on the full physical characteristics of that glamour as well. Now get dressed. You can put the kilt back on if you insist, or you can just Push the idea in the suit."

The Leviskin felt almost like soft leather, but was the weight of silk. It fit like a second skin. A small charge rippled across my body. I felt as if a thousand ants were crawling around my feet as the boots made subtle adjustments. In just over a second, the sensation subsided, and the boots fit perfectly.

The bug-out bag had a standard kit on one side: medical supplies, evidence kits, and basic field-gear-filled pouches. The right side was customized for me with a pack of chalk; two sets of dowsing rods; various crystals; and individually labeled packages of roots, herbs, and minerals, each dated. None were more than a week old. Weapons consisted of ten silver throwing knives, ten cold steel and ten ceramic blades. There were also several boxes of ammunition and spare magazines for my 1911.

Drea grinned smugly when I asked, "How long have you been expecting me?" No way was this all pulled together for me in a day.

"We set this place up twenty-eight months ago," she answered. "I'm the only one with your code, and I have kept your bags supplied with fresh materials. Let's head to the toy box."

I followed Drea with the bag in hand, now stuffed with my blades, Colt, and holster. My clothes were stashed in the locker. Our next stop was at the end of the hall where she swiped her badge. The doors opened into an armory that would have made a Klingon cry.

A tall, strong blonde rose from behind a well-lit workbench, where she was working on a small device. She wore one of the tactical bodysuits, modified to hold her tools of trade. Drea smiled at her. "Hi, Mel. Meet Grey. Grey, Melanippe."

Mel came around the workbench and looked me over. "Well, you have filled in well since the last time I saw you." I guessed she was one of the many that had come through when I had last been with the Daughters. "The suit fits well. I can adjust the others a hair to make them perfect. Fashion by Hephaestus." She leaned over to Drea and whispered, "Too bad it's not that time of year." I had no idea what she was talking about.

Mel began pointing and grabbing, acting like the flight instructor for the skinsuit, giving a briefing before takeoff. *These flaps here are for ammunition, these slips are for throwing knives, these slips are for the combat knives. An integrated rappelling harness, clip the D-ring here. This side pocket is for cash, cards, and IDs.* "Next, I can show you how to make any changes you need to the suit, including how to make modifications for your other gear."

Then the real fun started. Mel loomed four inches taller than me, and her build was obviously much stronger. The way she moved suggested that she was no stranger to using, as well as making, the tools of the trade.

"Let's start easy," she said. "Picture your favorite outfit. Now visualize wearing it." I felt a slight vibration and an indistinct, but not unpleasant, tingling sensation. The skinsuit instantly transformed.

"Nice." Mel looked pleased. "Okay, now the suit is also designed to become armor and nearly anything else you may need. It has a couple of basic modes, but you can change them up by how you visualize them." She walked me through the light, medium, and heavy versions. "One more thing. If you put something into the skinsuit, such as a knife, you have to include a pocket or access point for it in whatever you shift to." She demonstrated by slipping a large knife into a sheath on her leg. She shifted into a miniskirt so that her leg was showing. The knife was gone. "And now…" The knife and sheath phased into view on her leg.

"It comes in handy," Drea said. "It will get you past metal detectors. There are more subtle ways of finding out what you have on your person, but with experience, you can hide almost anything you can carry."

Mel took me to the wall with the personal blades and pulled out a long drawer. "Everything in this row is yours, tailored to your preferences. In addition to your usual selections, I've included a new type of ceramic that has a small hypodermic in it, which can release any number of combinations when you plunge it in. I figure you'll like the selection: holy water, iodized silver, vaporized cold iron. I can get you almost anything for the injector. Just let me know what you need."

She guided me to the next hall, which contained racks of small arms. Some of them had tags with names on them, presumably the owners. One table held a large selection of weapons. "I know you have the Colt 1911. Of course you can make any selection you like, but can I suggest you take these as well? Ammunition and magazines are here."

She had placed a Sig Sauer 226, an MP5, and a Bernoulli Tactical twelve-gauge on the counter. A few minutes later, she returned with what looked like a long, carbon steel sword of a design I had never seen before. I drew it from the Leviskin sheath. It had a nice weight and good balance.

Mel looked pleased with herself. "And what else would you care to see?"

I wanted to see a lot of things, two of which were in Leviskins. Okay, I had to ask. There were rows of weapons from nearly every epoch, and those were just the ones I could see. As best I could tell, if it had existed or been imagined, it was in here somewhere. "How about a Bat'leth?"

Drea rolled her eyes and punched me in my aching ribs. "C'mon, junior Jedi, we need to get a move on."

Mel was so excited, she almost bounced out of her skin. "One minute."

Drea grimaced when I looked at her. "Wrong universe," I said.

"What?"

"Jedis are from Star Wars. This is Star Trek."

Drea started to respond as Mel approached, holding a pair of long curved blades affixed to a second curving spar with mahogany handles that ran its length. She held not one, but two of the fictional weapons. The finely honed blades were sharp enough to shave with.

Mel looked at me for approval. "Based on your profile, I had these made just for you." She held one forward. "This one is carbon steel with a strong silver plate." She extended the second one to me. "And this is carbon fiber with several mystical alloys running through it. It won't go dull and will slice through steel. The grips for both are made of Leviskin and will integrate with your suit."

I loved this woman. "I'll take both, no gift wrap needed." I turned toward Mel and gave her a tackling hug. She blushed.

As Drea dragged me out the door with my haul, Mel said, "I'll try to have the light saber ready for next time."

"Really? She can do that?" My shopping list was growing rapidly.

Drea groaned.

THE ROAD WOVE around the seaside cliffs as we headed for Malibu. My fumbling experimentation with the skinsuit in the car provided entertainment for the hour-long drive. Finally, I settled on slate slacks and a white shirt with a matching slate sport coat. Drea had talked me into looking somewhat professional.

We pulled up outside a gated estate. From the front, the guardhouse looked understated, but closer inspection showed that at least the front wall was hardened and fortified. Some embassies didn't have this extensive of a perimeter. It seemed a bit much for a studio exec type.

Two guards approached the car. The one in the gatehouse looked familiar. I recognized him as a pro wrestler who had made a few B movies. The one that approached the driver's side was larger and carried himself as if he had been in the military. Both wore matching black suits, white shirts, and earbuds, and carried hidden submachine guns. Based on a quick look, they both appeared to be fully human. We had a brief exchange with them before we were cleared to go to the house.

The place was impressive. The dossier from Drea showed the estate to be ten acres, with a main house of over twenty thousand square feet. Two guest "cottages" were each around five thousand square feet. The landscaping suggested they had really given up the Woodland Clan ways. Only a handful of small trees stood on the entire property. The whole place had the look and feel of a faerie tale castle in Camelot rather than a Malibu party house.

The house was entirely built of stone, including a parapet and walk that overlooked the cliff. The front of the house had a courtyard that could easily hold a couple of hundred people comfortably. A circus tent had been erected on the front lawn, likely for the sweet sixteen party.

A black semi-trailer with slide-outs was parked on the side of the house. It was an FBI Mobile Command Unit. Four matching, government-issue Suburbans were parked facing the drive, ready to go at a moment's notice. That made sense for a high-profile kidnapping.

On parking the car, we were greeted by two FBI agents, led by my old friend, the very special Agent Girard Wynn. I had barely slid out of the front seat when he greeted me. "A pleasure to see you, Mr. Forrester. May we have a chat? Alone?"

It was clearly not a request. He was speaking to me in a tone that meant he was not thrilled to see me and probably a little shocked. We had not spoken since the incident in Canada. Agent Wynn had aged a lot since the last time I'd seen him. His hair was nearly solid white with flecks of pepper, and the bags under his eyes carried all of his case files. He was only in his early forties, but looked much older.

"Anything for the FBI," I replied.

Agent Wynn led me into the command center. The small tech center housed three big screens and hummed from the hardware and the chatter of the half-dozen agents at computers. We walked past the small kitchen into the conference room. A small table took up most of the room. Agent Wynn closed the door and immediately jumped into my face. "Why are you here? I want to know what you know, and now." Gone was any pretense of friendliness. His eyes had gone stone cold.

"Gerry—" was all I managed to say.

"Call me Agent Wynn. Why are you here?"

My patience was running thin, and I was getting annoyed. "I'm here because I was asked to be. If you'll excuse me." I tried to push by Wynn, but he grabbed my arm and shoved me back into a chair.

As it looked like I would be here for a while, I decided to get comfortable. I kicked my feet up into the chair next to me, blocking the door closed. "Is there something you have to say, or are you really that unhappy to see me, Agent Wynn?"

Wynn leaned over the table. "Last time I saw you was just as we were hit by a pack of werewolves and hellhounds. You were there, and then you were gone. I lost three men. Simmons. Wilde. Keas. When it was over, your friends Nicomedes and Dorian were pretty torn up. The only reason we survived was because the hounds and Weres started tearing into each other, and we pulled back. Nicomedes wouldn't say anything about you. I assumed you were dead or in on it. Dorian was in a coma. A week or so later, they just disappeared, and I haven't heard anything from them either. So would you care to enlighten me?"

What the hell? "Agent Wynn, I am not your enemy unless you want me to be. When the Weres hit, Dorian shoved me into a portal. I saw Nicky go down as I flew backward. I landed in the middle of nowhere Montana. Haven't seen either of them since."

Wynn looked confused. "A what? Portal? Why didn't he use it to get the rest of us out when we got trapped?"

I began to understand Wynn's frustration, but it was not like I had any idea. And the accusation put me on edge. "I can't answer that. The only ones who can aren't here. They abandoned me as well," I spat back. "So back off."

"So why didn't you contact us after you escaped?" Wynn asked.

I started to yell back, but nothing came out. That question was, well, logical. Leaning back in my chair gave me time to think on it. My first instinct had been to reach out to someone local. I'd assumed the reason I was dumped there was because of the close proximity to a friend of Dorian's—the person he'd told me to reach out to if I were ever in dire need.

Dorian's friend had stashed the Indian and the Blue Bomb, along with a small cache, on a ranch nearby. It had been their back door out, only they'd tossed me through instead of using it themselves. I'd taken what I'd needed from the cache and hit the road. "Wynn, as far as I knew, everyone was dead or worse. And it isn't like your unit is conventional FBI. Who was I supposed to call? I officially barely existed, and if it turned out you were all dead, what was I supposed to say?"

Wynn sat across from me, his arms crossed, looking exhausted. He sighed and leaned back in his chair as well. The look on his face indicated he was processing the information, but I didn't know if he was believing it. "I thought you'd led us into the trap after all of the time we spent together, much of that time here in this box. Simmons treated you like a younger brother. We trusted you."

Now it was becoming clear. Wynn had believed for years that I was dead, and seeing me alive made him believe something worse. I squared my shoulders and leaned toward him. "Then trust me again. The family asked me for my help. I'm here to give it. I'm going to find the kids. You know me."

Wynn paused. "Not if I lock you up for obstruction, for your protection. Do you have any idea who you're here with?" Wynn nervously chewed on his thumb. "And do I *really* know you?"

I had no choice but to come at him honestly, and no reason not to tell him the truth. "Priscilla called me in to help the family. I've known Drea since I was a teen."

Genuine concern showed in Wynn's eyes, along with something else I didn't recognize. I did not know if it was for me or himself. "So you signed on with Calypso Enterprises." His tone gave me pause.

I sighed then took a deep breath. "No. I'm not even sure what they do entirely. I owed Priscilla a favor, and now I'm repaying that debt. I hadn't seen them in years before yesterday."

Wynn studied me from across the table. His piercing eyes, which had broken the will of many suspects, bore down on me. They betrayed his effort to come to a decision, but as to what he was trying to decide, I did not know. "You may not have spent any time with them, but they were waiting for you."

"Yeah, that occurred to me as well." What would he think if he knew about how I had been equipped with the new provisions from their toy box? What else were they preparing for? They could equip a small army.

Wynn stood. "Odd the Amazons would bring a man into their ranks." Whatever his internal deliberations had been, they had ended. "I'll be right back."

"I'll be here," I quipped. Where exactly would I go? As Wynn went out the door, his statement hit me. Amazons?

AGENT WYNN RETURNED to the conference room with some paperwork in hand. "Here's the deal. You have two options." The stack of paper hit the tabletop. "Option one, we reactivate you as a consultant. You continue to work with the Calypso team as contracted, but you report back to me on a regular basis. You get a raise in daily rate, and under no circumstances do you disclose anything about this operation or our operational practices to Calypso."

"Okay, and option two?" I asked, with a pretty good idea of what was coming.

"We place you into protective custody until this is over and we have determined if you or any of your friends had any involvement in this or any prior incidents," he said.

After a microsecond of thought, I said, "Option one it is. You were saying something about Amazons? As in warrior women?"

Wynn shook his head. "You really should have a better idea of who you're hanging out with." He handed me a file folder. "Here's the dossier. Short version. Read it at your leisure later. Let's talk about the cases now and not keep your girlfriend waiting."

"Cases?" I asked.

Wynn directed me into the Control Center. Three agents sat at the six terminals in the room, monitoring the feeds from cameras around the property and current intelligence reports. The displays were mirrored on large-screen displays on both walls.

A spread of portfolios was displayed on the main screen—six missing girls, including Claire and Abbie. Wynn started his briefing. "They all disappeared within a couple of blocks of the same area. All wealthy. Six have gone missing in three incidents, always two at a time. No ransoms, no bodies, no signs. Any backpacks, handbags, or packages are dumped at the site. The only footage we have shows a hooded team of four throwing them into a nondescript stolen vehicle. Vehicle is found a short time later within a few miles and is burned to the frame."

"Do you have personal objects from them?" I asked.

Wynn pointed to six evidence bags. "Do your hoodoo."

The tension of the interrogation faded, and it soon felt more like old times. Wynn leaned back on one of the consoles while he silently observed me. Only one other agent was left in the room, and he paid no attention, looking as though he were impersonating a turtle, pulled into his tech shell.

I started with the first bag of evidence and did not bother to look at the name. The energy from the hairbrush, iPhone, and keys pulled my attention to the southwest. The connection was too weak to follow, despite my attempts. The second and third bags were almost identical.

As I finished with the sixth bag, I shrugged at Wynn. "I don't feel specifics. They're all alive and scared but not terrified. They feel like they're basically okay. I'm getting a pull to the southwest. If I had to guess, I'd put them out off the coast. A boat? An island maybe? They seem to be in roughly the same place."

Wynn showed relief and some disappointment. "That's more than we had."

"Can I go now?" I asked.

He held up his hand. "One more thing while I'm thinking about it. We picked up a case with a lot of cash in it a couple of days ago. One of our old tracers went off, and we came in to investigate. The box tripped all sorts of alarms. We traced it to a car buy. It looked like both parties were deceased. There was an odd note inside. Did you have anything to do with that?"

I smiled. "Glad you picked up the cash. It's possessed. Long story. Just stash it out of the way, and don't let anyone near it until I figure out how to destroy it." That was one check in the positive column for the day.

Wynn nodded. "Glad to know you're still looking out for the nasty stuff." He tossed me an envelope. "Credentials, secure PDA, and cell. A pouch of the new tracers as well. You know the routine. Stay in touch. Welcome back to the Longbow Initiative." The contents of the envelope found homes in convenient new pockets of my skinsuit.

Wynn pulled me in close as I shook his hand to leave. "Do not make me regret this," he whispered.

I LEFT WYNN in the Control Center. Our discussion had taken a little over an hour, and I was greeted by a displeased Drea leaning on the BMW, playing with her tablet. With an edge in her tone, she asked, "Shall we see the client now?" Without waiting for an answer, she walked toward a side door and glared at the agent who had been waiting outside with her. He was rubbing a sore hand. The grimace on both of their faces made it apparent they were not on speaking terms.

A tall, reed-thin woman with a sharply angled face introduced herself as Sonja, Mr. Underhill's aide. With grace that would shame a gazelle, she escorted us into Underhill's home office.

Mahogany bookcases lined the walls and were filled with texts, most of which were leather-bound. Some looked as though they might have come from the library of Alexandria. A few prized first editions were showcased on pedestals around the room. All of the artwork looked original and as if it belonged in the Louvre. Underhill rose from behind his desk, a pristine, ornate antique adorned by a laptop and a few folders. By the stack of files and papers on the conference table to the right of his desk, he spent most of his time there. But instead of seating us there, he led us to a corner, where several leather chairs surrounded a small table.

Underhill sank into a chair. He looked distraught and had lost most of the poise he had shown in front of Priscilla and his family. "So what do you need? How will you find my girls? The FBI says hurry up and wait. They have a circus in my back yard while I set up one in my front yard for a party that won't happen." Underhill seemed to be unraveling.

Drea tried to distract him. "When is her birthday?"

"June 21st. She'll be sixteen."

Her birthday wasn't for a week. I opened up my Sight and my Sense and focused as much as I could on Underhill. I had to use a lot of focus to cut through the façade and get a connection. Two threads ran from him to somewhere offshore. The stronger signal linked to Abbie. A cold floor leached heat from my body. Cramping muscles ached in a small space. The connection wasn't strong enough for me to see anything, but I felt others in the room. Abbie exuded anger and some defiance as she mentally fought against her captors. I took Underhill's hand and let him feel her presence through me.

He started to cry. "At least they're alive."

After a moment, he pulled himself together. "What do you need from us, from me?"

"I'd like a look at their rooms and to talk to the driver."

Sonja appeared on cue. "Please show them anything they require," Underhill instructed her.

Underhill was stooped over as he rose and shook our hands. "Please find them." The connection, no matter how small, seemed to have given him a little hope. "Anything you need. Anything."

On the guided trip through the house, we passed a banquet hall with seating for eighty people between two great oak tables. The large, open windows overlooked the courtyard and the party preparations. On the other side, a glass atrium the size of a mansion filled the space. It was three stories tall and opened to the sky. It contained what looked like a jungle.

Little Evan stalked us with curiosity as we went into the residence wing, but we pretended not to see him. Sonja opened the door to Claire's room. It was a teenage girl's dream. Near-fuchsia paint coated the walls. A king-sized, mahogany canopy bed held a place of

90

prominence in the center of the room. One wall was mostly taken up by a TV the size of an arena scoreboard. A large but tasteful workstation in the corner was neatly organized. Claire's laptop and a couple of books were the only items on display. I tried a quick hack on the laptop to no avail. "The FBI found nothing of consequence on the machine," Sonja said. Yeah, that was underwhelming.

Where most girls would have posters, Claire had enough memorabilia to open a Hard Rock Café and a Planet Hollywood with collectables to spare. A digital picture frame rotated through photos of the family and a few friends. Several of the shots were of Claire with Abbie. "How does Abbie fit in?" I asked Sonja.

She replied curtly. "Abbie is the daughter of the Mister's cousin and closest friend. He and his wife were killed in an accident when Abbie was a small child and Claire was an infant. With Mr. and Mrs. Underhill as her guardians, she and Claire were raised as siblings. Abbie is only a couple of years older than Claire and is set to start at the university in the fall."

The laptop in the corner had more emotion than this ice queen. "Thanks."

We headed around the corner to Abbie's room, nearly double the size of Claire's in layout, except it was painted a pale blue. Abbie seemed to share Underhill's love of texts and history over pop culture. Instead of props and costumes, her room was lined with bookcases filled with scrolls, leather-bound books, and ancient knickknacks. Fossils, rocks, and other objects acted as bookends.

Abbie's desk was slightly more cluttered than Claire's. Next to Abbie's laptop sat an unrolled scroll. The ends were held down by dinars. A notebook laid out the partially translated text. As I flipped through the notebook, I saw dozens of texts translated into Latin. They were full of charms, potions, and spells. I snapped a shot of the scroll with my phone. Other notebooks on her desk were filled with historical studies of magical practices. I did not find anything among the notes that was overly concerning.

"May we meet Robert, the driver?" I asked.

"Certainly," Underhill's aide said curtly. "Follow me, and I can arrange it."

Anya Underhill stopped us on the way back to the garage. She was dressed in yoga pants and a tank top with her blond hair pulled back, and she wore little makeup. She was ambling around the house and outwardly looked calm, but she reminded me of a mongoose on the hunt. "Evan tells me they're alive," she said. "Can you share this with me as well?"

I nodded. Anya was more open than Evan, and I was able to connect with her quickly. I could follow the thread to Claire through her. Claire seemed calmer than Abbie, maybe asleep. I took Anya's hand and felt the energy flow. Anya began to draw a lot of energy from me. I was frozen in place and couldn't break the connection. After a few minutes, Anya finally released me, and Drea eased me into a nearby chair. *What the hell was that?*

Anya thanked me dispassionately and walked away in a daze. Drea dropped to one knee in front of me and looked into my eyes as she gave me a cursory examination. "That took a lot out of you. Are you okay?"

I nodded.

Sonja appeared unmoved and a little bored while I recovered.

"Can we have Robert meet us at the scene?" I asked Sonja.

She nodded and escorted us to the door. I slowly made my way to the car. The encounter with Anya had left me exhausted.

Wynn approached the car as I slid into the passenger seat. He leaned in through the window. "Did you learn anything?"

"Yeah," I responded. "The Addams Family is alive and well in Malibu."

I PASSED OUT on the ride to Santa Monica. Whatever Anya had done to me was going to take a little time to recover from. Likely, it saved me some questions from Drea concerning my relationship with Wynn. An unknown energy touched the edges of my consciousness as someone, or something, tried to probe and Push their way into my mind. My defenses seemed to be holding even in my weakened state. A faint visage of the woman in gray from my dream was materializing behind my closed eyes when Drea nudged me. "We're here. Nap time is over."

I opened my eyes, but the fog in my head hadn't completely faded. Drea was calling Robert on her mobile. Across the street, a huge guy leaned against the back doors of an old panel van. A quick look with my Sight confirmed he was a Were of some sort. No one else around looked as though they could be part of his pack, and I assumed they might be on the prowl.

With the 1911 in my hand, I jumped out of the car. I was in a full run across the street before Drea's phone call was answered. The beefy man raised his hands when he saw me coming.

"Get down on the ground," I yelled at him.

The guy turned pale and screamed like a little girl—a high-pitched, crystal-vase-cracking kind of scream. He dropped to his knees. "Hey, hey, wait. Here's my wallet. Just don't kill me."

I stopped ten feet away and took aim at him. "You're a Were. Where are those kids? Where is the rest of your pack?"

Furor danced with fear as he started to change. His eyes widened and started to turn yellow. My curse binding my abilities shocked me just for thinking of shooting him preemptively. *I was just going to disable him. Really.* Whatever powers controlled my throttle jolted me again for good measure. When my vision cleared, the Were was curled up in a little ball. Well, a three-hundred-plus-pound ball of fur.

Drea jumped between us. "Wait. That's Robert."

Robert cowered, and his yellow eyes had gone beady. He was sweating, shaking, and whimpering.

Drea grabbed the barrel of my gun hand and lowered it. A few people were staring, but hey, it was LA. Drea leaned in and whispered in my ear "Calm down. He's okay."

"He's a Were of some sort," I said incredulously.

"Werehmmmmm," Robert muttered.

"What's that?" I asked.

Drea clarified. "He's a Were, um, hamster."

I burst out in a fit of nervous laughter. "How is that even possible?" I would've liked to have felt guilty for having laughed. With all of the bizarre things I had seen, a lot of which had tried to kill me, I did feel a little bad for the guy. Well, I would feel bad later.

Drea smacked me, and my senses slowly returned to normal. "Grey, you think you're no one's fool, and yet we adopted you to have a village idiot. Be nice. I remember Robbie. Priscilla helped him with his change. I'll fill you in later. Now, we need to get off the road. Let's walk the scene, and then we can go grab a bite and have a sit-down with Robert."

Robert was almost back to human form and sitting in the middle of the road. "Call me Robbie," he said to me. "And I'm a vegetarian."

I holstered the 1911 and offered my hand to pull him up. I hated LA.

ROBBIE SHOWED US where he had waited on the girls. Six overpriced boutique shops surrounded a small lot. It was a little corner of hell. High-end soccer moms and wealthy, fashionable teenagers darted from shop to shop like tropical fish on a reef. They stopped every time something shiny caught their eyes.

"I was waiting here by the limo," Robbie said. "I bring the girls down here a lot, sometimes to meet up with their friends. They went to the flower shop over there and ordered what they wanted for the party. Then they went into Garret's Gaming to rent a couple of retro game machines. They came out of Brenda's Bakery with a box of cupcakes. They even brought me a carrot cake one."

I wondered if Robbie had gotten the joke. Teenage girls could be cruel. Or maybe it was his favorite. Either way, he was happy.

He continued. "They dropped the box off in the car and walked across the street into Bella Donna's." Robbie pointed to a store on the corner. We retraced the girls' path with Robbie. "I walked in the store even though the place creeps me out. The lady at the counter said they had bought a couple of things and left through the back door. I followed her through the door where it opens up next to the caterers. I heard people shouting halfway up the block. I ran up there and saw Claire's purse and Abbie's backpack on the ground with a couple more packages. One of the people said they had seen four guys in masks stop in the street, grab the girls, and speed off."

We walked the long way around the block and stopped where he had found the bags. Even though a few days had passed since the incident, I opened up my Sense and my Sight to take a look. Fading ribbons of energy were still evident, and it appeared that whoever had grabbed the girls had been something other than human. Based on the energy, it appeared that whatever had taken the girls prowled the area regularly. I scouted around, but most of the shops appeared normal. Bella Donna's was the exception. Energetically, it was lit up like a Griswold's Christmas.

It seemed unusual that I wouldn't sense anything passively from a place with that strong of a signature. I wondered if Anya's touch had drained me more than I'd realized. "Robbie, please wait here."

Halfway across the four-lane street, the energy field from the store touched me like the glow from a gentle lamp. I was drawn in like a moth to a flame. Most stores put out an energy, usually one that tried to invite you in. This one pushed the idea of exclusivity, almost as if a person needed to be invited into the clubhouse. Drea stood a few steps behind and seemed to be trying to observe without disturbing me.

A large sign was hand-painted on the glass doors. A delicate hand held a rose with a golden stem and thorns. "Bella Donna's" was written in calligraphic script.

I peered in through the glass doors. Bella Donna's appeared as if someone had taken all of occult pop culture, thrown it in a box, and shaken it until everything looked purposefully chaotic. My Senses were bombarded the instant I crossed the threshold of the store. My Sight and Sense reflexively shut down on the edge of a total overload, and I was left impaired by an intense headache.

Plants in decorative pots were scattered all over the store. Books rested askew on antique bookcases. Jewelry and sundries sat on tables covered with mystical prints. A glass case held crystals, gemstones, and semi-mystical implements. Racks of clothes were staged around the shop. The music in the background was hypnotic and a bit gloomy. I guessed this was where all of the rich Goth-wannabe kids went for their *essence d'angst*.

A tall woman in a flowing garnet dress glided across the floor. Her skin was like porcelain, and her long black hair was coiffed with red roses. She was thin but very curvy, and she radiated warmth and desire.

She greeted us in a singsong voice. "Welcome. How may I serve you?"

"We're looking into the disappearance of several girls around here over the last few weeks. I understand that two of them were here just before they were abducted." I flashed a picture of the two girls.

Her singsong voice took on a dreary tone. "Yes, Claire and Abbie. They're regular customers. They had come in to order costumes for the upcoming party. The theme is an eighteenth-century circus. Have you found anything in the search?"

"We're still in the process of investigating," I answered. "Did you see anything, or are you aware of anything happening in the area?"

The woman's mouth turned down in a slight frown. "No, I didn't see anything from the shop. I've been warning our customers to take care since hearing about these horrible events."

"How long has your shop been here?" Drea asked.

The woman smiled. "Not very long, but we have been very fortunate with our business."

Drea handed her a card. "Please let us know if you hear of anything."

The woman gazed at me and took my hand. "My name is Daire. I have something that may help you in your search." She guided me to the counter and reached into a drawer. She pulled out a velvet bag and handed it to me. "Open it once you're outside, preferably while you stand in the ocean."

"Thank you." I slid the bag into a side pocket.

Drea led me out of the shop and back into the sunshine. Once we crossed the street, the hypnotic energy dissipated, and I snapped back fully to my senses.

Robbie was still waiting on the corner. "Did you get anything?" he asked.

"Creeped out," Drea answered.

My head was still throbbing. "Let's eat."

MY HEAD CLEARED as we walked around the neighborhood. A shot from one of the vials I carried with me speeded up my recovery. We found a small Indian restaurant just up the street from Bella Donna's. We ordered and started to talk.

"How did you get hooked up with the Underhills?" I asked Robbie.

"I came out here to be an actor," he said. "You know, I'm a big guy. I figured action films. How hard can it be? My first role, I played the Ibis-man in Mr. Underhill's production of *A Midsummer Night's Slumber Party Massacre*. It was fun, and then in *Frankenstein's Phenomenal Follies,* I got to be the monster. Except for the dance scenes."

Yep. Grade B *cinema de merde*. I hated to admit I had caught those on late-night TV, but sometimes I would have done anything to stay awake when the things that went bump in the night wanted to make sure I didn't wake up. And they were fun films.

"So, one day, Mr. Underhill's kids were all out on the set of *The Creature from Goat Man Swamp* and needed a ride home. I was done shooting for the day, and I offered to drive them. The next day, Mr. Underhill offered me a job as their driver and security when I'm not shooting."

"So any weird stuff around the girls or the family, especially of late?" It was a loaded question. Weird was probably normal in the Underhill house.

Robbie looked deep in thought, and I smelled burned tofu. I debated if the two were connected.

After a few moments, he nodded his head. "Well, there's been stuff since I became, well, you know. I figured it went with the life."

"So, Robbie, how exactly did you become… this?" I asked.

"I'm working on the set of *Swamp-man of Mars,* and—"

I interrupted. "Let me guess, you're the Swamp-man."

Robbie looked down. "Not this time. I'm Commander Austin. I'm killed by the Swamp-man in the third scene. Anyway, I was putting on my space suit for the shot and was bitten by a rat that was in my pants. I saw it run off. One of the crew caught it. It wasn't rabid or anything. A couple of days later, things started getting… weird."

"Did you change?" I asked. "And how does the hamster thing fit in?" I mostly held in my snicker.

"No," he responded. "The animal shelter was doing an adoption drive and fundraiser. Claire does some work with them as a volunteer. She wants to take all of the animals home. I was walking around and helping, and one of the cats went nuts in the cage. It jumped and hissed at me. I had a panic attack and collapsed.

"Claire drove me to the doctor, but a few minutes after we left the animal shelter, I felt fine. The doctor didn't see any major problems and thought I might be stressed. A few days later, I took Mr. Underhill to see Miss Priscilla. When we got there, Miss Priscilla thought something was wrong and sat me down with someone who looked me over. They said I was becoming a Were-rat."

"It looked like he'd been bitten by a carrier," Drea interjected. "Rats can carry the infection."

Robbie nodded again. "I didn't want to go crazy or hurt people. Miss Priscilla said we could change it so at least I could still be me."

Drea patted Robbie's hand and stared at me. I knew a bit about how Weres worked. Weres could be born, but they could also be made. It was part biological infection, a virus that made the host compatible. Then there was an energy imprint. The energy imprint seemed to be elemental. Vamps were similar, but with a different energy. "So, because it was a rat, she could use a similar animal, and the best she had was a hamster," I concluded.

They both nodded.

I guess a hamster could be seen as a step up. In the Were-world, Were-rats were the bottom dwellers.

"And since then?" I asked.

"I notice different stuff now," Robbie answered. "But I figured it was the life. What sucks is, before, I wasn't afraid of anything, and now I'm scared of my shadow." Robbie looked as if he could shrink into the chair.

EXHAUSTION SET IN. It was getting late in the day, but the sun wouldn't set for hours. "Let's head back to the ranch," I said to Drea. "I need to sleep for a few hours."

She smiled at me. "I have a closer option." We cruised a little way up the Pacific Coast Highway and pulled into the Athenian Palace Resort and Spa. Drea hopped out of the car and tossed the keys to a valet. "Come on," she said to me. I got out of the car and followed her.

The doors of the resort opened into a cavernous lobby. In the middle, a large shallow pool was surrounded by columns and greenery. Large koi swam above mosaic tile that made up the floor of the pool. Straight through the lobby, the beach and Pacific Ocean were framed through large glass panels. The spa was to the left. Drea marched into the resort hotel on the right as if she owned the place.

A concierge met us halfway to the elevators. "Your suite is prepared." We rode to the top floor. The concierge led the way to one of the two doors on the floor and quickly swiped the key card, opening the door. He handed each of us a key. "Have a pleasant stay."

Drea gave him a hundred. "Thanks, Dom. Always nice to see you."

The room had to be the presidential suite. It was large, spacious, and modern. Floor-to-ceiling windows overlooked a balcony that extended the entire end of the hotel with a great view of the beach and the Pacific. Drea pointed across the suite. "Your room is that one. Mine is over here." She disappeared into one of the four bedrooms and closed the door.

I opened the door to the balcony to get some fresh air. The breeze off of the Pacific was almost as refreshing as the view was impressive. A moment later, there was a knock on the door. I walked over to open it, and Dom rolled in a cart laden with fruit, cheese, various cold cuts, breads, and spreads. He told me the refrigerator was fully stocked and that he was at our disposal should we require anything. I took a bottle of water and a snack off the cart as he backed out the door.

Drea exited her room wrapped in a robe. "I'm going to the spa for a massage. Get a nap."

Light streamed in through the large picture windows in my bedroom, bathing it in afternoon sunlight. I opened the sliding door in my room so I could hear the gentle roar of the ocean. The king-sized bed beckoned, and I was asleep before my head hit the pillow.

I was again in the stone room, back in the castle. I stood on the open drawbridge, a warm and sunny day shining down on me. Through the entryway, the wooden doors at the back of the great room inside the building were totally blocked. Stones and sandbags had been stacked against the large double doors. More buttresses held up against the blockage. Even so, a dozen or so thin ribbons of energy crept around the frame.

My Sight was able to reveal more details. Through the blockage, the doors were still closed, and the lock was holding. But the doors were straining and warping with the pressure from behind. The only sense of what was beyond the doors was that of an intensive force. I turned off my Sight and touched the blockage. The charge that flowed through me left me tingling and energized.

From behind me, a gentle voice spoke. "Welcome back, Greyson."

The woman in gray appeared next to me. She motioned. "Walk with me."

We walked out the drawbridge onto a large grassy lawn. I got a better look at the castle. It was more of a keep: six stories tall, with a tower stretching into the sky. A light was on in a window of the tower.

"Where am I?"

"Please, sit," she said.

Two wooden chairs appeared as if they had simply grown out of the ground. So I sat. It felt very real, much more so than a dream.

The woman pulled her face veil around her throat and pushed back her hood. She appeared to be a very old woman, heavily wrinkled with white hair. Her eyes sparkled in a strange way. Something about her did not feel quite right.

"Who are you?" I asked.

With a crooked smile, she answered, "Your guide."

"And where am I?" I asked again.

With the same crooked smile, she said, "You would be better able to tell me than I you."

I began to feel frustrated, and she seemed to enjoy it. "What kind of guide are you?" I asked. "Guide to what? To where?"

"The guide to your path," she answered. "The guide to cater to your needs. What do you need, Greyson?"

I stood, threw my arms out in frustration, and screamed. I was shocked as a fireball flew from my hand.

"Do you feel better now?" she quipped.

"What just happened?" I snapped back.

"You threw a fireball," she said with a shrug. "Did you not mean to do so?"

I opened my mouth, but before I could respond, the fireball came around from my left and knocked me to the ground. A loud and embittered cry climbed from deep in my being. "Ahhhhh, dammit." I felt as though I was in a cartoon. Guides by ACME.

She stood over me and offered me a surprisingly strong hand and pulled me to my feet. "I see what you need."

She placed her left hand on my chest over the mark she had given me and placed her right hand on my head. A pale-blue aura around her grew into a bright glow. When it faded, she was again wearing the hood and veil.

I felt both energized and drained.

"You will need this soon," she said. She hung a leather strand over my head and around my neck. A brass skeleton key hung from the bottom.

Pressure was building in my head. Someone was trying to get into my mind. The gray woman stared at me. "You probably should do something about that." Then she faded from view.

I still stood in the grassy field, but noises were coming from the keep. I ran back in to see a glowing golden figure throwing sandbags from the inner door out of the drawbridge door. I had almost reached the figure when...

"Get up. We need to move. Two more girls were taken. One of them is Onyx." Drea stood over me in a rage.

"Moving," was all I said as I bounced out of bed and shook off the last of the fugue.

MY SIGHT SHOWED that the link to Onyx was strengthening. At the same time, Drea said, "She set off her transponder. It's coming this way."

Oh, yeah, technology. I forgot about it sometimes. But it tended to go on the fritz around some types of magical energy. A small screen with a local map and the transponder signal popped up on my sleeve. Her signal was two miles out and getting closer. I had to get to the road, and the stairs were the faster way down. "I'll cut them off. Call for backup and meet me."

Once they reached the road, they only had two options. If they were taking Onyx out to sea, the nearest marina was just past the resort. Otherwise, they had to cut straight up the coast. Either way, they would have to go through me.

People cried out as I burst out of the stairwell through the lobby. The signal was two blocks away by the time I reached the road and checked the map. They were approaching the T-intersection where I stood. Two dark Suburbans barreled down the road. I drew the 1911 and took aim. Half a block away, they saw me and slammed on their brakes, coming to a sudden stop in the middle of the road. One car angled left and the other went right. Both were fifty feet away from me.

Standard issue agents in black suits began to pour from the vehicles with their weapons drawn. Agent Wynn stepped out of the vehicle on my right. "I suspect this means I have someone who actually belongs to you."

I holstered the 1911 and closed the distance to Wynn. Onyx and another girl were trying and failing to look defiant while handcuffed in the back seat. Relieved, I shook my head. "How much for you to keep them?" I asked.

Drea pulled in behind me, driving a new SL600. She stormed to the Suburban, looked in, and saw they were fine. She spun on one heel to face Wynn and me. "Can I take them?" she asked.

Wynn grimaced. "After we talk for a moment. Is there somewhere we can meet?"

Drea climbed back into her car and waved offhandedly. "Around the corner. We can meet in the suite." She pointed at me. "He can lead the way." The scowl she wore cleared a path as she spun her car around.

I climbed into the Suburban with Wynn, and we drove to the resort. We pulled up out front, and a confounded valet was met with an unmoving agent.

"C'mon, Wynn," I said. "Let's get the countesses upstairs."

Wynn reluctantly handed his keys to the valet then let the girls out of the back of the Suburban. His shadow, a young female agent, followed us all into an elevator in the lobby, and we rode up to the suite in silence.

The door was propped open, and Drea was hanging up her mobile as we walked in. "So, what did the little darlings do?" she asked.

"We were just—" Onyx began.

"Shut it," Drea snapped.

Wynn was obviously as aggravated as Drea. "I had a couple of agents watching the area. We were following a couple of targets of interest when these two popped up like a shining beacon of entrapment. Our targets disappeared before we could get a good lock on them. Were you two out trolling as bait?"

Before Drea could answer, I stepped in. "No. No way." I looked at Onyx. "I guess you two thought you could use your teen charms to help find your friend."

Onyx was smart enough to stay quiet and nod.

Wynn looked at Drea and me. "We need to debrief you from your trip uptown."

Drea looked at the girls. "Go hit the spa and come back here. Do *not* leave the resort."

The young female agent with Wynn stepped to the side and let the girls pass. She then joined us at the table.

107

Wynn ran a hand through his hair. "What did you find?"

"Not much. There's some sort of focus down there, and whoever grabbed Underhill's girls and the others appear to be using it for a hunting ground. I could pick up a strong general sense, but nothing in particular. Unfortunately, the bait idea may be a good one."

Wynn surprised me. "We concur. This is agent Beth Raines. We would like to pair her with Miss Onyx."

Drea quickly piped up with her response. "No. She's a kid."

Wynn gave her a calm look. "A well-trained kid, who you have regularly used in your, ahem, own enterprises. It would make us much less inclined to look into some of your, shall we say, off-the-book activities." It was becoming clear that Longbow and Calypso had more than a cursory relationship.

Drea rose, the scowl firmly carved into her face. "I've got to make a call."

We all could have guessed who she was calling.

ONYX SLINKED OUT of the side bedroom. She had changed into a sundress and heels, and traded her blue spikes for a more modest hairstyle. "Let me present the new Beth," she said.

Agent Raines appeared in overpriced jeans, a pastel blouse, and leather boots. She carried a Louis Vuitton purse on her arm that probably would have cost her two months' salary. They both had become the epitome of rich Malibu teens. And they looked almost like clones of the missing girls.

I opened my Sight. Many of the people in the area designated as the hunting grounds had been marked by a sort of energy thrown into their auras—very subtle, but distinct. Neither Agent Raines nor Onyx showed any indication of having been tagged. Drea had been during our short visit, and I studied the pattern. With a crystal from my pack, I waved it around Drea a few times and vacuumed up the energy. It gave me an idea of how to make the bait a little more attractive.

Magical beings all have unique signatures in their auras. People who didn't know they weren't entirely human—usually some variety of half-Fae—had a unique phosphorescence. I thought of this as a signal of potential.

With some reluctance, I pitched my plan to Drea, Wynn, Onyx, and Raines. Fifteen minutes later, a chalk circle dominated the middle of the room. Onyx went first. I scattered various crystals around her and Pushed a little Will into it. A short incantation released energies within the energy circle, and her aura started to shimmer. Her energy shifted to be more Fae-like. I broke the field and released Onyx. Once the stones were cleared and the circle was reset, we repeated the process with Raines.

We agreed Raines needed to stay in the suite and bond with Onyx overnight. The fishing expedition would have to wait one more day. Wynn headed back to the local command post to make final arrangements. Drea wandered off to her room to sleep. As it was pushing midnight, it was my time to work.

A shower rinsed away any residual magic. Drea had apparently arranged to have a couple more Leviskin skinsuits, bug-out bags, and other gear brought in and stashed in the closet. The suite was starting to look as if I was moving in. After dressing in one of the clean suits,

109

the process of re-equipping myself took some thought. My knives found their sheaths, and on a whim, I decided to carry the Sig. It was a little smaller and would be easier to conceal around Santa Monica.

With some chalk, a few potions, and a couple of the new-and-improved Holy Hand Grenades stashed into my thigh pocket, I was almost ready to go out into the night. With a little Push of Will, I changed the suit to jeans, a cream T-shirt, and a jacket.

As I came out of the lobby, the valet rushed over. "The Miss said you might need a ride for the evening. They just delivered it a few minutes ago."

He pulled around a Harley Softail, which looked as though it had been through a few of Kizzy's modifications.

The valet handed me a helmet and a note.

Hey Grey,

Made a few changes just for you. There is also a small cache in the storage compartment. Her name is Ktesippe, or Special K. Introduce yourself. Don't scratch the paint.

Kizzy

I felt the love.

I CLIMBED ONTO the Softail, grabbed the grips, and slipped the helmet on. "Hi, Special K." I felt a little odd speaking to my ride.

A tingly, happy wave flowed through me, and I hoped it was a good sign.

As "we" pulled onto the Pacific Coast Highway heading toward the Santa Monica hunting grounds, a Heads Up Display appeared in my helmet. I almost crashed as a voice purred in my head. "I've never been ridden like this before." I felt another happy wave.

"Hi, K. I'm Grey. "

The voice purred back like a possessed GPS. "Hi, Grey. You have two messages."

"Um, okay. What are they?" I asked.

Kizzy's face appeared up in a small screen in the corner of my helmet.

"Hey, so as you might have noticed, Ktesippe is special. If you think it, she'll respond faster than you can. She can also change based on your thoughts. She operates the same way as the skinsuit. She has a layer of Leviskin covering nearly her entire body. Be nice to her, and she'll be nice to you. Keep my home-girl K safe." The video faded.

Next, Drea's face rolled onto the screen. "I figured you'd sneak out. If you need help, think it, and a distress signal will go out. Like what Onyx did. I hope you like Kizzy's loaner. If you aren't good to her, Special K gets bitchy, and the ride is a lot less smooth. And Kizzy will bitch at me. Oh, yeah, and she will beat you senseless. Happy hunting."

"Hey K, do you have a stealth mode? How fast can you go?" It didn't seem to surprise anyone that I had sneaked out for a look at night when magical energies were at their strongest.

A throaty laugh came through the speakers in my helmet. "That's more like it. Where are we going?"

I told her the area in Santa Monica I wanted to visit.

The next thing I knew, K was driving, and I was clinging on with a death grip. My skinsuit adhered to K, and the ride smoothed out like a Sunday drive… at a hundred miles an hour. When we reached a mile out, she let me have control again.

Special K chirped in my ear. "Backseat driver."

I must have been cussing more than I thought as we zipped around traffic and through red lights.

When we arrived at our destination, I parked a couple of blocks away from Bella Donna's and asked Special K to go stealthy. She disappeared in a blink. A few bars and restaurants were still open. People, mostly in their twenties, roamed the sidewalks, oblivious to the predators I Sensed nearby.

I climbed onto the roof of the shopping center and activated my Sense. I reached out across the area a few blocks in every direction. The skinsuit seemed to boost my abilities. I immediately sensed a couple of hotspots in the area. Bella Donna's was by far the strongest. It felt even more energetic at night than during the day. That made some sense; it would be stronger without the sun to wash away any residual energy. The essence from the predators permeated the routes around the neighborhood more strongly. Nothing specific was coming across about them, other than their instinctive need to hunt in the same area once they had selected a grounds. It felt much more territorial than I would have suspected. Four places they had abducted people stood out even though I was aware of only three events, six people in total.

The dark trail of the predators was soaked into the neighborhood from their repeated pattern of prowling in the road. I looked up and down the street. The party seemed to be dying down for the night. I jumped down and roamed toward Bella Donna's.

The boutique effervesced energy. I saw it, felt it, even smelled it on the currents. It was intoxicating. I activated a small shield spell, enough that I could still Sense the world around me, but not be overwhelmed again.

The door was unlocked, and Daire stood ready at the entrance. "Welcome, Greyson." I stopped and was pulled into a welcoming hug. I almost melted into the floor with desire. I trailed behind her as she led me into a back room. A circle of a dozen people sat around, mostly women. "We expected you a little sooner, so we got a head start."

"On what?" I asked.

"Finding the girls, of course," Daire cooed.

"And how'd you know…"

She cocked her head. "Did you not come here for my help?"

I looked around. Nothing seemed out of place, at least nothing except a witches' circle. I didn't have any other leads, and I wasn't in a position to question her motives too deeply… not yet. But something more was going on than just a concerned shop owner at play.

She nudged me to the center of the group and seated herself in the open spot. A map of the greater LA area was spread on the floor. She touched a ring on the map drawn in salt, and an energy wall formed. It was one of the strongest I'd ever seen. "You may begin," Daire said to the group.

Everyone in the circle around me closed their eyes and began to meditate. "You can open yourself now," Daire said. "I believe you can follow the trails from here to where they were taken."

A bit dubious, I took my place in the circle, crossed my legs, and closed my eyes. I slowly dropped my shield. The room sat in dead silence. Even the practitioners around me gave off the shallowest of breathing.

I reached into my pocket and pulled out a small silver nugget on a string. I dipped the nugget into a pouch of charcoal dust, muttered a few words, and focused on Claire. After a few minutes, the pendulum began to move. It stopped over the shop, dropped a small pile of charcoal, then traced a line up the street. Following the navigation on the map, a thin trail of charcoal led to a second spot. The pendulum dropped a second dot. The brief scene of someone departing a vehicle flashed in my mind.

The trace continued up the map a bit further and stopped. Another little pile of charcoal dust dropped where the van was torched. The line began to move again and ended at a small marina up the coast, leaving another dot. Finally, a thin line wove across the map and ended at a small spot out in the Pacific. No island was on the map, just open ocean.

I repeated the process focused on Abbie, and it followed the same path. It looked like both had ended up in the same place on the map, and the trail ended there. I tried a couple of other incantations, but nothing new came to me.

Seeing I was finished, Daire waved her hand. The field around the circle dropped, and the circle broke up. People began to depart. She thanked each of them individually as they exited.

"Why are you doing this?" I asked her after everyone had left.

She smiled at me. "Why are you?"

That was a question to which I had no good answer. It was more than just a debt to Priscilla. This whole mess was going to dig me a deeper hole for the Inquest. Somehow I doubted everything I was doing for this investigation counted as low-profile.

Since I had not responded, Daire said, "Maybe this little quest is important to your journey. Or maybe you're the moth to the flame, rushing headlong to death. Either way, you probably should get moving."

Having been dismissed, I thanked her and headed for the door.

MY FIRST STOP from the map was an establishment I was very familiar with. The Gin House was a pub that catered to the supernatural types around LA. It was owned by Mr. Obi Ramla. I had done a few odd jobs for him and his family, including digging up the possessed cash for Henri and Katie. Obi had sent me a message the old-fashioned way for that job—by text. I had not been to Obi's place in a while. I hoped Fifi the Pomeranian was not on the loose again. I didn't have time to hunt him down.

No sign was visible outside. People either knew the pub was there or not. I knocked on the door. A slit opened, and a pair of eyes popped out on long stalks. They looked me up and down then glanced up and down the street. "Whad'ya want?" a gravelly voice asked.

I flashed a chit. The small metal disc was a deep golden color with the azure sigil of the Ramla family emblazoned on it. The door opened, and I stepped through the door. Six tentacles slammed me to the wall and frisked me.

"No weapons," the bouncer grunted. From the dark recess where it stood guard, I saw a big toothy smile and a lot of tentacles. I was pretty sure Lovecraft's nightmares could have never come up with that one.

All it found was the Sig. "You can have it on the way out," it said in a bored tone.

Lazy fans stirred the air over a teak bar that ran the length of the back wall. Packed tables were scattered about, and at them sat a mix of everything dreams and nightmares could provide. An angel shot darts in the corner. He looked bored, throwing a bull's-eye every time. A satyr was doing body shots off a well-endowed vampire. A two-headed being argued with itself on the flavor of tobacco for the hookah. And two zombies staffed the bar with Alvin the pukwudgie. All in all, it seemed like a regular packed night at two a.m.

Alvin slid a house stout in my direction before I reached the bar. He greeted me with a fist bump. "Fifi lost again?" He was a little over three feet tall with mottled brown skin, a full head of black hair, and observant, beady eyes. He wore a pair of black pants, black shoes, a white shirt, red suspenders, and a very dirty apron.

"Nah," I said. "Or at least not as far as I know. Obi in?"

Alvin nodded toward the back.

The first sip of the cool stout cleared my head after the visit with Daire. "I'll catch you on the way out."

Alvin waved and nodded at my beer. "It's on the house, but you could tip for once."

It was slow, maneuvering through the crowd to the office. Obi Ramla opened the door on my second knock. A little under six feet and dressed in a three-piece suit, he was a middle-aged Mediterranean businessman. He grasped me by my arms and gave me a gentle squeeze. "Wonderful to see you. What brings you by?" he asked in his odd little accent.

A tug pulled at my leg. Fifi was looking for attention. Fifi was small, even for a Pomeranian, and he could have been in an eighties hair band with the coif he sported.

Obi snapped his fingers. "Fifi. Enough. Go to your spot."

Fifi ignored Obi and continued to paw at my leg.

Obi rolled his eyes and sighed. "I really want to kill my brother for this."

Fifi had been a gift from Aqil, Obi's brother. A bit of a practical joker, Aqil had enchanted Fifi to live as long as Obi so that he would have an eternal companion. The Ramla family had a long history in the magical arts, based on what little I had been able to learn.

Fifi also had the ability to open portals and loved to play hide and seek. Thus, occasionally the call would come in to track him down. Obi's revenge against his brother had been to name the dog Fifi. From what I understood, Obi had sent a pair of Siamese cats in return. For each one that died, two more appeared. Last I'd heard, Aqil had a house of thirty cats.

I was a little apprehensive about what I was going to ask, but I was still happy to see my old friend. "It's good to see you're well."

Obi closed the door to his office and motioned for me to sit. Fifi unceremoniously flopped into my lap.

"Obi, I'm looking into the disappearance of a number of girls around the area. I've traced at least one of the kidnappers here immediately after one grab."

Obi stared at me quite gravely. "We've had more than our usual out-of-town visitors as of late. Some have been from much further than others. I've felt a dark working underway."

"What kind of dark working?" I asked.

Obi shook his head. "I'm unsure. Even the seers have had little luck. Several of my regulars complained of unusual happenings that were making them uncomfortable, so I started checking into it. My feeling is that someone is trying to reopen one of the old portals. A hellmouth, possibly. Even I have considered going to visit Aqil for a while in Atlanta." Obi pushed a map across his desk. "These are the sources of the disturbances we've been able to map."

Several sites scattered around the LA area were marked on the map, including one well off the coast. It was in the same general area in which I had marked the girls' destination. One of the markers on the map looked quite close to the Underhill estate.

"Can I take this?" I asked.

"Certainly." He rose. "It may be fortuitous that you're here on such an errand." Obi opened the side door to his office. A small, ancient Asian man shambled in and sat down. A pair of Pixiu, which looked like Doberman-sized dragons, were barely visible as they lay at his feet. I stood.

Obi introduced us. "Mr. Forrester, this is a friend and business associate, Oh Phuk Xiang."

Xiang shakily rose to his feet and bowed as best he could. I returned the gesture.

Obi continued. "Xiang's granddaughters, Ling and Meihui, were taken earlier today. I believe by the same people you're investigating."

Xiang looked at me with a pleading stare. "I will do anything to find the girls. Longwei, their brother, was injured in the abduction, but he was left behind."

"Do you have any personal effects of the girls?"

Obi handed me a bag with two hairbrushes. "I was going to take them to Sibillya, but since you're here…"

Xiang nodded. "I must check on Longwei. Mr. Forrester, I would be most grateful for your help. Name your price."

I bowed to Xiang. "I'm on the case already. Let's just call it a favor."

Xiang nodded as an agreement had been reached and shuffled toward the door. The Pixiu followed him closely but were only visible when my Sight was focused on them. They looked as if someone had put dragon heads and eel tails on hairless chows with lion feet. Feathered wings were folded on their backs. I tried to glance at Xiang through my Sight and was rewarded by a blinding red flash.

Another immensely powerful being had missing family.

Obi took my hands in his. "Please let me know what you require in the search."

"Thanks, Obi."

ALVIN PUSHED ANOTHER stout toward me as I chose a barstool and sat down. "I see he roped you in."

I rubbed my head. "Didn't have to. I'm already on the case. They just added a few more victims." I sipped at the stout and looked around. "Hey, Alvin, have you seen anything strange lately?"

He waved at the patrons. "Care to be more specific?"

I motioned for him to come closer. "Obi mentioned you're getting a lot of out-of-towners," I whispered. "Three days ago, a little after two o'clock, right after one abduction, one of the kidnappers came in here."

Alvin looked pensive. "Yeah. The Fomorian over there. One of his buddies came in about that time and checked with him." He grabbed my arm as I moved to make the Fomorian's acquaintance. "Remember to take it outside."

"Alvin, I just want to talk to him," I said.

Alvin smiled. "Sure. I've heard that before."

I slapped one of Priscilla's hundreds on the counter.

"About time," he said. "Hey, wait. That had better be a tip and not trying to pay for damage in advance. That won't cover a barstool."

"Stay mischievous, Alvin."

I scanned the bar as I walked toward the Fomorian. He was throwing a glamour to look like one of Hollywood's finest—a nice, tan, Armani suit, blond hair, and black loafers. It covered up the nine-foot-tall horror underneath.

I knew a little Fomorian history. The story was that thousands of years ago, they had invaded Ireland, but it didn't last long. According to some legends among the Veiled, the Fomorians split

120

into two groups after they landed. The first group saw a conflict coming and left Eire to unknown pastures, but they were rewarded with beauty. This guy obviously belonged to the second group. The ones who stayed and fought were driven back to the sea, resuming a life as pirates. And they did not get the beauty charm.

Based on what was visible underneath the glamour, he was not purebred. He was too short. And though I'd never seen a Fomorian in person, he didn't match what I'd been told in stories from when I was growing up. Under the glamour, he reminded me of a Minotaur, but with a goat's head. He was very muscular, and his scars revealed a hard life of combat. He sat at one of the scarred wooden tables with a hookah and an unidentifiable drink.

"Hi. Can I take a seat?" I barely ducked out of the way as the hookah flew by my head and crashed into one of the zombies behind the bar.

"I said take it outside," Alvin yelled.

I yelled back. "What do you think I'm trying to—"

The Fomorian reached over, grabbed me by the throat, and hurled me at the bar as easily as he had the hookah. In the flight across the room, I felt the skinsuit stiffen for the impact before I knocked over a table and slammed into the bar. The Fomorian ran out the front door.

Scrambling to my feet in the spilled mess of drinks from the table, I followed him through the door. The bouncer tossed me the Sig as I ran by. His toothy grin flashed in anticipation. Maybe he got to eat the loser.

When the Fomorian dropped the glamour, I realized I had been very wrong about his appearance. He stood more like twelve feet tall, and he easily reached an arm up and pulled himself onto the top

121

of the building. I used all of my speed to keep up in the chase. On the ocean side, the complex ran for three blocks with small gaps in between. I slapped a magazine of silver-coated rounds into the Sig.

"Can't we talk this out?" I yelled to the Fomorian.

He responded by hitting me in the chest with an air vent he'd ripped from the top of the building. The skinsuit Pushed into armor and took most of the impact, but a trickle of blood ran down my neck.

The Fomorian resumed running. From a Weaver stance, I fired three rounds into his thigh. He fell for a brief second before standing up again. Then he turned and began marching toward me with a limp. "I was supposed to let you live," he uttered in a gravelly voice. He tore an air conditioner from the top of the building. The Leviskin shifted to become heavy armor. I doubted it would help.

An arrow appeared in the Fomorian's left shoulder. He dropped the air conditioner and let out a small yell. With a grunt, he snapped the shaft of the arrow and began to run again. This time he looked a little more concerned, but not because of me. A glimpse of movement drew my attention to the shadow of a figure on the roof forty feet away. It ducked before I got a good look.

Relieved that I wasn't under a ton of metal, I got a second wind and chased after the Fomorian. He was rapidly losing me with his long strides, but the wounds in his leg were slowing him down. He jumped from the roof and landed with a crash on the beach. My landing was less graceful as I flailed more than rolled.

I had run fifty yards down the beach and was rapidly losing ground when a shadow hit me in the chest and knocked me onto my back. As I hit the wet sand, a huge black hellhound jumped through the space where I had just vacated and overshot me by fifteen feet.

A small black furball stood on my chest. It looked like any other small black dog with curly hair. But no hellhound had the kind of glowing blue eyes that gazed back at me. It let out a woof.

I felt as if an elephant used my chest as a springboard when the small dog leapt over my head. Several more hellhounds ran up the beach toward me. I sat up and shot the one that had nearly decapitated me, watching its red eyes fade as it fell.

The little black dog snatched one of the hellhounds by the throat and ripped as it dove. I watched in horror as another of the hellhounds grabbed the furball in its mouth. I shot the hellhound in the head and kept moving forward.

I emptied my gun into the approaching hounds then slapped another magazine home. As I emptied that one, the remaining two hellhounds closed in. The Sig landed in the sand as I drew two of the silver throwing knives. Each of the blessed blades found their marks in a hellhound's head, dropping them. As I looked around, the furball lifted a leg and peed on the head of the dead hellhound that had tried to snack on him.

An outboard engine roared to life another hundred yards up the beach. The silhouette of the Fomorian driving a skiff jetted into the open ocean. There was no sign of the archer. The furball jumped into the ocean. Brushing off the empty Sig, I replaced the magazine and holstered it. The small, wet black puppy limped over to me. Thirteen pounds of fury had saved me. His bite wounds bubbled from the ocean water.

Drawn by a sense of dread, I scanned the night around me. Scar stood fifty yards up the beach, covered in fresh knots and open wounds from his dip in the ocean the day before. A lump swelled up in my throat. I couldn't reason how he had survived, but there he stood. If a gigantic hellborn dog could flip you off, I swore he did as he melted back into the shadows.

The furball happily jumped into my arms. He looked as if he had been through hell. I suspected he had.

THE TIDE DRAGGED one of the hellhound bodies out to sea. I retrieved and cleaned my knives then dumped the remaining carcasses into the surf. The tide would take care of them pretty quickly. I limped back up to The Gin House. Squid boy did not bother to pat me down as I walked back in. Reclaiming my seat at the bar, I glanced at Alvin, who was giving me an annoyed look about the dog I was carrying. "That doesn't quite look like Fifi."

I glared at him. "Ice in a towel, a stout, and something for the furball."

Alvin returned with an icepack, a towel, an herbal tea, a bowl of water, and a hamburger. "New friend?"

I told Alvin about the furball saving me and the evening exercise. "Did anyone else follow us out of the bar?"

He shook his head. "No one that wasn't back in here two minutes later when they realized they would have to walk to see the fight. But I can't be sure."

"Thanks. Any idea where Fomorians would nest these days?"

Alvin pursed his lips. "On this side of the Veil, they mostly stick to water. There are a few hidden offshore outposts. On the other side, who knows what realms they haunt? Pirate villages move pretty frequently."

Tell me something I don't already know.

The furball wolfed down the hamburger that was almost as big as he was and shook his tail.

Alvin's eyes lit up when another hundred landed on the bar.

"Thanks, Alvin," I said. The furball hopped off the bar and followed me to the door.

Obi commented as he watched us leave. "It appears you have a new guardian angel. Allah has a sense of humor."

Great. We wandered back to where the Harley was hidden. Special K faded into view, and I slipped on the helmet. An unhappy voice bounced around in my head. "What's that, and what are you doing with it?"

"Hi, K. We have a new member of the family. Got a place for him to ride?"

Instantaneously, a little basket appeared on the back of the bike. The bigger miracle was that she did it without a snarky comment. The furball jumped in, and the back tire dropped. K let me know she was not entirely pleased by giving me a less-than-pleasant electric shock to my balls when I slid on. "He had better not leak on me," she said tersely.

Even though my mood motivated me to go back to the suite, we followed the map to the last stop on land near the marina. With all of my Sight and Senses stretched, I could only make out faint traces of residual energy leading out to the ocean.

I decided to take a look at my new canine companion. As an overlay to the small black dog was a huge white hound with the same mesmerizing eyes. "Woof." No wonder K was unhappy about the new passenger.

Using my compass and GPS, I mapped the direction of the energy signature. I got back on K and turned toward the suite. Halfway to the resort, we stopped and took a second set of readings.

Upon arrival at the resort, the valet took Special K, and I picked up the furball. No one said a word as we went upstairs to the suite. From the balcony, I took a third set of readings. It would give me enough information to plot an approximate location, but I was betting it would come to that same spot on the map.

From one of the lounge chairs on the balcony, I sat and watched through my Sight as the energy traces faded, washed away by the rising sun.

I went back in and got a bowl of water, put it in my bedroom, and whistled for the furball. I tossed him on top of the bed and stripped. After a quick shower to wash off the night's adventure, I crawled into the bed for a few hours of sleep.

I WAS DREAMING a recurring dream. Bríghid Sinclair and I sat on top of a hill. We were teenagers. She spread a picnic between us. Her red hair and fair skin stood out in the moonlight against her flowing green dress. She was my Celtic goddess rising out of the green hills.

She leaned over to give me a kiss, and everything went still. Large hands grabbed Bríghid, snatching her away from me. Something hit me on the back of the head. The world grew dark as rough hands grabbed me as well.

I awoke alone in a cell. Kids from my village, as well as some I didn't know, were locked in similar cages. A gruesome goat-faced head appeared, staring at me through the bars. Did I remember him as Fomorian? He spoke to an unseen figure behind him. "He doesn't look all that special to me."

A fist flew between the bars toward me, and all went dark again.

My vision gradually cleared. I felt more lucid as I discovered I was lying on top of a hill. A small path stretched down toward the keep. The trail led a short way into the distance, ending at a set of gates. Curiosity pulled me to the outer gates, but nothing was perceptible beyond them. I turned and walked back to the edge of the lawn overlooking the keep. Shadows moved in the lone light of the upper tower.

The entire building seemed to stress, as if a great pressure was building inside and threatening to explode. Nearly the entire outer chamber was full of debris. A golden blur seemed to be trying to clear the breach, but it was losing as it dashed in and out.

A mild compulsion drew me to assist in the efforts to clear the debris. With two of us working together, we started to make some headway. After what felt like years, we had cleared much of the room. The source of the wood and stone debris became apparent. A portal in the ceiling was dropping the material.

A thought came to mind. I conjured a blue energy ball and shot it toward the opening. The golden blur zipped out of the front of the keep. I had to duck and dodge as the energy ball ricocheted around the room, finally bouncing out the door. Debris was rapidly piling up again.

I envisioned a net over the portal and threw another energy ball. It reformed as a net over the opening and slowed the flow of debris. Then it began to stretch and threatened to rupture. The vision of a

127

steel door formed in my mind and materialized over the opening. Within moments, it started to buckle under the weight behind it. The golden blur entered the room and shoved a tree trunk under the steel plate to block the portal closed. I glimpsed at the beautiful smiling face.

Behind me, a gentle woman's voice said, "You may now start your lessons."

The woman in gray was waiting for me outside. "Follow me," she said. We stopped in the middle of the field. She turned to look at me. "Conjure a fireball and hold it."

I envisioned the fireball. After mere moments, it began to burn my hands.

The woman in gray nodded at the fireball. "It's your energy. Don't let it hurt you." She hurled a fireball at my head. I blocked it with the one in my hands.

"Good," she said with a sly cackle. "It's coming back to you. Let's see how you do with this." A tree trunk flew from the forest like a missile. Partway, it splintered into a thousand spears.

I threw up a shield around me and braced for the impact. The smaller spears ricocheted off the sphere surrounding me. Behind the initial rain of wood, the core of the trunk became visible and hit the sphere, sending me rolling like a giant cue ball. I dropped the shield and tumbled to the ground.

She looked disappointed. "Tsk. You'll have to do better than that."

An invisible hand grabbed me and flung me high into the air.

"Wake up, Rip Van Wizard." Drea slapped me. "It's noon."

Groggy, I muttered something even I didn't understand.

"And your new pet made a mess on the carpet," Drea barked in her drill sergeant voice. "Lunch is up. Get moving."

The furball hopped on my chest. "Woof."

I WAS READY in five minutes. I'd dressed in a clean skinsuit and had a furball on my heels. The mess it had made was indicative of something much larger than the thirteen pounds of fury that followed me.

Wynn, Raines, Drea, and Onyx sat around the dining room table, studying the map of the area we now referenced as the hunting grounds. Mel opened the door, and a train of concierges rolled in three carts laden with lockers.

A stack of sandwiches sat on the counter, and I grabbed one as I half-listened to Wynn. "We have units in each of the locations flagged in green. Remote cameras are in the spots marked blue, including the lines of sight. Tactical response units are parked in these locations."

I took a bite out of the sandwich. "Fomorians," I said with a full mouth.

The entire room stared at me.

"Say again," Wynn said.

I leaned against the counter and swallowed. "Fomorians. Hired freebooters from the looks of it. They're operating from off the coast."

"How do you know?" Wynn asked.

"I chased one last night through most of the hunting ground area. Shot him a couple of times, but it barely slowed him down. I played fetch with a pack of hellhounds while he took off in a runabout. Didn't your surveillance teams pick that up?"

Wynn sat in stunned silence.

Mel looked excited. "Sig or Colt?"

"Sig," I replied. "Nice handling."

Mel rummaged through one of the lockers and tossed me six small boxes. "Explosive rounds. Let me know how they work. And try these cold iron blades."

Fantastic. I was a beta tester for monster-killing ammo. I hoped I would be around to give it a five-star review.

Wynn was on his phone, yelling at people to start reviewing video.

I waved at him to get his attention. "Tell them to look for an archer. I didn't get a good look, but the Fomorian took off with whatever load Robin Hood shot him with."

A pawing at my leg distracted me. I grabbed a steak sandwich, pulled out the meat, and placed it on a small plate on the floor. The furball gulped it down.

"And where did you find the poop machine?" Drea asked.

I tossed him another piece of steak. "He saved me from the hellhounds."

"So if everything around you is saving you all the time, what are you here for?" Onyx snipped.

Teenage girls. Proof that hell existed. "I've chummed the waters. Now you two head out and play bait."

I got busy loading magazines with the new ammunition. "I'm ready to go pirate fishing."

WE SPLIT UP on arrival at the hunting grounds. Wynn met up with his team at their mobile post. Drea and I took up position on the patio of a bistro down the street from Bella Donna's. Mel was parked on the other side of the block of buildings. Onyx and Raines wandered in and out of shops, looking like a pair of giggly teens. At least they could make it look natural to snap pictures with cell phones if they saw anything they thought looked suspicious and text in regular updates.

I opened my Sight and Sense, watching the streets for anything unusual. The challenge was that this was still LA. Everything was unusual. I would get burned out pretty quickly if I kept my abilities wide open, so I switched them off and on.

Drea and I sat in the café for hours. The continuous refills of liquid caffeine were making me jittery. Onyx and Raines were on their fourth lap of the block, somehow still looking pretty fresh, as if they were just starting their day's shopping excursion.

Drea pointed out two people sitting in the back corner of the café. It took me a minute to realize she was star-struck. Apparently, the women were two hot young actresses who were supposed to hate each other. From the way they were behaving, they seemed to be friends. I guessed it was more hype for their careers. A dozen other people were scattered at tables, all in their own worlds.

We watched Onyx and Raines as they meandered down the block. Onyx texted me a picture of a passing van. I opened my Sight back onto them and noticed something not right. They had been tagged with a different energy from what we had seen before. A third of the people on the block were tagged in some way, but they were the only two I had seen with that signature.

I sent a text to Wynn. "It looks like we have a nibble. They've been marked."

I heard Wynn's announcement to the team in my earbuds. "Heads up… It looks like we are active."

We watched as Onyx and Raines continued to make their way up the block. Several more minutes passed, and they neared the corner. I was starting to think it was a false alarm. Then, from behind us, one of the bistro tables flew up and hit Drea.

A flying chair knocked me sideways, so I continued the fall, rolled over on the floor, and drew my 1911. Six Fomorians stood behind us where patrons had sat just a moment ago. In their true forms, they were a gruesome sight. All of them were at least nine feet tall or more. The low ceilings forced them to crouch, which worked to our advantage. They had more animal-like heads than human, and their skin was mottled and lumpy. They drew bladed weapons and marched toward us.

The two starlets transformed into Woodland faeries. A couple behind us transformed into werewolves. I realized that everyone in the bistro had changed into either a Fomorian or something that really didn't like Fomorians, except for a middle-aged couple that sat

132

next to us. They wore badges from some convention. Their nametags read Dick and Betty.

I pointed to the mobile command van at the end of the block. "Run there now." Then I said into my mic, "Wynn, two inbound your way. Code green in the bistro."

"Hulkbusters en route," Wynn squawked.

Wynn loved his little inside joke. Any supernatural in its real form was a Hulk—big, green, and likely to cause a mess. And, in his opinion, Hulks should be sent back to the realm of fantasy.

The couple dashed safely into the street. The wife said something about how they shouldn't have left Iowa City.

My attention returned to the Fomorians. *No time like the present to try out the new ammo.* As they approached, we started hammering them with bullets before they could get close enough to attack us.

"Apprehend them all, alive if possible," Wynn squawked.

One of the Fomorians must have seen me turn because he threw one of the faeries at me. She slammed into my chest, knocking us both to the ground. I swore and shoved her off to the side and fired two rounds into the Fomorian's shoulder. His right arm was blown off.

The now one-armed Fomorian fell to the ground, bellowing in pain. One of his friends seized the loose arm and started swinging it like a club. The fight rolled into the street, which gave the Fomorians an advantage with their size. Wynn arrived with four of his agents from the command post.

Onyx and Raines screamed. They were being pulled into a van. Drea and Wynn tried to contain the fight behind me as I chased after the van, but it sped off before I could get there. "Mel… gray van… stop it!" I yelled into my mic.

The remaining Fomorians gave up the fight and ran for a second van. One of them stabbed One-Arm in the skull then began to run. As it became clear he wouldn't make it to the van, one of the other Fomorians aimed a blunderbuss at him.

I lined up my shot and emptied my magazine into the van. Luck was on my side. I hit the shooter, and the blunderbuss went off, blowing out the top of the van as it sped off.

Now stranded, the remaining Fomorian turned to attack. I threw one of the cold iron blades into his leg, and he crashed down with a roar. Wynn and team moved to secure the Fomorian, and I ran for Special K. She was already running, ready for me.

Mel was pursuing the van with Onyx and Raines and fed me directions. Wynn had a couple of teams following behind. Nearly flying in and out of traffic, K was helping to balance and weave between the cars and obstacles.

Mel's Audi came into sight a block ahead. She passed through an intersection and was T-boned by another car. I blew by and hoped that everyone was okay. "Wynn, we have an accident. Mel is down, and civilians involved." Chatter indicated that help was en route.

The van was a little further ahead and close to the pier. It crashed from the road onto the pier and slid sideways, blocking the entrance. People scattered. Two Fomorians came around from behind the van, aimed grenade launchers, and began to fire at me.

Special K threw a shield of Kevlar around me and most of the bike. Only a thin slit was left open for me to be able to see. One of the grenades landed just to my right and blew Special K and me into a parked car.

I sensed she was hurt, damaged, or both, but she released me from the Kevlar cocoon. Sore and a little shaken from the explosion, I found cover behind a car. While the Fomorians reloaded, I rammed a fresh magazine of explosive rounds into the 1911 and started shooting. At a distance of sixty yards, I was not much of a threat, but they took cover anyway. I reloaded and darted forward. At twenty yards out, one of the Fomorians leveled the grenade launcher at me. I fired first and saw the Fomorian drop with several large holes blown into his chest. His partner turned and ran down the pier.

The last Fomorian paused for cover behind the van then jumped into a cigarette boat and immediately shot out into the open ocean. A small ski boat sat running, tied to the pier. I jumped in, cut the moorings, and followed him into the Pacific.

The borrowed boat did not have the power to keep up, much less catch him. I was ten miles offshore as the sun set on the ocean. The Fomorian boat was a dot in the distance. It disappeared completely in a green flash as the sun dipped below the horizon.

They were gone.

I TIED OFF the ski boat at the pier. Some Malibu type was talking to one of Wynn's agents, pointing and yelling at me. I guess I'd borrowed his boat.

Wynn stormed directly to me with Drea on his heels. "What the hell happened?" he asked.

"You tell me. You have agents and surveillance covering the entire area."

Drea pointed at us both. "You pulled Onyx into this."

Wynn was furious. "You didn't know that no one in the café was human except for a couple of conventioneers?"

My adrenaline spent, I fell to the ground exhausted and leaned on a pylon. "Half of LA isn't fully human. They don't come with flags to tell you what side they're on."

Wynn received a message through his earbud. "I knew I shouldn't have trusted you," he said to me. "This isn't over." He stalked back toward a group of his people.

Drea leaned down beside me. "You're bleeding."

I waved her off. "How's Mel?"

Drea breathed deeply. "Okay. Pretty banged up. She's back at the suite, being attended to. The driver of the other car is in better shape."

"And Ktesippe, how's she? She saved my life when we took the hit."

"Bad," Drea said. "She's a mess. Her personality is there, but the hardware is… mangled. And you saved her. You're the one who threw up the bubble. She just pulled something out of the bag of tricks."

Drea pulled me back up, and we walked over to the Mobile Command Center. Wynn's medic, a small brunette named Rebecca, had patched me up in the past and started doing so again. Wynn returned and looked as if he'd cooled down a bit.

He assessed me. "How are you? You look like you had your ass handed to you."

"He'll live," Rebecca chimed in. "But I'm running out of fresh places to bandage."

Neither Wynn nor I was in the mood. And that was not what he was asking.

"I'm pissed," I said.

Wynn stared me down with steely eyes. "Good. Now maybe you'll stop holding back. Debrief at twenty-two hundred. Your place." Wynn turned away and resumed barking orders.

"Drea, let's get out of here." We had an hour to get back to the suite, clean up, and be ready for Wynn.

Drea ushered me into the passenger seat. She started the car, rolled out of the lot, and stopped. A mix of law enforcement agencies had things cordoned off for blocks. "How much of a history do you have with Wynn?" she asked, staring straight ahead.

I debated how much to tell her. I was not really in the mood, but it would come out anyway if she didn't already know. "I spent six months with his team. Dorian, Nicky, and I were consulting for them when things went bad in Canada. Wynn was leading up a special operations team, investigating some out-of-the-box stuff. Dorian has known Wynn for probably twenty years. Because I reappeared, Wynn assumes I had something to do with what went down up north."

"Did you?" she asked. "Did you have anything to do with what happened?"

It felt like an accusation. "If you're asking if I led them into a trap then, and if I led us into a trap now, the answer is no. And if you believe I did, let me out now." I was fuming. I was angry with Drea and more so with Wynn. Things were falling apart quickly, and trust was running short all the way around. If we couldn't pull together in a hurry, then bodies would continue to pile up. Soon, those bodies would belong to people we cared about.

Drea did not give me an answer, but she pulled out and drove toward the suite.

DREA DROVE QUIETLY the entire trip back to the resort. She marched straight into her room when we entered the suite. I sat next to Mel, who was bandaged up and lounging on the couch. The little black furball curled up on the couch next to her.

I tried to keep it light. "I see the mummy has risen."

Mel was obviously drugged, but lucid. "I don't think that a couple of wrapped cracked ribs and a head bandage quite make me the mummy."

I scratched the furball's head. "I'm sorry about the crash."

She smirked. "In no way are you responsible. I was driving. I pushed it in the chase. Some days you win, and some days you come up craps."

A shower did little to wash away some of the day's confusion. How could I miss a room full of Fomorians? Their ability to do a glamour was pretty basic. The average person wouldn't notice, but anyone with an inkling of talent should have noticed something.

My wounds from the fight with the hellhounds the night before had all but faded. Fresh cuts and big bruises from the brawl and chase with the Fomorians had taken their place. I pulled myself into a clean Leviskin and Pushed it to become a pair of jeans and shirt. I took a couple of healing potions from my satchel and drank one down.

An argument had erupted in the living room and temporary command center. Drea and Wynn were having heated words in the kitchen but stopped when I came out. I tossed the other healing potion to Mel.

Ignoring the accusations that were flying around, my appreciation increased for the resort life. A huge spread was laid out on a couple of carts. I made a sandwich and looked at the map and still pictures from the fight.

A series of videos was queued on a laptop.

Wynn called us to the table. "Here's what we know. At 7:45 this evening, we were hit from multiple sides. The Fomorian team in the café was just one of several. A second group was in the Koffee Klatch around the corner, and they took out Surveillance Team Four. A third group was roaming around. Surveillance Teams Six and Seven got into a running fight with them. All in all, I have nine casualties, including four dead, four wounded—two critically, and one missing. In addition, Miss Melanippe was injured, Onyx is missing, and eight civilians were injured, including your werewolf and faerie friends from the café. It was not our best day."

"What about the Fomorians?" I asked.

"Eleven dead and two injured and captured, including the one you took down," Wynn said. "There were also a few others, but we don't know who or what yet. The unknowns and six Fomorians holed up in a warehouse and burned it down with themselves inside once they failed to fight themselves out."

"It doesn't make sense," I said.

"Care to elaborate?" Wynn asked.

I recalled stories from old histories I had read. "So, the Fomorians have a history of being pirates, going back to the days of early Ireland. Depending on the text, they're either demonic creatures, or more likely, the creations of the old dark gods. One of the old, more reputable texts placed them as demigods, which makes the most sense. Once they lost their foothold on Ireland, they stuck to the sea."

Wynn had a disbelieving look. "Demigod pirates?"

I guessed it was time to ante up. "So, there's a lot of confusion about the old gods. I'm not talking a supreme being, boss to the angels and like. Not exactly. There's a myth from one of the ancient texts that talks about certain times when God was so saddened he cried. When Lucifer revolted, the days when Adam and Eve were kicked out of the garden, etcetera.

"These tears sometimes fell to earth. If there were people around, and if they believed enough, those tears could sometimes manifest a deity. That deity would have some of the abilities of God. The more people believed in them, the stronger they would become. When the deity fell out of favor or was forgotten, it didn't die. Sometimes they would reinvent themselves and find new people to worship them. Other times, they would hide or even go into a state of torpor, waiting to be reawakened."

Wynn paled, and I saw the wheels in Drea's head turning.

I continued. "So, in time, some of these deities procreated—sometimes with other deities, and other times with people or other entities."

"Demigods," Wynn said.

"That's the story. If I had to guess, these guys are several generations away from being a full-blood. A full-blooded Fomorian is supposedly twenty-five, thirty feet or taller."

Wynn replayed video of the Fomorian boat disappearing. "So, if the Fomorians are demigod pirates, where are they hiding out, and what are they up to?"

My allegiance to Wynn and Longbow only went so far. Not knowing how much Wynn or the government knew about other realms, or how much I was talking out of school, I shared only the barest necessities. The Accords were murky in reference to people who had been awakened to reality. "Just a guess, they're across the Veil. The question is where."

Something seemed to click for Wynn. "You mean like a pocket dimension."

It sounded as though he knew more than I did. "I guess. It's a reality very close to our own. Sometimes it looks just like this side of the Veil. Other times, they can be really bizarre."

Wynn nodded. "Our people have been theorizing about how they work. We've even been to a few of them, unofficially of course. How do we get there?"

"'We don't. I do. Or at least, I try to. When I get the lay of the land, we can figure out the next step. I'm not even entirely sure which realm they're in."

Wynn protested. "They have one of my people."

"I'm going," Drea said.

I looked at both of them. "No. I may have a few ways to get myself in, and hopefully get out. I can't guarantee they'll work for me, much less for others. No, if I can get over, I'm not stranding anyone else. Besides, Wynn, I don't think this is in your jurisdiction."

He gave me a frustrated look. "So, what's your plan?"

That was a good question. "If I'm right, we know exactly where their portal is located. I try to use it and see where I wind up. I find out what I can and do my best to get back here."

"What do you need?" Wynn asked simply. "And when can you be ready to go?" Hints of resignation and desperation laced his voice.

I LAID OUT a list of what I needed for Wynn and Drea to acquire. It would take them a few hours to get the necessary supplies, so I opted to meditate and ready myself. I must have fallen asleep in the process.

I found myself flying through midair and a fireball hurling directly at me.

"We were not done yet," the woman in gray hissed from the ground.

Using an energy shield, I deflected a dozen incoming missiles of fire, ice, wood, and stone. A rib cracked when I landed hard on the hill and rolled. Vines shot out of the ground and tied me down. I managed to wriggle free and found myself naked except for a pair of shorts. I immediately visualized armor and a shield, and it manifested just in time to block a hail of arrows.

A legion of nightmares stood at the top of the hill. Some looked almost human. Some had four, six, eight, ten arms, legs, and appendages I couldn't fathom. Some wore armor, and others looked as if they had exoskeletons. Another round of arrows flew. One caught me in the side, but the armor took the worst of it. Still, blood ran down my leg. The archers pulled back, and the horde charged down the hill. Reflexively, I began pitching fireballs. The demonic horde took them in stride as if they were mist on a summer day.

I realized I was an idiot. I tried ice spears. They melted just before hitting the horde. I telepathically launched trees and rocks. The wood became ash on contact, and the rocks harmlessly bounced away. I tried to buy time by manifesting walls between the horde and me as I ran for the keep. It slowed them down just enough for me to get into the keep and raise the drawbridge.

Something new had manifested in the hall. The debris was gone, and a circular staircase spiraled into the tower. Following the corkscrew, I climbed to the ninth floor, which opened onto the roof of the tower.

The horde had surrounded the keep and were shouting and beating drums. The tower vibrated from the noise. Archers took pot shots that bounced off the walls, and the horde dropped bridges and ladders to cross the moat and climb the walls.

In a desperate attempt, I manifested rain and hail. It slowed the horde down, and the water appeared to create discomfort, but they were still advancing and would soon breach the gates. Conveniently, my rucksack sat on the wall near me. One lone Holy Hand Grenade was perched on top. While levitating it, I envisioned it growing. It reached an unbelievable size and floated above the castle just as the horde reached the top of the keep. I exploded the grenade. A deluge crashed down, and the horde began to dissolve.

When the water cleared, the woman in gray stood next to me on the tower. A mixture of frustration and acceptance rang in her voice.

"Crude, but effective. Why do you keep holding back? You could have handled the horde with ease."

I was taken aback. "With ease? Where did they come from anyway?"

Instead of answering, she faded from view. I walked back downstairs to the ground floor. The wooden double doors were still barricaded. The staircase vanished after I moved off the last step.

Ribbons of light streamed around the door and through any crack it could find. The door was straining. An unknown force was holding back whatever was behind the door. I feared it and knew it would destroy me.

The voice of the woman in gray echoed in my head. "You are not the weak being you pretend to be. You will have to face them someday. They are already bleeding into the world."

Someone rubbed my shoulder, snapping me awake. "I'm back with your requests, my liege," Drea said.

I looked into her eyes. "What did you say?" I was still foggy.

She frowned. "It's a joke. I'm running around like your errand girl. What's with you?"

I felt as if I was going out of my mind. "Nothing, just stress, I guess." I took her attitude to mean I was working my way back to her good side.

EVERYTHING WAS PREPARED for the tracking spell except for some ocean water. I walked down to the beach and put my bare feet into the Pacific. A gentle warmth radiated from my pocket. I had forgotten the velvet bag Daire had given me. Opening it and removing the shard of crystal, I studied the refraction of the sunlight through it. It held a powerful energy that I had not sensed until now. An iridescent glow slowly spread around it, forming an aura.

A voice boomed from behind me. "Got Fomorian troubles?"

I spun around to see a huge man. He looked to be around fifty and was near seven feet tall. He was barrel-chested with a huge bushy beard that was flecked with gray. He stood there, wearing shorts and undoubtedly the ugliest Hawaiian shirt I had ever seen in my life. The ridiculous scene was completed with the undersized Gilligan hat that floated on his mane of hair. He leaned against a walking stick and took a drink from a mug.

"I said top of the morning to you," he boomed.

I must have been hearing things. Maybe I was finally going crazy. "Morning to you as well," I yelled over the wind and surf.

Returning the crystal to the velvet bag, I slipped it back into my pocket and filled the water bottle from the ocean. I flicked my Sight toward the man and saw sparkles of power unlike any I had seen before. I stood and walked over to him. "Hi, I'm Grey."

The man reached out with more of a paw than a hand. "I'm The Dag. Nice to meet you." His voice was a deep baritone with hints of an Irish brogue and southern England accent. I felt a warmth flow from The Dag as I grasped his hand.

He offered me his cup. "Care for a snort? Bloody Mary cures a lot of ills."

"Rain check?"

The grin on The Dag's face grew. "Absolutely, lad. Tata!"

As I returned to the suite, I hoped to live long enough to have that drink. I sensed that meeting The Dag had not been a chance encounter.

Wynn was in the suite with Drea when I returned. Mel was up walking around, looking almost healed.

Wynn was stone-faced. "We need to get this right. I think you need support going with you."

I leaned against the bar counter. "I'm not going to be responsible for your team." I looked over at Drea. "You, either."

Wynn slammed his fist on the table. "If this goes south and we lose you, we don't have another option. You are the only key in." He left it unsaid that he did not entirely trust me.

I sat down at the table. "Gerry, if this goes south, I can leave you another way to get in. It won't work until I've been gone for twenty-four hours, but I can give you a back door—a portal on this side, and one on the other. If I can't get out, I can give you a way in. And if I need help, I can set up a signal."

"Walk me through it," Wynn said. After an hour or so of intense discussion, he unhappily agreed. "We have a secure holding facility not far from here. It's empty and should meet your requirements."

I shook his hand. "I need an hour." I went into the empty closet in my room and drew out the portal to my dimensional spider hole.

Standing in the middle of the circle, I muttered, "Home, Jeeves."

In a flash, I was stepping out into my workshop. I hurriedly grabbed supplies, dumped them into my rucksack, and loaded up a spare pack as well. With my few spare minutes, I skimmed an old text on portals and wards.

146

My hour was almost up. I looked around the lab as I stepped into the portal ring and again debated hiding in the old leather recliner in the corner, but I knew that wasn't really an option. "Off to be the wizard." I stepped out of the closet and nearly erased the sigil out of habit. Instead, I cast a protected glamour and hid it.

I carried my rucksack and the second pack into the living room. "Can someone grab the bug-out bags?"

We carried everything downstairs and loaded up into a couple of Wynn's Suburbans then rode over to what looked like a two-story industrial building. Inside, we were greeted by a security detail, which led us into a central holding area. The idea of a trap briefly crossed my mind.

Wynn waved. "The place is yours."

I spent hours mixing concoctions and drawing portals in each of the individual holding cells. I raised wards and defenses around each. When I was done, I had them close all of the cell doors. They would work as temporary portal gates. I used a small room at the end to give them a sort of control room that would let them activate the portals. It also had an option that would, if necessary, let them destroy the portals in an emergency.

Wynn, Drea, and I piled into one of the Suburbans and headed for the marina. Wynn had arranged for use of an old Coast Guard cutter. It towed a smaller landing craft. I grabbed my rucksack and the two bug-out bags and headed for the vessel.

"I'm dropping you off and bringing the cutter back," Drea said.

"No," I argued.

"Non-negotiable," Wynn said. "Do you know how hard it is to get one of these?"

147

The skiff was serviceable, but small and underpowered. It couldn't get me there in time, and they both knew it. "Let's go."

Drea piloted while I did a last check of my gear. I Willed the Leviskin into an armored diving suit with buoyancy bladders, just in case. The sun was dropping rapidly. We were twenty-one miles off the coast when Drea slowed the boat. "We're here. Good luck, and hurry back."

I slid into the smaller craft and cast off from the larger boat. My suspicion that she was trying to force herself along still lingered. "Get to a safe distance," I yelled. "If this doesn't work, I'll need a ride."

Now to find the exact portal. I took out a bottle of locator potion I had made for Onyx and doused a cotton ball. It floated in the air until I whispered, "Seek."

The ball glowed pink, did a few circles in midair, and dashed a hundred yards in front of my skiff. The sun was minutes away from dipping beneath the horizon. I opened my Sight and my Sense. A portal was forming. I gunned the boat and aimed for the swirling mass.

A green flash came over the sea as the sun dipped under the horizon. I looked around me. The cutter was right behind me, and lights flickered to life from the shore. I had missed the window. Drea was not on deck to help me recover the skiff when I pulled up to the cutter. When I boarded, I discovered her tied up and unconscious on the floor of the wheelhouse. Before I could draw the 1911, I felt a shock then a tingling sensation. Everything faded to black.

I WOKE UP lying on the floor of a dark stone cell, with a splitting headache. My hands and feet were cuffed. A thin sliver of light showed underneath the cell door. With a couple of movements of my hands and a Push of Will, the bonds fell free, but it took more effort than I would have thought. The world around me spun when I tried to stand, and I fell onto a bench.

Shuffling came from outside, and an observation slit opened in the door. It slid shut just as quickly. I heard more shuffling, then a door creaked open and closed. A few moments later, I heard the door again, then more shuffling. My cell door opened, and an ogre waved at me. He stood eight feet tall and had leathery green skin. A smattering of sparse wiry hair covered his bulbous head, and he wore a rumpled gray uniform. "Follow me," he grunted.

We stopped in front of a small office around the corner. Bureaucrats looked and worked the same way throughout the universe. The guy behind the cheap faux mahogany desk looked almost human, but his proportions were not quite right. Everything was longer and thinner. He looked as if someone had put him in a taffy puller. He wore a cheap suit and had the standard bored look of an office worker.

Los Angeles was visible out of the windows… but on further inspection, I realized it wasn't LA. I was in LD.

"Reason for visit to Los Diablos?" asked a monotone voice.

Oh, damn. We'd made it through the portal. Where the hell was Drea? "Vacation. LA has too many tourists this time of year."

A semi-grin barely passed over his lips. "Anything to declare?"

From somewhere, I channeled Foghorn Leghorn. "Well, I say, I do, I do declare you are vexing me."

149

No longer amused, he pointed to my bags in the corner. "Are those yours?"

"Indubitably."

He shook his head slightly. "How long will you be staying?"

I clued in. Even hell had customs agents, and this was the devil's vacation spot. "A couple of days. A quick getaway for me and the missus."

The customs agent stared at me. "Next time, stop at the office in Los Angeles and get a visa in advance. Please obey all laws, and try not to get killed while you're in town. The paperwork is quite invasive to any disembodied spirits here, and there is quite a backlog, as you would imagine. Here is your estimated tariff. Have a pleasant stay."

In a move I barely followed, the customs agent stamped and shoved the documents in my face. He also handed me a pamphlet on getting a pre-approval for future visits.

Obviously dismissed, I grabbed my bags and paid the tariff with one of the remaining gold coins. A small amount of change hit the desk. Half was pushed toward me, and the rest landed in the agent's pocket. I shuffled out of the building. Drea sat outside the doors.

She took one of the bug-out bags from me. "I've already gotten the boat out of hock. Why didn't you do customs in advance?"

I frowned at Drea. "You're not supposed to be here. I'm sending you back."

Drea looked quite pleased with herself. "I thought you had a single-use portal," she snipped. "Are you sending me back without anything useful?"

"You can take the ferry," I snapped back. "I didn't know they were hiding out in Los Diablos. This is the tourist trap of the hell realms. It pulls in magical and demonic alike. Their slogan is, 'Come to town and make a little mayhem.'"

Drea gave me a grave stare. "Look, I'm here. Let's go find them and get out of here. And what do you mean by 'take the ferry'?"

I pointed up the road from the Customs House toward the pier. A large sign read, "Ferry to Los Angeles. Leaves every hour, on the hour."

"I'm not going back without them," Drea stated with resolve. "So where are they?"

I breathed deeply and counted to ten. "Okay, if you are staying, it's one hundred percent my rules. No negotiation."

She nodded.

"First, we need to get somewhere quiet. I need to whip up a few things. I know a place we can go."

"And second?"

"This is a dangerous place, but I doubt they're here. I suspect they used it as a stopover. I should have figured it out when they disappeared in the green flash at sunset, but there are a number of places you can go with that power. The good news is, I think I know where they went."

She looked hopeful. "Okay, great. Let's get moving. Where are they?"

"A place that makes beings want to come here for vacation." I'd hoped the subtle hint would be enough to get her to take the ferry, but I should've known better.

I hailed down an armored cab, and we loaded everything in. The driver was tall for a goblin, just short of five feet. All I could see over the seat was the little gray head and wisps of white hair. "Whar to?" it grunted.

Against my better judgment, I went with the only relatively safe place in town that I knew. "Gin Hole. You know where it is?"

A grunt came back. "Aff course. Not a place for tourists. I can take you much better place."

I smacked the window. "Good thing we aren't tourists." It was time to see Obi's nephew and the local dive he owned.

A small grunt. "As you wish."

"And take the east route."

We pulled out from the Customs House. I'd directed the goblin to take a route I knew pretty well, but I hadn't traveled it in a while. I avoided this place unless I absolutely had to come down, but it was a handy hiding spot for some of the more unsavory types. The jobs I'd been taking had led me there around four times a year. I didn't know if the east route was still a good route to take, but it would give me a feel for how Los Diablos was now. At least LD was more honest than LA.

Off in the mountains, a sign read, "HELLYWOODLAND."

I pointed to the sign. "Drea, look over there. At dawn, the sign becomes just 'WOODLAND,' and the Fae come out to play. At night, it's 'HELLYWOODLAND' and the demonic… well, they do their thing."

The east route turned out to be better than it had been the last time I'd come through, but as we neared the north quadrant, it got rougher. A street brawl was in full swing between a unit of Ba'als horde and what looked like some of Enke's warrior monks. Both sides looked to be having way too much fun. Someone had roped in a pack of wereoxen, and they seemed to be ripping through both sides with equal zeal. Hundreds of wounded and dead floated on a sea of blood and effluvia.

Drea paled a little at the gratuitous slaughter.

With her watching the fighting, I took to the opportunity to broach a subject I had been avoiding. "I thought Amazons were great warriors."

She stiffened at the mention. "There are very few of us left. We fight for cause, for honor. This is... senseless. A waste."

I had to agree, but I knew where some of these entities came from. This was still a vacation in comparison with their homelands. I figured I would continue to push my luck. "I would have thought you would have found someone by now. A partner."

We rode in silence for a few moments and watched as the mayhem outside got worse. Unfortunately, The Gin Hole was in the middle of the north district. The fighting got worse as we drove, but fortunately, cabs were usually considered neutral ground.

"We do not take mates, except to ensure another generation," Drea said. "Once a year, some of my sisters choose a mate. I have not elected to do so because of my other duties. The children are raised where they're safe and can be brought up in our ways."

"You mean the girls. What about the boys?" I knew I had hit an uncomfortable subject.

She winced. "In the past, they would have been abandoned. Over time, though, we have found ways to mostly produce female children. If a male is born, sometimes the mothers have raised them outside of our society. Usually, they're adopted out."

"And what about you?" I asked. "Will you eventually select someone?"

She didn't speak for a long moment. "I thought I had found someone," she finally murmured. "But he still appears to be pledged to another."

"Who?" I asked. "Who's the lucky one?"

"The only son to become an Amazon." I could barely hear her whisper.

WE PULLED AROUND to the back entrance of The Gin Hole. A garage door opened when I punched in my personal code. I was a little surprised it still worked. The goblin backed into the garage, and I shut the door.

Buziba Ramla, Obi's nephew, came down a half set of stairs into the loading dock. "Greyson, my friend, how are you? You should have called. I could have had a driver pick you up."

Buziba looked much like the rest of his family: Middle Eastern, short, thin, but well-built and mannered like a sultan. Unlike much of the rest of the family, he always dressed in a plain black suit, ready to either fight or party. In this neighborhood, open warfare could be considered a party as long as libations were provided. His eyes still showed the yellow fire of his youth. He came over, and we clasped in a tight bear hug. One of his men came down and started unloading our bags.

I let out a false laugh. "You know how those last-minute trips are. You never know where you'll end up. Buziba, meet a close friend, Drea."

Drea looked uncomfortable as Buziba hugged her as well. "Come on in and relax," he said. "I'll have your bags taken to your old room."

My attempt to pay the cabbie was rebuffed. Nervously, he tried looking anywhere but at me. "Iz on the house."

"Um, thanks." I dumped my change from the Customs House on the seat for a generous tip.

Buziba led us into the sin den he called an office, and shooed a couple of half-naked females out. One of them was a Woodland elf, but I had never seen anyone like the other before. Her upper body was built-out, almost human. Her legs looked to be thick, but deer-like.

Tapestries covered the stone walls of the round room. Buziba favored depictions from the Kama Sutra. The floor sank into a round red leather couch, with a small stair breaking the circle. I knew the stair could be flipped over to form a complete circuit, and I had no desire to know the kinds of rites he performed there.

Buziba took his place on the couch. "You like the fawn? She came from the Summer Fae. She will mature in a year or so and go full deer. Or at least that is her current choice."

The Woodland elf came running in, carrying a tray with the strong coffee Buziba preferred.

He started fixing cups for the three of us. "So, what brings you to paradise?"

I leaned back on the couch. "Looking for a bunch of kidnapped girls."

He nodded. "Obi said you're on some fool's errand, like usual."

Drea started to get angry. "My sister—"

I stopped her in mid-sentence. "One of those taken is a dear friend. Fool's errand or not, I will see it through."

Buziba leaned back and kicked his feet up onto the table in the middle of the circle. "I suspected as much. I have a bit of information that may be helpful. I believe I've done a little business with the ones you seek."

I knew Buziba well. "What is it going to cost me?"

Buziba mocked being hurt. "I owe you many favors, Greyson, my friend. Consider it repaying a debt."

Aw, damn, here it comes.

Buziba pretended to be modest, something he never has been. "But if you're going anyway, I would consider it a personal favor if you could collect their outstanding balance. And a collection fee for you, of course."

"How much are they into you for?" I asked.

He waved dismissively. This wouldn't be good. "Three hundred thousand Imperial, give or take."

I started calculating. "What have you sold to them?" At that rate, he had either ripped them off magnitudes worse than his usual customers, or...

Buziba shrugged. "You know, the usual: food, weapons, clothes, building materials, everything you need for a campaign."

Double damn. This was much bigger than I had imagined. "Deal," was all I said. Negotiating would take time I doubted we had.

Buziba picked up a tablet from the bench behind him and tossed it to me. "Here's their location, the materials I've sent, and their estimated strength. They're camped on the Molan Sea. Give or take three hundred strong, based on the materials I sent."

"We'll need to use your back door," I told Buziba.

He grinned. "Feel free."

I LED DREA upstairs to a room I'd used before. Our bags were stacked outside, and one of Buziba's men stood guard. He looked as if he were a relatively young vampire, a few years since being turned at most. He was built like a tank and stressed the seams on his size fifty suit. He said nothing as I waved my hand in front of the wards on the door. The walking wall of a guard opened the door and carried all of our bags inside. As soon as the bags hit the floor, he left and closed the door.

"Chatty fellow," Drea snipped.

I did not want to tell Drea that Buziba had been known to find the biggest, dumbest guy in a bar, have his tongue ripped out, then have the poor bastard turned while dying. He used them for in-house security. Like most vamps in Buziba's employment, the guard wore sunglasses to cover up the fact that he was under a serious compulsion. They weren't much more than powerful zombies.

I waved my hands again at the wards, and a lavender light filled the room. "We can talk now," I said to Drea. "The room is secure."

She looked concerned. "How much time do you spend here, and how well do you know your friend downstairs?"

I shook my head. "I've only been here a half-dozen times. I know Buziba's family pretty well. One of his uncles arranged for me to hide out here for a few weeks one time, right after Canada. I occasionally do find-and-retrieve jobs for his uncle, Obi, to find out where Obi's dog, Fifi, is hiding. Usually, it's here. If you have something or someone you want to stash with no questions asked, Los Diablos is the place."

A puzzled look crossed her face.

"Don't ask," I said. "I don't trust Buziba. He's usually working a deal from both ends. As long as we have a common goal, or if it at least brings him more benefit than trouble, we should be okay. And Obi would be displeased if something were to happen to me, I think."

Drea frowned. "You really know how to instill confidence in a girl."

"Look, you wanted to be here, and you're here," I said with a serious tone. "If you want to head back and take the intel to our people and Wynn, now is the time to do that. I can port you back to LA from here. Otherwise, I need to ship what we have to Wynn, and we need to move within the hour." I was on familiar ground, and I wanted to be in Los Diablos for as short of a time as possible.

The resolve in her eyes won out over the fear. "I'm all in. They have Onyx."

Having her there made me feel more comfortable, but I was also terrified for her safety. I'd never known she had feelings for me. She was one of the most beautiful people on the planet, and I cared for her. But I couldn't let it go beyond that, especially if this went badly. One more reason not to tangle her up in my mess.

I opened the folio on the tablet and memorized the major details. "Prepare for cold. Cold that makes the arctic look like the tropics. Be ready for long range and hand-to-hand. And most importantly, we'll need to travel fast."

She thought for a minute, and the next instant, she stood in a white bodysuit with mottled gray flecks. It looked armored and warm.

"So, how real is the construct around the Leviskins?" I asked. "I can tell it's much more than a glamour, but how much?"

A moment later, she stood in jeans and a T-shirt again. "Very real. The Leviskin pulls material from the ether, or somewhere. You can construct most anything you can imagine, within reason and the natural laws. Maybe even more."

I toyed with the options in my own suit until I found a workable combination. The package for Wynn contained a note, instructions, and the tablet with the intelligence info. I drew out a circle and symbols that were tied to one of the portals in the secure facility, then placed the package in the middle. I Pushed a little Will and said, "Fly, my pretty." The package disappeared.

Drea looked at me with amusement. At least, I hoped that's what it was.

"Time for us to fly," I said.

We each finished our load-outs and packed what we could carry. The rest stayed there. I lowered the wards and raised them again after we left the room.

Buziba's back door was his own personal portal facility, a lot like what I'd built in Los Angeles earlier in the day. But his was larger and much better equipped. The big block room had portals in each individual cell block. The main difference was that the room was made of three-foot-thick granite, and all of the light came from torches. The cell doors were constructed of heavy, cold iron. Most importantly, each of the circles was permanent and had built-in wards. They were made of a variety of materials—gold, silver, iron, copper, crystals—which varied depending on the target location and purpose. Each had the four elements integrated in some shape or fashion.

The portal that connected to the Winter Lands of the Fae landed in a very public spot. I chalked in a few small changes so we could go in unnoticed and away from any watchful eyes. I'd put in a private stop a few years back when I was tracking a lost Yeti. Fifi had adopted it.

The Winter House had been controlled by the House of Edur for millennia. They held sway over weather, including rain, snow, and sleet. If it could fall out of the sky, they had probably done it. Fomorians had been aligned with Winter as far back as I knew. Hell wouldn't have them, so they had to eke out an existence in the next-worse spot.

I pulled Drea onto the circle with me. "You ready?"

We both Pushed ourselves into the winter wear. She nodded.

"Off to Hoth."

An instant later, we stood in a cave. The walls had a thick coat of ice, but it sat over a geothermal hot spot, leaving the floor damp. Up ahead, a small opening was visible. The wind howled and whistled like a thousand wolves. Within seconds, a thin coat of frost had started to form on our clothes and exposed skin. I visualized a mask and goggles to cover my face. Drea did the same.

Over the wind, I heard her chatter, "Cold." She bulked up slightly more.

I have found that in the Fae realms, I have the ability to do short teleports as long as there is line of sight or it's somewhere I've been before. Based on the maps and the shifting landscape, I estimated that we needed to go thirty kilometers. I had never been to the Molan

Sea, but expected it to be as unpleasant as the rest of this Winter Land perdition.

I held onto Drea and made the first hop. The move was meant to get us out of the cave and onto the hillside. I wasn't sure if it was from the wind or the shock from the hop, but Drea fell and took me with her. We rolled a little ways down the hill. The wind and snow were blowing so hard that a small snow bank started to form against us before we could stand. I grabbed Drea's arm and bounced us down into the valley below.

We landed in a soft snow bank. The wind was still strong but more manageable. I'd failed to take into account that the solstice was days away. In the north, it was the summer solstice, but in the south, it was still winter. The solstices were the most powerful times in the Fae realms because those were the times when the power peaked on both sides. That meant our whole trip would be a rough one, but the further we got from the central Winter Court, the more it would settle down.

I held onto Drea and continued our hops across the landscape. How could anyone, much less ocean-going Fomorians, move through this mess? It took nearly two hours and a couple of more falls to reach the shore of the Molan Sea, where we stopped on a high cliff overlooking the water. Huge waves carved deep into an old mountain, which had been worn down to a cliff. The wind was still strong and cold, but for the most part, the snow had stopped falling. Even with the heavy clothes, we were both nearly frozen.

We could see a campsite about a half mile up the shore, so we gradually worked our way closer to the top of the hill overlooking the encampment. A high stone wall surrounded eight old stone longhouses, and a small keep sat in the middle. A reinforced set of double gates was the only visible entrance. A dozen iced-over Quonset huts encircled the permanent settlement walls. Six stone guard towers, a double chain-link fence, and barbed wire protected the whole camp. Dire wolves patrolled in the gap between the fences.

Smoke rose from the chimneys of most of the buildings. I turned on my Sight and saw the energy patterns that flowed around the entire encampment. There looked to be two ways in. The front gate was well defended. I pulled out a set of binoculars. A dozen longboats were docked on the shore near a stone pier. A few larger ships tossed in the turbulent seas off the coast.

Drea's voice barely managed to drown out the wind. "Any ideas?"

"Not any real good ones. I'm going to take some pictures to map the site. Stay here. If I'm not back in an hour, use this." I handed her a rock of smoky quartz. "All you need to do is hold the crystal and ask to pair it up. The other half of the crystal is in one of the ports in Wynn's warehouse."

Searching for a hidden spot facing the front gate, I found a copse of dead tree trunks and boulders. I ported into the spot and ducked down quickly. The fence was much larger than it had looked from below. The chain-link fence stretched thirty feet into the air. Razor wire was threaded into it and along the top. The keep was straight ahead, up a gravel road. The top of the tower was visible over tall stone walls that sheltered the buildings inside.

The dire wolves stalked toward the main gate, sniffing around. A quick jump to a snow hill on the far side of the camp helped confuse my scent and gave me a good look at the pier. I sank into the thick snow.

The Quonset huts were just on the other side of the fence. They stood twenty feet tall and were covered in a thick coat of ice and snow. The dire wolves turned in my direction. I ported to a small hidden spot on the pier. A thin coat of ice covered the pylons, and icy waves crashed and lapped over the stone walkways.

The closest longboats were loaded for an invasion. I took a few last pictures then ported back to Drea and handed her the camera. "They're gearing up for war. It's more than just raiding. Get that back to Wynn. I'm going to try to port in and get out."

Drea shouted a string of words over the wind that I chose to interpret as, "Be careful."

If I were being careful, I'd be sitting in a pub somewhere drinking a pint or holed up in my lab. I just gave her a thumbs-up.

My focus was on the top of the keep. No movement was visible in the tower. I crouched down to make myself as small of a target as possible. With my right hand, I took out an MP5 loaded with explosive rounds, and I pulled out a cold steel blade with my left. Then I visualized the landing.

As I ported over, an energy field surrounding the camp sprang to life. I rematerialized, flying through the air and barely had time to envision being surrounded by thick airbags. I hit cold, hard ground and bounced. Mercifully, I was knocked out on the first impact.

I STOOD OVERLOOKING the now-familiar hill and the keep from my dreams. I was starting to think of it as mine. A light snow was falling and had spread a white coat a few inches thick across everything in sight, capturing my footsteps as I moved toward the castle. Around me, the air was absolutely quiet and dead still. A shadow moved against the dim light in the tower. Ribbons of power started to trickle out of the windows and portcullises. The stream of energy rolling out of the front drawbridge was getting stronger.

I walked across the drawbridge. The inner doors appeared to be at their limit. Cracks had formed, and someone had added more buttresses and reinforcements to hold the door closed. I touched one of the ribbons of power and was thrown off my feet.

A sharp rock stabbed me in the ribs, rousing me. I lay on the floor of a small stone cell. This was becoming too much of a habit. Deflated airbags surrounded me. Some of them looked like they had burst on impact. Others had definitely been slashed.

I Willed the balloons to disappear. As I sat up, I could feel that any weapons in my outer gear were gone, but I could still feel the others connected with the base skinsuit. From the looks of the cell, I was in the main keep. It may not have been what I'd planned, but I had gotten in. Porting through the door of the cell failed. I bounced off with a resonating thud that brought a guard to the door. He was a thirteen-foot-tall Fomorian, mottled green and gray, with scales and bony plates like an alligator. Dressed in heavy leathers and furs, he looked to be more full-blooded than the ones I'd seen in LA. He had more of a goat head, horns, and dull red eyes. A wooden club almost as tall as me hung from his side. A broadsword was stuck in his boot. On him, it looked like a dirk.

The guard opened the cell and looped a heavy noose around my neck. Several things became very clear. One, I was going where he wanted me to go, for now. Two, he could easily snap my neck like a chicken's if I resisted. Three, someone wanted to see me.

I looked up, way up, at the guard. "If I'm a good puppy, will you scratch me behind the ears?"

In answer, he shoved me along toward a stone spiral staircase. The several cells we passed on the way were empty. The steps were built for much larger beings than me, but my captor was kind enough to help me climb by pulling me up by the rope around my neck. The Leviskin formed a collar that braced the rope so the help from my escort did not kill me.

We must have climbed forty feet up, using twenty stairs. The guard banged on an equally huge door, which opened with a shudder into a short corridor that emptied into a large hall. Tables and benches, which looked big enough to suit medium- and full-sized Fomorians, filled the room. But the hall was nearly empty. The walls were lined with long red banners, emblazoned with curved black swords. Whole tree trunks burned in fireplaces the size of cargo containers.

Other than the guard, a Fomorian sat in what I assumed was a granite throne. If he were standing, I would have guessed him to be twenty-five feet tall or more. He was an imposing figure, dressed in heavy leather clothing and furs and a breastplate the size of a car. His skin looked reptilian with overlapping plates running up the sides of his arms. His head looked like a giant bull's, with long, curled horns and more overlapping plates for skin. His huge red eyes pierced me. I searched and failed to find a weak point.

A small figure about my size stood on a ledge near the head of the throne, right next to the ear of its occupant. He looked like a dark elf and was dressed in the formal armor of an advisor to the Winter Court.

My guard dropped the rope but left the noose around my neck. The sheer weight of the rope alone almost brought me to my knees. The large doors behind me slammed shut with an echo as the guard left. I managed to struggle out of the noose. "Howdy."

The elf said something to the imposing figure, who let out a huge laugh. The reverberation beat in my chest. The elf slowly and fluidly made his way down a staircase to approach me.

He was lithe and stood a bit over six feet. He was malignantly beautiful, dressed in a simple black cloak with red trim. Pale-blue skin and ice-blue eyes stood out against his raven hair. In an oddly light and airy voice, he spoke a singsong stream of phrases I couldn't understand. I caught a few of the words in elven, but decided to play dumb. The elf turned back to the enthroned beast.

After a moment, the elf turned back to me. With a smug look, he spoke in singsong English. "Wizard, for what do you darken my lord, Chief Bren's, door?"

He'd gone straight to business. This could be good if it were just a simple raid for profit. It would explain taking supernaturals, who would have value here. "I believe your lord may have possession of some people from my realm. Some of his lesser soldiers have been raiding our side against the standing Accords. I am here to negotiate their return."

The elf turned to look at Bren. Telepathic communication? A moment later, the elf turned back. "Whom do you represent? Who are you looking to have returned?"

That was simple. "All of them."

The elf looked again to Bren. They both burst out laughing. "That will be quite expensive," the elf said to me. "We have some unique specimens here."

I smiled. "I represent some quite wealthy and powerful parties. May I inspect them?"

The dark elf smiled cruelly. "Certainly. You may refer to me as Drake. I shall escort you."

We walked out of the keep into the bitter cold. Drake stopped and stood for a moment, taking in a deep breath of frigid air. He slowly opened his eyes and cut me a sideways look. "Refreshing, isn't it?" His skin deepened to near cobalt.

We entered one of the stone longhouses. The walls climbed to a shallow arch overhead. Four guards, clones of my friend from the keep, sat around a table, gambling in some sort of dice game. Most of the light in the room came from torches at the front. One of the guards met us. He and Drake looked to be having a silent conversation.

The longhouse was a simpler structure than the keep. More of the huge fireplaces ran at intervals down the length of the building. Scattered torches provided minimal light outside of the entrance. Six twenty-by-twenty-foot cages, three on each side, ran down the middle of the hall. Each cage housed six to eight people, with forty hostages in total. Most of the captives were girls, but I saw a few boys as well. Minimal bedding was thrown in each cage. I opened my Sight. A compulsion appeared to have been placed on each cage, keeping the occupants in a state of near-torpor.

I began inspecting each cage individually. Onyx and Raines were in a cage with two others. Claire and Abbie were in another. Drea was bound in chains in the last cage. She barely looked up at me. *Damn, she's been captured.* At least all the prisoners appeared to be in good health, albeit a bit dirty.

"I believe we can make a deal on the entire lot," I said.

Drake gave me a waspish grin.

I matched his energy signature to the compulsion spell on the cages as well as the fields around the entire base. That kind of energy meant he was a dark elf mage. *Joy.* I had heard of them, but this was the first one I had ever met. They were pretty rare.

Drake's color slowly returned to a pale-blue as he warmed next to the fire. On the walk back to the keep, his skin darkened to the shining cobalt color.

Moments later, he led me to stand before Bren again. Drake announced with great flair, "My lord, the wizard has an offer to make for the entire lot." He turned to face me. "Wizard, present your offer."

I nodded at Bren. "In deference to your great power, I extend an offer of four million Imperial."

Even on a bad day, this was a reasonable offer. I was a little shocked when Drake and Bren howled with laughter. "You amuse my lord," Drake said. "Thus he offers not to lock you with the others and give you as a bonus to the next buyer. For that price, you may have four of our choice or one of yours."

I spoke before I thought. "Name your price." No way would I leave any of them behind, but binding deals were a tricky enterprise.

Bren and Drake had another silent conversation. "The deal is this, wizard. This is an order placed by another buyer. If we sell to you, we will have to compensate the other buyer and find yet another way to fulfill their request. Forty million Imperial in one day hence. Plus, you must find a way to amuse my lord. Fail to do that, we will take the money and give you as a bonus to the other buyer. Fail to return, and we will find you and sell you to the powers that seek your head, Mr. Forrester. If that is not agreeable, you may flee now with your head, back to the hole from which you crawled."

Bren and Drake howled again.

A pit formed in my stomach as the realization hit me. The entire deal had been a setup, and I had been played hard. They knew who I was, and that I was coming, maybe even before I did. Obi's bastard nephew had double-crossed me. It was the only explanation. Not that it mattered. I had only one choice, and they knew it. "Agreed."

Drake took my hand and Pushed a little energy into me. "The deal is sealed. This will also keep a timer in your head of how long you have left. We will port you and the ransom here in twenty-four Earthly hours. It would be a lot for you to carry, so we shall save you the trouble."

Faust had gotten a more even deal with the devil. *This keeps getting better and better.* The good news was, if they killed me, it would deprive my people at home of the pleasure.

Drake escorted me to the outer gate. I thought it was more to take in the cold than to safely see me out.

He gave me a malevolent smile. "See you tomorrow."

Seconds later, I stood in the middle of the café in LA on the spot where Drea and I had sat, talked, and staked out the hunting grounds. Crime scene tape stretched a block in each direction.

One of Wynn's Suburbans sat parked down the street.

I SHIFTED INTO a black tactical suit from the winter gear before I walked down the street and knocked on the window of the Suburban. Agent Hicks rolled down the window.

Before he could say anything, I climbed into the passenger seat. "Have Wynn meet me at the suite. And can you give me a ride?"

"Hi to you, too," he said. With sirens blaring, we raced to the resort.

I sent Priscilla a text to meet at the suite as we drove off.

169

When we arrived, Hicks followed me up to the suite. Mel sat at a table, working on a weapon. She looked as though she was mostly healed. Wynn stared at his laptop.

"Where's Drea?" Mel asked.

Priscilla stormed in right behind us. "Yes, where would she be?"

I related the short version of the events since we had taken the boat out.

Wynn pointed at Hicks. "Go get the boat from Los Diablos."

"I assume you have another plan?" Wynn asked me.

"Yes. We rescue the hostages and blow the bastards up."

Mel gave a grim smile. "I'm up for that plan."

"You remember that box you picked up a few days ago in Vegas?" I asked Wynn. "I'm going to need it. And is your team in for a little off-dimension action? It could be a one-way trip."

Wynn leaned back with his hands behind his head. "They have one of ours. We'll have plenty of volunteers."

I nodded. "Keep it small. Tactical units only." I looked over to Priscilla. "Well?"

She leaned against the counter, fuming. "Bastards. I cannot go into that realm. Mel and Kizzy can. I can get a few others. What else do you need?"

I needed to go visit a friend. "We will meet at the secure facility in eight hours. I have a couple of stops to make."

I locked the door to my bedroom and stepped into the circle, which was hidden to everyone but me.

"Grey's House of Horrors."

The lab materialized around me, and I shoved anything I might need into duffle bags. A couple of old resource books found their way into the pile for good measure.

It took effort to maneuver myself onto the stack of bags on the portal. I took one last look around and wondered who the lab would pass on to, if anyone. "Going back to Cali."

My bags tumbled out of the closet, dumping me along with them. After several trips of carrying books, I finally had the whole pile stacked in the living room. "Can someone transport these over to the facility? Thanks."

I headed out the door before anyone could answer.

THE VALET HANDED me the keys to Drea's car and opened the driver's side door. I found myself pulled to the Underhill's estate as if guided by an unseen hand. Party preparations had continued, and the grounds now looked like a full-blown Cirque du City of Angels theme. Wynn's Mobile Command Center was still running, though operations had mostly moved to the secure facility.

Sonja greeted me coolly at the door. "I'm sorry, but Mr. Underhill really is not up to visitors. Do you have news I can relay?"

I was running really short on time and temper. "Yeah, tell him I've seen both girls."

Evan Underhill rushed around a corner and pushed Sonja aside. "Really? They're alive?"

"Can we talk in private?" I asked.

171

Underhill led me by the arm into his office. Sonja tried to follow, but he closed the door. I waved my hand, and a light-blue hue overtook the room. Underhill looked terrified. "Relax. It just means we can talk without eavesdroppers."

Underhill sank into his chair. "How are they? When can we have them back?"

I opened my Sight and my Sense as much as I dared and gazed deeply into the man's eyes. "Do you have any idea what's going on?"

Then I saw it. There was more on Underhill than whatever whammy they had put on his family so they wouldn't remember. There was something else. The only word that came to mind was befuddled. More than one force was having an influence on his mind.

Underhill broke down. "I only know someone has my girls…"

He was not sleeping. His clothes were disheveled. He was on the verge of collapse from the internal struggle.

Something else was not right. I searched the room and looked at all of the family pictures. All of them were of Underhill, his wife, and the girls.

"Where's little Evan?"

"Who?" he asked. I saw the question increase the conflict in his mind. The compulsion that hid his identity and built his false life was coming apart, and his sanity was going with it.

I dropped the veil on the room and rushed to search the house. The little bastard's shadow lurked in a corner, still watching me. Sonja was on my heels. "What did you do to Mr. Underhill?" she was yelling.

I ignored her babbling. "Little Evan. Come out and play."

His shadow ran down a hall and jumped through an open window. I followed, rolling less than gracefully when I hit the ground. The kid ran directly at me, and I missed tackling him as he jumped up and grabbed my head, knocking me off my feet.

His mouth was close to my ear as we flew through the air. "Let's take a little trip," he said in a creepy voice, sounding like an old man speaking through a small child.

I tucked and rolled as I landed then crouched low to the ground, looking for the miscreant. He glared back at me like a wounded predator and began to change and grow.

Seconds later, Little Evan morphed into a Woodland elf. He was long and lithe with pale golden skin and platinum hair, and he wore a green and golden cloak. His green eyes penetrated my soul as he drew a dagger and dove for me with a shrill scream. "Where is my daughter?"

I raised my hands and began to back up. "Wait, what?"

The elf moved faster than most vamps I had seen and shoved me to the ground, pushing a blade to my throat. Rage boiled in his eyes. "I Sense their mark on you, Winter slave."

His glare bored into my eyes. Something about the idea of an angry elf started cracking me up, and I started to laugh. He got angrier. And I laughed more. With a little Push of Will, I shoved the elf off of me then put my hands up. "Wait just a minute. Let me talk. And if you don't like the answer, you can try to kill me then."

The elf straightened. "I can do one better. I'll leave you here in the hunting preserve."

The grass was green. Green like you do not find in nature. And the plants were huge. And it was hot. *Dammit.* Little bastard pulled me into the Summer Court lands.

As an act of good faith, I sat down on the grass and crossed my legs. Woodland Fae took that position as a sign of respect to bond with the living world. "Tell me who you are first."

He crouched to the ground. He kept a wary eye on me. "I am Anraoi, Chief of the Woodlands and former Lord of the Summer Lands."

"Former?"

He looked stoic. "Conchobor, Chief of the Hunt, and his queen took rule as Lord a few years back. What's your role in this?"

I wish I knew. "I'm Grey, limping wizard. I was asked to help find a couple of missing kids, and I walked into some sort of ancient conflict. Based on what I've seen in the last few days, I expect there will be open warfare here within the week."

The elf looked surprised. "You're not with Winter?"

I laughed. "Hell, no. They marked me to bring the ransom back. I think they're hoping I don't come back with it so they can drag me back screaming."

The elf must have believed me. He sat down cross-legged, facing me. "You really have seen my daughter? Claire?"

The look on my face must have been one of shock. "Claire is your daughter? Not Underhill's? So what is really going on?"

Anraoi visibly struggled with his response. "I will trust you, for now. Betray me, and you will pray for death at the hands of Winter."

I nodded.

He paused then started to speak. "My queen, Dáiríne, and I are Woodland. We embraced balance. We held power for millennia. We worked with Queen Mairsile of Edur to maintain that balance. There must be conflict between Summer and Winter, but there can be parity and harmony. Abbie, or Ailbhe, was the same age as Claire. She was sent to be held as a noble hostage for the negotiations. We sent my son Drake in trade."

With my eyes closed, I focused on Drake. His face favored his father.

Anraoi was lost in his own pain. "During the negotiations, Conchobor, led by his queen Mave, stormed the Summer Court, killed my queen, and wrested control. I believe there was treason in our court. In the last moments, I told our most trusted aides—my queen's champion, Carlyn, and my head of guard, Aindrias—to take the girls and keep them safe until order was restored. We sent them to a friend in your world—"

"Priscilla," I interrupted.

"Yes," Anraoi said. "She gave them new lives and protection. A wizard friend of hers, Helena, helped to create their new lives and locked away any memories that could expose them."

I looked at him. "Helena Forrester."

"Yes."

"My mother."

Anraoi's eyes grew wide. "And that makes you…"

I nodded my head. "That's me. And I'm the only one who can save your daughter, if you still trust my family."

Anraoi calculated his options. Finally he spoke. "Your family has protected mine in the past. I believe a Forrester will do so again, and I will be doubly in your debt."

That made it harder to tell him the next part. "I think I also met Drake."

Hope bloomed in his eyes, and I dashed it quite hard. "It's his mark of Winter you Sense on me."

Anraoi was devastated. "Are you sure?"

I felt for Anraoi. "I can't be positive, but a dark elf mage named Drake is supporting Bren's army. And he favors you."

The news crushed Anraoi. After a few moments of silence, I helped him rise. When we parted, we were again standing outside of the Underhill house.

"Come with me," I said.

ANRAOI CHANGED INTO a more conventional form as we drove. I explained the plan in part, and he told me more about the two major factions of the Fae. He also continued to study the energy that Drake had used to tag me as though I was a free-range bear on the Discovery Channel. He seemed to be starting to accept the fact that his son had changed sides.

He was concerned that crossing into Winter territory would be an even bigger act of war for his people, but he said he had something that would help. A moment later, he ported away.

My next stop was to see Obi.

I parked on the sidewalk in front of The Gin House. I was still a little pissed, and when Tentacle Boy opened the door, I slammed it into him instead of taking a pat-down. For the unwarranted attack, I felt a jolt go through my body, but it was worth it. Obi met me before I got to his office. "What is the meaning of this? You know I will have no violence in here."

Alvin reached for something from behind the bar. I could only assume it was his sawed-off shotgun.

As calmly as I could, I looked into Obi's eyes. "Your nephew set me up. And you put me on a bad path."

Anger and betrayal flashed in a blue surge behind Obi's eyes. Betrayal by family was an offense not taken lightly. "Let's pay him a visit. You can apologize to Ichabod later."

Ichabod? Squid Boy was named Ichabod? Either I was walking into a trap or Buziba was about to get a demotion. My instincts told me to trust Obi as we walked into his office. Fifi jumped into my arms. He knew where we were headed, I think. We walked into a small closet that filled with mist as soon as we entered. A moment later, we exited from a similar closet in Buziba's club.

Buziba stood up, half-naked. Eyes stretched wide when he saw us. "Uncle," he cried. "Uh, Greyson?" Somehow, I did not think he'd expected to see me alive. The fawn from earlier took a quick clue and sprinted for the door, buck-naked. *Maybe that should be doe-naked.*

Obi reached out into the air, and Buziba soared across the room into his hand. Buziba was gurgling as Obi spoke to him in a menacing tone. "I hear you may have had some involvement in issues our dear family friend encountered. He came into my club so angry, he assaulted Ichabod."

Buziba's face paled with fear, and this time he looked as if he might be frightened of me. "He hit the Kraken and lives?"

I was going to have to do something really nice for my friend Ichabod. *My good, close friend Ichabod.* He had such a gentle way with those tentacles when he patted people down.

Obi's eyes flashed a deep blue. "Focus. Did you send Mr. Forrester into a trap?"

Buziba stumbled over his words. "He was going there anyway. I just asked for a favor since he was on the trip. I didn't—"

"Enough," I yelled. "They knew who I was and that we were coming. You were the only one who knew." I was aware that a wave of energy had passed from me through the room. An unpleasant tingle reminded me to check my temper.

Something clicked in Buziba's mind. "Boris. It had to be Boris." He nodded vigorously.

"Who's Boris?" Obi and I asked simultaneously.

Buziba was nearly in a panic. "One of the vamps I use for security. He unloaded your bags and watched your stuff. He must have overheard us."

I stormed out the door, looking for Boris. He was unfortunate enough to be close by. He had likely been listening through the door. As he turned to run, I speared him through the heart with the leg of a chair that was conveniently next to the door. My violent actions didn't sting me in the least. I guess undead monsters didn't count toward my penance. Boris fell face-first to the floor, lifeless. His body lifted up and floated into Obi's other waiting hand.

I slammed the door behind me and erected a quick privacy field. When I was confident Obi had the vampire under control, I pulled the stake out of his chest.

Boris started to thrash in Obi's grasp until Obi looked at him. "Calm," Obi said. The compulsion immediately stopped his thrashing. Boris's mouth sagged open, and Obi looked disgusted by the lack of a tongue. Holding both Boris and Buziba by the throat, he regarded Buziba. "You can speak for him."

I was oddly fascinated to watch Boris's and Buziba's mouths synchronize.

Obi looked deeply into Boris's eyes. Boris seemed to be in some sort of trance.

"Can you hear me?" Obi asked.

"Yes." Boris's mouth moved, but Buziba voiced the word.

"Did you inform anyone that Mr. Forrester and his associate would be coming?" Obi asked.

Buziba struggled for a moment. "Yes," he finally uttered.

"Why?" Obi asked.

Boris started shaking uncontrollably. "Because they asked," Buziba mouthed. "They're in our heads. They had us place something in the wizard's bags."

My Sight revealed thin tendrils running into the ether. They did not look active, but I recognized Drake's energy signature.

"Winter's mage. Drake. I see some leftover energy around the club. And on the tongueless wonder."

Obi nodded and looked to Boris again. "Did Buziba know? Is he tied to them?"

Boris smiled. "No," Buziba mouthed. "He is too foolish and arrogant. He isn't worth their time."

Obi looked back to me. "Do you have any questions?"

"Nope. I'm good."

Obi flung his nephew into a corner like dirty laundry. Boris started to smoke and burst into flames in Obi's outstretched hand. He grinned for the minute or so that he burned. He looked happy to be free. From the screams around the club, every other vamp, and maybe others in the place, had burst into flames at the same time. They didn't sound as happy to be fired by frying.

I looked at Obi. "I'm sorry to have accused you."

He shook his head. "It is I who owes you an apology for the betrayal of my house. You do owe Ichabod an apology, though."

I nodded. "I'm assuming he likes sushi?"

Obi smiled. "Very much. Do you require anything else while we're here?"

I nodded and headed for the door. On my way out, Obi began speaking tersely with his nephew. "You will clean house before I return. I have started that job for you. Now…"

By then, I was out of earshot. I dropped the wards to the room in which I'd stayed on my previous visit and ran in. Knowing what to look for, the subtle energies clinging to the bags came into view clearly. A wave of my hand cleared Drake's subterfuge. I tossed a fireball into my room to cleanse it and shut the door. Then I raised the wards so it wouldn't burn the whole place down. Yet.

Customers and staff had all cleared out of the main bar. A number of scorch marks and ash piles were scattered around. Obi had vaporized thirty or more in an instant. When I walked into the office, carrying the packs, Buziba sat in the corner on the floor, looking like an admonished child.

"Are you ready to leave?" Obi asked me.

I nodded and walked into the small closet.

Obi pointed a long finger at Buziba. "We are not done."

180

Buziba looked terrified.

Obi stepped into the closet, and the fog surrounded us.

OBI PROMISED ME he would meet me at the secure facility later in the day. I was pretty sure Wynn no longer considered it secure, but that was a problem for later. On my way out, I apologized to Ichabod and promised to take him for sushi. A big toothy grin and a tentacle pat on the back were the response. As I left, he gave me a little nudge. His love tap was enough for me to know he could make me into a pile of goo in a heartbeat if he so desired, but I was forgiven.

With the bags secured in the trunk, I climbed in the driver's seat. I sent Wynn a message, and he confirmed the cursed box was in a locked room by itself. Next stop, I needed to find Melvin the Muse.

I had not seen Melvin in a while. He was an angel. After the war in Heaven, Melvin was depressed and came down to help rebuild the universe. He was a tinkerer. He was also flaky, even for an angel. If he were human, he would have been classified as clinically insane. He also used to make me the coolest toys when I was a kid. If anyone could help me make the box work, it was him.

Melvin owned a small watch-repair shop, but was usually flitting all over the universe. The good news was, he usually answered his cell when I called. His signal was good pretty much anywhere.

181

I drew a sigil in the air, which left a thin golden line. I focused on the sigil. "Melvin," I yelled.

John Malkovich appeared in the seat beside me, wearing white slacks, a light-blue shirt, and sandals. "Grey, man, how's it going?"

If I didn't know better, I would have sworn he was stoned. "Melvin, what's the deal?"

He shrugged and screwed up his face. "I was watching *Being John Malkovich* and decided to give it a try."

I rubbed my temples. I really loved Melvin, but he gave me migraines. "Good to see you, Melvin. Can you please be… you?"

Melvin shrugged. He shimmered in a golden light. When the light disappeared, the Melvin I knew sat there. Still in the same clothes, this Melvin was perfect… beautiful, even. He was tall and muscled, not a hair out of place, with blazing blue eyes and a chiseled jaw. And one dimple.

The clock in my head was down to seventeen hours, which meant I had an hour and a half until I had to gather everyone up at the secure facility. Melvin started playing with the radio.

"Melvin, I've got a puzzle for you. I need you to make something work."

His eyes glowed like small suns. That happened when he was intrigued. "Cool. What is it?" Shiny objects and small children also triggered that reaction.

I told him everything I knew about the cursed box, which wasn't much. I also ran through my plan to see if he thought it was feasible. When we pulled up to the facility, the security detail looked less than thrilled with all of the "guests" coming through, especially considering this place was built to imprison the kinds of beings I was bringing in for help. Melvin was like a kid in a Lego store as we toured the facility.

A guard stood on each side of the door that Wynn had directed me to. "Sirs," one of them said. He opened the door for us to walk in. I flipped on the lights as the door swished closed behind us.

For a moment, I thought we were looking at the wrong device. A clay jar, four feet in diameter and covered in a variety of scripts, sat on the floor.

"I haven't seen this in millennia," Melvin yelled excitedly. "Wow."

"You know what this is?"

He walked around it, studying it from all sides. "Of course, man. I designed it with Hephaestus."

Of course he had.

I stared at Melvin. "What is it?"

He took out a pair of magnifying glasses and put them on. He looked as if a giant spider had built a web on his face. Lenses of all colors of the rainbow flashed by as he swapped them around. Once Melvin settled on the correct lenses, he studied the container at a distance.

An old branch appeared in his hand. It was always eerie how he could manifest things. He used the branch to gently lift the lid, then he looked inside. Flipping the lid the rest of the way open, he poked his head in.

"Melvin?" I asked after a beat.

He raised his head and scowled. "It's broken."

"What does it do?"

Melvin walked around the box and changed lenses. He squinted and flipped lenses a few more times then poked a spot on the box. "Gotcha."

I found a chair in the corner. "Melvin?"

He leaned against the wall, studying the jar and looking as if he'd just smelled something rancid. "A cheap hack on my work. I'm not sure who built it, but it was poorly done. We made the box a long time ago as a gag for Pandora."

I was becoming frustrated as precious seconds ticked off the clock. "How did it become a soul-sucking machine?" A vision of Katie Clouse in the clutches of the power of the box, rolling around in its former contents, flashed in my mind.

Melvin snorted. "It didn't, not really. Zeus wanted to make a point with Pandora. Hephaestus gave me a call, and we built the container to hold a few lesser demons. We trapped a few—Gluttony, Jealousy, Envy, and a few others—and shoved them in the jar with a cherub. We hung a little 'Hope' banner on him. They put a big 'Do Not Open' sign on it. She couldn't take the curiosity of course, and when it popped, it was like one of the fake peanut cans with rubber snakes. She waited it out longer than we thought she would, so by the time she opened it, the cherub was a little miffed. Cherubs have nasty tempers. In revenge, he told her she had released all of the ills on the world. It was a lie, of course, but she bought it for a long time.

"It looks like someone tried to repurpose it," he continued. "They pulled a greed demon back into the jar. Reading the history, I'm guessing someone used it as a lure in a casino. The box is designed to learn. I guess over this length of time, it learned a lot and got really out of whack."

I took Melvin by the shoulders and spoke slowly. "Can you fix it? Will it do what I asked for?"

Melvin rubbed the side of his head. "Um, hmmm, no, no… *yes!* Give me an hour."

I was beyond terrified. Melvin would go out of his way to put a wing back on a mosquito, but he would accidentally break universes in the process. But as options went, this was my only one.

He seemed to have read my mind. "If I blow the world up, we can rebuild it. Better. Faster. Stronger. I have the technology." He raised a hand, and with his best 'mad scientist' look, he manifested a white lab coat.

"Thanks, Melvin." At least if we broke the universe, I would not have to go home to stand trial. I shook my head. I had the feeling that Drake and Bren might not get the shot to kill me. My friends would do it first.

WYNN PAGED ME and asked me to come downstairs. The clock in my head was counting down, and I had thirteen hours to go. Wynn and five other agents I recognized sat around a conference table. Hicks sat at Wynn's left. Melanippe, Kizzy, and Obi sat on the other side of the conference table. Surveillance maps were projected on the walls. It looked as though they had been discussing strategy for a while.

Priscilla opened the door. "I have help." She smiled, just a little too proud of herself.

The Dag, Dorian, and Nicky strode through the door. *Oh, damn.* This really meant the world was ending.

Dorian was… older. Silver lined his temples, and his dark hair was specked with gray. He moved a little stiffly, but the old spark was still behind his eyes. He opened his arms and gave me a fatherly hug. "Greyson." He smiled.

Wynn looked uncomfortable, but it seemed he had gotten to speak with them in private.

Nicky looked exactly the same. Tall, lean, and with a freshly shaved bald head. The disdain on his angular face was stronger than normal. In his peculiar accent, he greeted me as only he could. "I always knew you would be the death of us. He does not listen." He waved toward Dorian.

The Dag was dressed in shorts and a gigantic T-shirt from the movie *300*, leaning on a gnarled walking stick and knocking back a giant mug of what I hoped was coffee.

"Hi, Nicky," I said. "Nice to see you as well." I took The Dag's hand and shook it firmly. "Hi, Dag. Welcome to the party."

Priscilla smiled at my confusion. "The Dagda is an *expert* on Fomorians."

We made a full round of introductions. I reviewed what I'd seen of the fortress during the encounter.

The Dag leaned back. "It sounds like the Sons of Balor. Mostly half-breeds. Their chief is the only one somewhat close to full-blood. After we booted them out of Ireland, they took to the sea. They're part daemon and part animal. They're not of the Divine races but are the result of a cursed deal. They can breed with most anything. Any more, they're pretty much a mindless horde. The few full-blood Fomorians will have nothing to do with them. Usually, the full-bloods kill them on sight. Worst of all, they have no direct lineage back to Balor."

"So, how do we kill them?" Wynn asked.

The Dag laughed. "Same way you kill anything. It just takes more of it. They particularly do not care for cold iron. But large explosions work just as well."

We spent a few hours working through a plan and a contingency. I pointed to the map. "All of you will stage here. I can port you directly there. Stay low. If I can drop the field that Drake has raised, blow the outer gate. Blow the inner gate. Secure the longhouse. Get the prisoners. Head back out the front, and Nicky can port you home."

"And if you can't drop the field?" Wynn asked.

"We return here and prepare for whatever they're planning," Dorian answered.

"What about you?" Wynn asked me.

I shrugged. "I'm on my own. I'll trigger the diversion and run like hell. Then I'll try to meet up with you at the longhouse or outside."

"And if you can't?" Wynn asked.

"Simple," I said. "I'll be dead, or worse."

"So, what kind of diversion do you have planned?" The Dag boomed.

I looked to the room upstairs. "I'll let you know as soon as I know."

I left the rest of the team to plan their specific tactics. The less I knew, the better, in case I was caught.

On returning to Melvin, I found him deep in thought, tinkering away, so I left him to his work.

I went to my makeshift lab and worked on a variety of potions that might be helpful. It was more to burn time than anything else.

187

Dorian came in. "It's been a long time, Greyson."

I nodded. "What happened to you? You look…"

Dorian gave a contemplative smile. "Nicomedes and I had agreed in advance that if you were in jeopardy, we… had an escape plan for you. We were all caught unaware in the woods, and things went badly quickly. We activated that plan then tried to find Wynn. Instead, we found Simmons. He had been bitten and was dying. We got him to safety and resumed our search to assist Wynn's team.

"We found the area where most of the team was holed up in a defensive position. It was bedlam. We managed to get out with the surviving team, but I too was injured and incapacitated for a short time. When I awoke, we rushed to get to Simmons. He was going through the Change. We took him to a pack that would help him and bring him into the world civilized, not feral.

"I was still injured and at risk. Nicomedes tried to get me somewhere to recover, but it didn't go as planned. Instead, we wound up… well, somewhere unpleasant. It took a lot to return to the world, and for me to heal from the experience. Even immortals have their weaknesses."

"I've been looking for you in some unpleasant places," I said.

"So I've heard. I will give you the details at a later time."

"Any words of wisdom?" I asked.

Dorian sighed. "The choices are never easy. Do what it takes to bring everyone back." He turned toward the door. "I am proud of what you have become. And what you will be, if you can stay the course this time."

"This time?" I was talking to empty air.

MELVIN TINKERED AWAY at the device. We were down to six hours. "Melvin. We are on a clock." I remembered one time when I was a kid, Melvin had made adjustments on an old clock in the house for three weeks because it was a millisecond off. I knew that rushing him never helped.

Wynn and team had finished their final briefing and were in the process of checking their gear and weapons. Ever the professionals, they all just nodded as I stuck my head in the room.

Obi sat meditating in a corner. "Is that accursed insane angel having any luck?" he asked as I started to walk away.

I gave a fake smile. "Making final adjustments."

He snorted in reply. Apparently, Obi and Melvin had met.

The holding room had become a spectacle. Kizzy and Mel were dressed identically in white bodysuits with built-in armor. The capabilities of Leviskin kept impressing me. On top of it all, they wore silver breastplates and back shields, bracers on their left arms, and armor on their thighs. All of it was covered in delicate filigree. In the dead center of the breastplates was the shield-and-bow symbol of the Amazons. Their helmets and shields sat on a table to the side, along with swords, bows, and quivers of arrows, which were tipped with cold iron. Both Kizzy and Mel had a Sig.45 and a Kalashnikov rifle.

The Dag stood in heavy leather armor with a Gladius hanging on his side. He leaned on a nearly seven-foot-long, solid wooden club. His beard was braided, and he wore a huge smile.

Dorian and Nicky sported the Longbow tactical snowsuits. Dorian carried his broadsword and usual assortment of weapons. Nicky had his scimitar and sidearm, and was pacing around the room. He was setting up a portal big enough to not only take them over, but to bring the large group back.

Priscilla sat in a chair, wearing jeans and a tunic, looking elegant, and holding court. Under the calm demeanor, her frustration radiated. She wanted to be going with her people.

The rest stood around the table, drinking from a copper cauldron cast with Celtic knot-work around the top. They laughed and joked about battles from the past. The Dag dipped a cup from the cauldron. "Drink, son."

I took the cup. Whatever the concoction was, it wasn't too bad. But I felt sure that if I drank more than one of them, I would be curled up and passed out in a corner.

The Dag raised a cup. "To our fearless leader. May we have a successful and glorious day in battle."

A round of cheers erupted. Nicky grumbled as he continued to work the circle.

I figured it was my job to give the rousing speech. Instead, the best I could do was raise my glass and say, "Thank you to my friends and my family. May we bring everyone home safe."

That brought another loud cheer and another round of drinks.

Everyone fell into more small talk and more stories of glorious days and fallen friends. I hoped none would fall this day, but I doubted that was a reasonable expectation. It was more likely that we would all be killed. We had roughly a dozen people going in against hundreds of powerful creatures on their home turf.

We were four hours out.

Nicky nudged me. "It's ready."

I knocked on the door of the room where Wynn and his team were fidgeting. "It's time."

Shortly, everyone stood in the middle of the circle. They all looked solemn and ready as they stared at me, looking for direction. "If you don't have a signal from me in eight hours' time, abort. Come back for plan B."

A few nods came in response. More looks said "like hell." They saw this mission as do or die.

I gave the signal to Nicky. He gave a little wave, and then Priscilla and I stood there alone.

Anxiety and doubt were replaced with resolve in her face. She hugged me. "Have no fear. Your course is not to die today. Make sure the rest of them share the same fate." She walked out the door without looking back.

I checked my load-out of weapons. Underneath my bag was a large box wrapped in a dainty bow. With it was a note in Mel's delicate script. "Today is not a good day to die."

I opened the box. Wrapped in tissue paper sat a finely crafted Damascus steel saber. It was sharp enough to shave with. The handle was wrapped in Leviskin. I grasped it and felt a charge jump from me to the weapon. It was made for me to use as a focal point for magic. I clasped it to the back of my skinsuit, and it melded in like any other weapon.

I equipped myself with everything I could carry while still being able to move. The rest was shoved into a duffle bag. Anraoi appeared with an hour to go. "I can't stay. Take this. You will know what to do." Before I could look at what was in my hands, he was gone. I laughed to myself. *So much for a secure facility*. Maybe they could turn it into a supernatural flea market or the new transit station to the other realms.

He had given me a delicate necklace. I did the only thing I could think of and slipped it over my head. Then, I paced. Thirty minutes to go.

"Melvin, how's it coming?" I marched into the room where Melvin was working. A delicate box was stacked on a pile of gold. I estimated fifty million Imperial.

I cocked my head at him. "Isn't that overselling?"

He ignored me. "When you're ready, open the box, but not before. It's a one-trick pony."

I asked the dumbest question that came to mind. "Have you tested it?"

He raised a hand. "Give me a high five."

I slapped his hand. "What's the deal, Melvin?"

He grinned at me. "Like I said, one-trick pony. But it'll work. Trust me. See you on the other side." He disappeared into the ether.

I still had no idea what would happen when I triggered the box, if anything. I knew Melvin's comment was meant to instill confidence. Instead, I felt pretty sure it translated into seeing me when I had wings and a harp… or a pitchfork.

What the hell. I stacked two duffle bags on the pile and sat on top, careful not to touch the box.

The worst thing was sitting and waiting for the action to start.

Do not touch the box.

Do not push the big red button.

Do not be Pandora.

It was so shiny. I hoped Bren thought so too.

Fifteen minutes to go. I was so screwed.

I WAITED IMPATIENTLY. Drake had an evil streak. At the strike of twenty-four hours, an alarm bell went off in my head. It was a cross between an elementary school bell, an air raid siren, a werewolf dragging its claws across a chalkboard, and a crying baby on an airplane. It was a little annoying after a minute or so.

Five minutes passed. Mercifully, the alarm stopped.

Fifteen minutes passed.

With all of the terrors I had faced, nothing was worse than waiting.

Thirty minutes. I wanted to pace. One of the security detail stuck his head in the door. He nodded to acknowledge my presence and walked on.

Fifty-eight minutes in, I closed my eyes and yelled in frustration.

When I opened my eyes, I sat in Bren's court. The whole pile had transported over. In the process, some of the stacks of gold coins had tipped over from the slight movement.

Drake stood before me with his slender hands folded in front of him. A sly smile crossed his face. "Are we in a rush?"

One glance told me the room was well packed with Fomorians of all sizes and shapes. They all roared. I took it to be laughter.

Eyes from all around the room stared at the pile of gold. I opened my Sight and saw thin tendrils drift from the crowd toward the gold. Everyone but Drake was drawn in.

Drake looked to Bren for a moment then back to me.

Drake smiled like a snake about to take a mouse. "It looks like you have more than provided the payout. Impressive in so short a period of time." He appeared suspicious and a little annoyed. Then he raised his hands and played to the audience. "But you still owe an amusement to my lord and his subjects."

I looked past Drake to Bren. "I brought an extra ten million to pay for whatever amusements your lordship desires. And I did get a laugh when I came in. I'll be taking my cargo now."

Drake glided over to me. "I believe our audience is laughing at you, not with you. I feel sure you have something much better for my lord and his court in your bag of tricks, wizard."

I gave a plastic smile to Drake. "Does your lord prefer stand-up or card tricks?"

Faster than I could follow, Drake doubled me over with a punch to the solar plexus. A long thin blade pressed against the back of my neck. Drake had bloodlust in his eyes. "An execution, then?"

The crowd roared again.

Coughing and fighting to breathe, I pointed to the box on top. "Take the box to your lord," I wheezed out.

Drake nicked the back of my neck, and a thin drop of blood rolled down. He sheathed his blade and slithered to the pile. Delicately lifting the box, he examined it. Then he started to lift the lid.

Still wheezing, I tried to stand. I pointed to Bren. "For your master's eyes only."

Drake carried the box in one hand and stopped in front of me. "A trap, then," he whispered. He kicked me in the stomach, and I folded on the floor. The dark mage slowly, deliberately glided across the floor.

A large paw grabbed me from behind, yanked me to my feet, and shoved me forward. "Walk," a grumbling voice muttered.

I shuffled forward ten steps behind Drake and followed him up the stairs to the stone landing.

Once I crested the top, I watched as another guard escorted someone up the stairs from the other side and handed her off to Drake. Behind the throne, another doorway was visible.

Drake turned to the woman. "Let me present my master."

She lifted a veil from her face, and I stifled a gasp when I saw it was Claire. She dropped Drake's outstretched hand, and a thin ribbon of energy ran between them. Claire appeared to be in a trance, her eyes stretched wide.

"Greetings, wizard." She reached out to me. "You have brought my war chest. Are you to join me as well?"

I tried to hide my surprise. "Princess, who is this little army for?"

She smiled and gently shook her head. Apparently, she thought I should have already understood. "Everyone. The forces of Winter kidnapped me and brought me here. It was an act of war. We shall rebel and unite both Summer and Winter. The war shall finally end. And I shall be queen. For all."

She was crazy. Or at least whoever was pulling her strings was crazy. I took a good look at the princess. She looked as if she had been ripped from a fairy tale. Her long red hair was curled. She wore a billowing green dress, trimmed in golden thread. Her creamy skin glowed in the torchlight. And I saw her brother's power through her eyes. A porcelain doll as a ventriloquist's dummy.

The delicate necklace warmed against my skin. She reached out and touched it. I removed it and held it out to her. "A gift for my queen."

She bowed her head and allowed me to place it around her neck. When she rose, I felt Drake's power weaken in her. Her eyes started to clear.

A voice echoed in my head. "The box. Don't forget the box."

Melvin sat on the edge of the dais. I must have been the only one who could see him. He held a box of movie popcorn and a drink. "I'm here for the show," he said.

I took the box from Drake before he could object and offered it to Bren. "A gift for your troops. The entertainment I promised."

Before Drake could stop him, Bren accepted the box. It was tiny in his huge paws. With a flick of his fingernail, he threw the box open. Nothing happened.

"Have him set it on the floor," Melvin said in a stage whisper.

I channeled a little bit of Henri's stage showmanship. I bowed and waved my arms. "My lord, if you do not mind being my assistant, place the delicate instrument on the floor."

Bren handed the box to his Master at Arms, who placed the box in the middle of the floor. Fountains of golden sparks arced high into the air. A tiny golden dragon trailing sparks flew out and circled the room. Another one followed it. And another. Soon, a stream of hundreds of tiny dragons chased after them. They danced in loops and spirals. They began to merge; two dragons became one, and the one grew larger. The patterns grew less intricate as the dragons merged, until only a few large dragons danced and fenced with each other. It was an amazing display.

Melvin gave a little snort. "Get ready."

I looked at Melvin. I tried to be subtle as I whispered, "For what?"

Melvin responded as if I were totally clueless. "To run. And I would take the princess with you."

I glanced at the box. Shadows flowed out of it, along the floor and up the walls. He'd boxed up demons to go. All of the smaller dragons had merged into two large ones. They breathed small puffs of fire at each other as they danced around the room. None of the Fomorians had noticed the shadows as they were entranced by the show overhead.

Melvin kicked his feet like a little kid at the circus. "Go!"

I grabbed Claire by the hand and yanked her from Drake's grip, half dragging her as we ran for the back stairs.

The last two dragons merged into one and rose to the peak of the room. It did one final dramatic loop and flew directly into Bren's chest. He exploded in a gooey mess over his troops.

I flipped a couple of powerful explosives onto the stairs as we ran. We made it nearly halfway down before Drake got back up to pursue. Loud sounds of battle and cries of terror reverberated off the walls. A shadow tackled Drake, and the stairs exploded as we hit the bottom step.

Claire was knocked over and fell to the floor. "Where... where..." Drake's hold over her was fading fast.

I pulled her to her feet. "We need to move. Come with me."

The back door opened onto the courtyard. Fomorian soldiers stumbled out of the longhouses at the sounds from the keep. The shock of the cold gave me focus and seemed to break the remaining hold Drake had on Claire. We ran for the longhouse where the prisoners were being held. Behind us, the top of the keep vanished in a loud blast, and stone debris rained around us. The golden dragon flew out and strafed the grounds. Outside the main wall, an explosion ripped the outer gate open. Several Fomorian warriors were blown apart in the blast.

The door to the longhouse that held the prisoners was firmly locked. I planted the last explosive charge I carried on the front of the door and took Claire around to the side of the building. The rest of the explosives I had were sitting in the keep on top of the gold, or whatever manifestation Melvin had conjured up. I couldn't go back in there for anything I might need.

Claire leaned on the side of the longhouse. She was terrified. "What's happening? Where am I?"

"It's a rescue, princess. Stay down."

The charge on the door at the front of the building detonated with a sharp crack.

I circled back around to the door. It was charred and smoldering but still solidly locked.

One of the Fomorians saw me as he staggered out of the next longhouse. He drew his sword, and I drew my 1911. It took most of a magazine of explosive rounds to drop the warrior. Wynn and Hicks rounded the corner and greeted me at the door. Hicks placed shaped charges against the charred wood.

I left Princess Clueless with Wynn and Hicks and dashed to the main gate.

Mel and Kizzy had taken up positions in the main tower and launched waves of arrows almost as fast as I could fire the Colt. Wynn's men operated as two-man fire teams and swept the gate with rifle fire as more Fomorians tried to charge through.

Dorian and Nicky were swinging blades, mostly hamstringing and slashing Fomorians as the pair dashed between the lines of soldiers. The smallest warriors were more than twice my height.

The Dag looked downright gleeful. He was swinging the giant club, taking two and three down at a time.

Obi was nowhere in sight. The element of surprise had passed, and time was running out. Fomorian warriors streamed out of the longhouses in a greater number than Buziba had indicated, and they were getting organized.

I gave the order to fall back to the longhouse with the hostages. We needed more time. I emptied another magazine into the oncoming Fomorians.

Hicks had blown a man-sized hole through the door of the longhouse. Fomorians blocked the hole and held us back by swinging pikes.

I stopped and focused. A fireball formed in my hands. It grew until it reached the size of a basketball. I directed it through the hole. It engulfed the Fomorian that waited on the other side of the door in a roiling ball. More cries came from inside.

Before the warriors could block the hole again, I crashed through, waving my Colt. I slipped in something soft and warm on the floor and stopped just short of the cages. The gore and remains of the warrior who had taken the brunt of my blast covered the floor. Six singed and really pissed Fomorian warriors stared at me. I took aim at them. The 1911 cracked loudly in the small space, and two more of the brutes fell. The others cautiously approached me with swords drawn.

I reached back, and my hands found the saber. A surge of power jumped from me into the blade when I grasped the handle. The blade sang with energy as I swung at the first Fomorian. I sliced through his sword into his gut and through his thigh. He went down. The blade vibrated as I pulled it free.

I did a full rotation to build up the next swing. On the uptake, I sliced the Fomorian from his groin through his chest and separated his leg. He fell with a loud howl.

Wynn and Hicks charged in, dropping one warrior apiece. I swung the blade and removed the head of the still-screaming Fomorian.

Wynn pulled Claire inside. She was in shock. Kizzy and Mel ducked in through the door. They were bleeding from small cuts but appeared fine otherwise. Dorian and Nicky strolled in, covered in gore but unhurt. The Dag pushed through right behind, looking downright gleeful. The rest of Wynn's men stumbled in and used Fomorian bodies to block the door.

"Has anyone seen Obi?" I yelled.

Everyone gave me blank looks. The Dag shook his head. "He headed into the main castle when the gate blew."

Damn.

Kizzy and Mel assembled more arrows from their bags and reloaded their quivers.

Hurriedly, we unlocked the cells. As each door opened, I sensed the power fade. The occupants began coming out of their stupors.

I opened Drea's cell. Relief flowed through me as the light came back into her eyes. She smiled at me. "Did I miss the party?"

Looking down at myself, I realized I was covered in Fomorian blood and guts. I smiled. "No, just the happy hour."

We took a few minutes to get everyone organized. Claire crawled into the cell to rouse and hug Abbie.

I tapped Nicky on the shoulder. "Can you port them out from here?"

He shook his head. "Too much magical residue. And I feel the mage's shield starting to energize again. We don't have long."

A bluish ball of fiery plasma flowed through the blocked hole in the door. A thousand candle flames danced and took shape. They coalesced into Obi. The last flames to die were the ones burning in his eyes. "Greetings. I see the first half of the plan has gone well."

I HUDDLED TOGETHER with Dorian, Wynn, Drea, and Obi in a corner. "Obi, what did you see before you came in?"

Wynn raised a hand. "Wait a minute. What in hell kind of demon are you?" He stared directly at Obi.

Obi looked slightly offended. If we hadn't been in the middle of a slaughter, he might have vaporized Wynn where he stood. Obi glared at Wynn and spoke with a bite in his voice. "I am most certainly not of the realms of Satan. I am Djinn. Please provide me the respect I afford your short mortal existence."

Well, that answered one of the questions on my bucket list. I needed to do some research. Obviously, Djinn were not a blue cloud on a carpet. "Obi," I said.

201

He greeted me with a grim look. "I do not believe we will be able to leave via the front door. Reinforcements have arrived. The demons unleashed in the keep have done a lot of damage but are still tied to the box. It is slowing their progress, and I am unsure how far their reach can stretch from it, or if eventually they will entirely break free from its hold."

"How far out are the demons covering?" Dorian asked.

"They are no longer contained within the keep," Obi said. "Their range extends outside of the main wall on the far side and covers most of the inner wall on this side. It is expanding rapidly. When I entered, it had nearly reached the door to this longhouse."

"Any chance you can port us out of here?" I asked.

Obi shook his head. "No. I am relatively weak here. I am unsure I could port myself outside."

Wynn was making notes on a map. "What about the reinforcements?"

"The entire camp is surrounded by Winter forces," Obi said. "I do not believe they are entirely friendly to the Fomorian goals, and a heated battle has started on that front. I believe they are going to adopt, as you would say, a scorched earth policy."

"I'll be right back." I tried porting to the cliff overlooking the camp but was unable to summon the energy. It took a lot to get through the field, but I finally mustered enough vigor to stand on top of the longhouse. I hoped I could get back inside.

The barrier Obi had described dominated the Fomorian garrison. The demons were gradually stretching their field, mauling anything in reach. Little more than darting shadows could be seen from my position, but it would be enough to give me an eternity of nightmares. It reminded me of the event horizon of a black hole. Anything it touched was sucked in and destroyed.

A couple of dozen full-blooded Fomorians and a dozen frost giants stood outside near the front gates. They ranged from over thirty feet to nearly fifty feet tall. A mix of smaller figures wore the armor of Winter and looked to be in command. We were surrounded on land. All of the Fomorian forces were being driven by the demons behind them into the front lines of the Winter armies at the front gates.

On the pier, most of the boats had been set afire. The larger ships offshore were blazing and foundering. The seas raged and inundated the pier.

"Melvin!" I yelled.

The demented little angel appeared next to me, looking playful. "What did you think of the box?"

"What were you thinking? You brought a demon portal into the Fae realms?" I found myself shouting at the top of my lungs.

He shook his head. "No. They brought a demon portal into their realms. It's temporary. All you need to do is close the box. What did you think of the light show?"

My jaw hung open. "Melvin, we can't get to the portal to get out of here. And how am I supposed to get past *that* to close the box?" I pointed at the swirling mass of shadows.

Melvin shrugged. "It's your plan. I told you it was a one-trick pony. Worked great, didn't it? I figured you would get the box closed."

"I didn't know I would need to close the box."

Melvin nodded. "You do now. I've got to go. See you when you get back. Can you bring the box back to me so I can finish fixing it?

203

We can't leave a hellmouth down here. That wouldn't work out so well for someone." He faded out.

My first urge was to strangle Melvin, but I had more immediate problems. I took a detailed survey of the surroundings. The demon storm had reached the front of the longhouse. Winter forces were closing in from all sides. Several of the Quonset huts were burning or had collapsed.

A couple of small longboats were visible near the front of the pier. They looked as though they might be serviceable, at least enough to get us away. And it was shaping up to be our only option. Now, I just had to get everyone out of the longhouse and to the pier safely.

I needed most of my remaining energy to get back into the longhouse. I was barely able to stand after I materialized. "Everyone. Get to the back wall. The demon storm is at the front door." A few shadows flickered in and out as they made their way through the wall.

Getting everyone's attention took the last ounce of energy I had in me. Everything went black.

Blue skies shrouded the green field overlooking the keep.

The woman in gray sat in a chair of vines. It looked like it had grown from the ground. A tea set sat on a similarly grown table. She waved to another chair and sipped her tea while waiting on me.

I refused to sit. "Do you know what's going on out there, in the real world?" I asked after a moment.

She took another sip of tea and shrugged nonchalantly. "You assume it to be the real world. What does that mean? Is this not real?"

"I don't have time for this."

"Yes, you and those you are responsible for there are about to die. Unless you do something, of course."

"Do you care?" I asked.

A cold but gentle laugh floated from her lips. "Of course, dear. Why else would I be here?"

I shook my head in frustration. "So why are you here? And where is here?"

She shook her head. "You are impatient and quite dense. That's what will lead to your demise." Her cloak ruffled as she rose, took my hand, and led me into the keep. Her tapered fingers grabbed a few of the ribbons of energy streaming out around the buckling door, which she slammed into my chest over the mark.

I screamed as a searing heat surged through me.

I opened my eyes and stared into Drea's. She looked at Dorian and Wynn. "He's awake."

I SAT UP. The wave of demons had only made their way a foot into the longhouse, so I couldn't have been out for long. The Fomorian bodies stacked in front of the door had disappeared, but there was little risk of anyone coming through the open hole. Now trapped, nearly everyone had been led to the back of the longhouse and away from the horde. An occasional form manifested at the edge of the diabolical storm.

Now energized, I pulled Drea, Dorian, Wynn, Obi, and The Dag over to a quiet corner. They stared at me as if I were a madman. "We have one shot. We need a back door to get to the pier. There are a couple of longboats that may be serviceable. It looks like all of Bren's forces are being driven to the front of the camp and into the fight with Winter."

Dorian raised an eyebrow.

"All we need to do is get far enough up the shore for a portal," I said. "I'm listening if anyone else has a better idea."

Obi spoke softly. "I have been speaking with Nicomedes. He believes with your help, the three of us can open a portal from the pier itself. The rough seas should cause enough interference to block Drake's shield."

I sighed. "It'll interfere with our powers as well."

Nicomedes walked over. "Targeting our arrival in the Longbow facility, I think we can raise a quick portal since we have a ready destination. With all of us working together, we should have enough power."

I nodded. "We have a plan B and a plan C. Now we need a door. Wynn, what do you have left in explosives?"

Hicks shook his head. "I don't think we can make a dent in this rock."

"May I see what you have?" Obi asked.

Wynn and Obi went with Hicks to one of the fireplaces near the back.

Drea had changed into one of the skinsuits. Onyx had as well. They were armored up and carrying weapons. Mel and Kizzy must have brought them in the spare bags.

I took Drea in my arms. "I'm sorry I left you behind."

She smiled. It was the warmest, gentlest look she had ever given me. "I'm sorry I got caught."

Hicks tapped me on the shoulder. "The Obi fellow says he did something to supercharge what we have. He wants to talk to you."

Obi and Wynn stood talking and looking at the wall as if it were a piece of fine art.

"I've done what I can," Obi said. "If you hit it with enough energy, I think we can get through the wall."

"What are you going to do?" I asked.

He looked at me in his fatherly way. "I believe Nicomedes and I can put up enough of a barrier to protect everyone else from the blast. You must be outside of the field or risk disrupting it, so you will be on your own."

Shaped charges formed a circle on the back of the alcove of the last fireplace in the longhouse. With the wall behind me as a barrier, I was looking at forty, maybe forty-five feet between me and the explosion. The brief distance almost guaranteed I would be incinerated, along with everyone else in the building.

Then I did something I didn't do often enough. I looked up. I saw the sky, and a prayer was answered. "Hey, Wynn, got any rope?"

A few minutes later, Wynn, Hicks, Obi, Dorian, and I stood in the fireplace, looking up. Drea came over and looked up the shaft. She looked back at Melanippe. "Hey, Mel, do you have the rope ladders?"

Hicks gingerly removed the supercharged explosives and put them into a bag. With a few minutes of effort, Obi cut the bars that closed off the chimney. I grabbed two rope ladders and ported up the fireplace. *Gee, I've always wanted to be a Jolly Old Elf.*

Shooting up the fireplace was much easier than porting through barriers. The bars had held some enchantment, which had been removed when they were cut. With the ladders secured to the top of the chimney, I dropped them down. Wynn's team climbed up one side, and the Amazons on the other. They secured the rooftop and watched for anything hostile coming our way. Bren's troops were thinning rapidly. The Winter forces had taken the entire outer gate. The demon horde was still stretching our way and had taken up the front third of the building.

The back path to the pier was still open, but it wouldn't be for long. Silently, we rushed everyone else up the ladders to the roof. We paired five captives each with either one of Wynn's men or one of Drea's team. We had thirty-nine hostages in all, not including Onyx and Raines, who was now also decked out in her own skinsuit.

Wynn, Dorian, Nicky, and I took point to clear the path. The Dag, Obi, and Drea would cover the rear. Everyone else was in the middle.

The gap at the gate was closing rapidly by the time we reached the ground. I moved along the wall toward the gate. A couple of Fomorians were hidden in an apse, trying to find their own way out. Dorian and I incapacitated them with our blades. The rest of our group caught up to us just in time to see the demon portal grow and block the gate.

We pulled everyone back to the inner wall, away from the swirling cloud. At this distance, nightmarish shapes were visible, taking form fleetingly in the cloud.

I pulled Drea, Dorian, and Wynn aside. "I'll be back. I've got to close the gate. When the demon wall pulls back, head for the pier. If you can't port out, take one of the boats."

Drea took my hand. "I'm going with you."

I shook my head. "Not this time. Get them out of here."

Before she could object, I focused on the blown-out top of the keep and ported.

THE BATTLE RAGED on but was winding down. I had an excellent view from the crumbling remains of the walkway at the top of the keep. Two groups of Fomorians were still putting up a solid fight, but it was only a matter of time before they were defeated. The snow was dark with the carnage and gore that lay in every direction. From where I stood, the outer wall of the demon horde looked like a swirling mass a couple of feet thick. They had shredded everything living behind them.

Through the gaping hole in the roof, the floor of the Great Hall was directly below. The delicate little box sat in place on the floor, still open. Shadows occasionally continued to slip out of the top. I ported down next to the box and slipped in the thick pools of muck that had been Fomorian warriors. Before a shadow could slide out-of-the-box and add me to the mire, I leaned over and flipped the lid closed. *Could it really be this easy?*

My answer came too soon. The lid flew back open, and a gentle pull tugged at me. A shadow was dragged back into the box. Then another. And another. The pull accelerated, and the pool of blood and gore was slowly sucked into the opening. The gentle breeze rapidly strengthened as forces from the underworld recalled their minions. I ported back to the top of the keep before it became a full gale. A glowing red swirl was sucking the storm back to hell, and the tide of death was swirling down a shrinking whirlpool.

Long talons on a sharp black claw wrapped around my leg and dug themselves into my calf. One of the demonic horde had tried and failed to escape through the roof and now clung to me. Mottled, flayed, and desiccated flesh hung off the mostly solid upper body that phased into an etheric gray mist. Burning eyes locked onto mine. The demon's spiny grin said if it was going back to hell, it was dragging me down with it as a prize.

The pull was intense. On the third tug of the thickening maelstrom below us, we were pulled into free-fall. The snarling hellion lost its grip, and I was barely able to port myself back to the roof before falling through the demonic portal. The horde shrieked with fury as they were unceremoniously recalled.

A quick scan of the battlefield showed Bren's remaining forces retreating to the remains of the keep behind the horde. They would soon be captured or more likely executed. I ported back down as the storm pulled back from the entrance to the gate. The stone was scarred by the countless claws and talons that had passed over its surface in that few minutes.

As soon as the horde had receded enough that we could safely open the gate, Wynn led the group into a dead run. I stopped short just as we cleared the gate. Twenty dripping mermen stood guard at the pier. That had been one of the reasons Dorian had been concerned about exiting by sea. Merfolk from the Summer side were the sexy ones, or so I'd heard. These guys, not so much.

These mermen from the Winter side were covered in blue-green scales. Heavy plates shielded their spines, and crests rose over their heads like dinosaurs. Their webbed hands ended in long talons. The ones on land stood about five feet, and a hatred for land-dwellers rolled off them like the waves in the stormy sea beyond. More mermen swam in the waves, waiting for someone to be thrown over. The group was armed like gladiators with tridents and nets.

One of them hissed at us, and I responded with a daisy chain of fireballs down the middle of the pier. The mermen scurried away and dove off the sides of the pier for the relative safety of the sea.

Nicomedes rushed to the middle of the pier and made preparations. The waves kept breaking over the pier and washing away the circle. A spell from my childhood that we had used to create a shelter when it rained came back to me. We rushed everyone inside the ring, and I raised a dome. The downside of this spell was that the person raising the shelter always had to get wet. I was trapped outside. I wouldn't be taking this ride home.

The mermen figured out that they were still able to get to me and began pelting me with stones. I deflected most of them, but the force of the waves crashing against the shield was weakening me rapidly. I yelled at Nicky to hurry.

I sneaked a look back toward the keep. Most of the fighting looked to be over. The demon horde was no longer visible. It had pulled back to the inner walls of the castle and would soon be gone.

A group of Winter forces moved our way.

I nearly lost the shield when a huge wave crashed over the pier and knocked me over, soaking me to the bone in the icy waters. The mermen worked the waves as their weapon.

A welcome warmth spread from my pocket. It was the velvet bag from Daire. I pulled the bag out and found the small sliver of crystal inside. I clenched it in my right hand and felt a surge of power unlike anything I had ever encountered before.

Incantations flowed through my mind like a rushing river. I grasped onto one and repeated it. The energy field I had cast on the circle hardened into a translucent dome.

Another spell let me throw walls up around me to slow the oncoming troops and protect me from the waves. Lastly, I froze the waves around the pier as protection from the merman incursion.

The shard dissipated. More than fifty people were crammed into a small ring. I touched the dome. It was as solid as diamond. And there was no way I could get through.

The Winter troops hammered against the wall behind me. Finally, Nicomedes nodded at me. I waved to them all. I met Drea's eyes, and she screamed as they faded out.

What the hell. I'd promised to get Melvin's box anyway.

Releasing the incantation blew down the wall behind me. For a moment, the thought of taking the Winter troops head on crossed my mind. The crystal had me charged with energy to burn. Instead, I opted for the ever popular, "Take me to your leader."

The troops surrounded me at a healthy distance and escorted me to the remains of the central keep. We entered through the gaping hole where the back door had been. I thought the demons had done damage clawing to get out, but it looked as if they had been very motivated to stay out.

The hellmouth was down to thirty feet in diameter. The demonic horde was fighting hard to escape, but it was obviously a lost battle. The mass was almost solid black, with small streaks of gray to break up the monotony. The view just reinforced my idea of how the event horizon of a black hole would look. Maybe they really were the universal gateways to hell.

The throne and platform had been reduced to rubble. Barely a thread was left of the tapestries from the walls. Only a few torches were still perched high on the walls to cast any light. I threw a fireball into the air, nearly to the top of the keep, and it hung there. It was almost like daylight.

The Winter warriors drew weapons but fell back to protect their eyes. The bright light sent the last of the horde diving through the gate and pulled the box lid closed.

The little wooden box again looked fragile, as if the mere act of touching it would cause it to fall apart. Gently, I leaned down and picked it up. It felt lighter somehow. The one-trick pony had been ridden.

An exquisite voice carried across the devastated hall. The woman in gray from my dreams drifted across the floor, floating just above the blood-slick and around the debris to stand across from me. "Impressive. You still manage to rain down mayhem and destruction without opening your own power."

Something deep down screamed at me to be terrified, but I was too tired to care. "So you actually exist. Who are you? Really."

The woman in gray shifted form into a cloud and blossomed to over eight feet tall. Her viscous form solidified into a lithe and supple figure with azure skin. She wore a long sheer gown with cobalt trim that matched her flesh. Long white hair flowed down her back like a snowdrift. Her ice-blue eyes drew me in as if I were staring into a frozen abyss. She was a beautiful and exquisite creature. She also looked as cold and deadly as the arctic.

I chuckled. "Queen Mairsile of the House of Edur, I presume. Queen for the Winter Lands."

She gave a gentle smile and a slight nod of acknowledgement.

"So, why the subterfuge to get me here?" I asked.

"It is not my doing," she said. "All I did was give you a nudge to be prepared. A queen's first duty is to keep order and ensure her subjects are secure."

My mind flooded with questions. "What's the mark you put on me?"

She shook her head and looked at me with an icy smile. "You still seek your place in the order of things. I only made your mark visible and helped you remember who and what you are. Nothing more. My sister on the other hand… I think she gave you a bit of a lift."

I crawled out of the fog and realized how out of my league I was. "Daire is your sister? Queen Dáiríne of Summer?"

She nodded gently. "She is not queen at current, but the opportunity may present itself to regain her crown."

A commotion rose behind me. Two huge humanoid mountains of white fur dragged Drake toward us. He looked as if he'd had a rough day. Most of his clothes were shredded. His deep blue skin was bruised and bloody, but none of his wounds appeared life-threatening. *Too bad.* The two frost giants lifted Drake up in front of us, spread-eagle. Each one held an arm and a leg. I waited for them to make a wish.

Mairsile smiled at Drake in a way that could freeze time. "Our host has arrived. Lovely to see you are able to join us."

Drake sneered at Mairsile and spit up a bit of blood. "Queen Bitch."

With the smile still on her face, she motioned for Drake to be placed on the ground. I barely perceived the blur as she slapped him to the floor with a sickening thud. "Have a little respect for your queen."

Drake struggled to sit up on the floor. "You are not *my* queen."

Mairsile ignored the comment. "There is this little matter of the violation of the Accords. One for which the punishment is death." She pointed to the box I held. "Anything of the Divine in these realms is dangerous, but an opening to the demonic forces is cataclysmic on any scale."

Drake pointed at me. "The abomination, he brought it here."

Abomination? Little old me? I smiled. "Actually, he brought it here. At his own request."

The box sailed up in the air, and I reeled as I was slammed to the floor.

Mairsile caught the box quite gingerly. The lid lay open. "What is this device?"

"It's Pandora's Box. It reflects the desires of the one who opens it. Bren wanted a light show. Ducky over here wanted to unleash hell. I wanted a distraction. We got a three-fer."

Mairsile turned to Drake. "For the crimes of sedition, attempted coup of the crown, and violation of the Accords, I sentence you to death, to be executed immediately." She waved to the frost giants.

They leaned over and reached for Drake. He grabbed a broken blade from the floor and dove for Mairsile, plunging the blade deep into her side, and dropping her to one knee. Drake leapt away from Mairsile to a spot on the floor, whispered something, and disappeared.

I rushed to Mairsile's side. She waved me off and rose to her feet. Fascination, and a touch of horror, held me as she pulled the blade from her side. Bloodied, she dropped it to the floor and scorched it out of existence with a blast of energy. I dove for the portal Drake had used, but it was gone.

Mairsile stood supported by one of her guards. The rage on her face outweighed the pain. She glared at me. "Greyson Forrester, I hereby pardon your crimes. There are three conditions. First, bring me Drake, alive if possible. Second, you are to ensure no harm comes to my daughter, Ailbhe."

I nodded.

"And finally," Mairsile said, "get this damnable box out of here."

I took the box from her hands. The energy of a binding agreement touched me and chilled me to the core.

Mairsile left with her guard. Within moments, the keep was empty.

Oddly enough, the only things untouched in all of the mayhem were the pile of faux gold and my two bug-out bags. I took the two bags and walked out the front door.

Within the main walls, the devastation was almost absolute. A greasy slick covered every surface. It was all that remained of anyone who'd met with the demon horde. The longhouses were cracked open. Two of them had been reduced to rubble.

The view from the front gate was not much better. Everything outside of the old walls was smoldering rubble. The fences, Quonset huts, and guard towers were all gone. A few dozen of Mairsile's army wandered around, setting funeral pyres, but they paid me no attention.

I entered the copse where Nicomedes had made his circle. "There's no place like home."

I STEPPED INTO absolute chaos. The formerly secret and secure Longbow facility had become a madhouse of triage. Some of the

216

former captives sat on makeshift tables, being examined for injuries. Others waited their turn. Ignored, I dropped my bags into a corner.

I checked around on my team. Claire and Abbie waited in one of the side rooms. Abbie appeared dazed, but unhurt. Claire hugged me. "Thank you. When you put the necklace on me, I started to remember who I am. Who I really am," she whispered into my ear.

"It will take a while to adjust, but there are friends around who can help." I left her to care for Abbie.

Wynn's whole team was in the locker room in the process of being checked out and bandaged up. Hicks had a nasty slash down one side. Davis had broken ribs and a concussion. Raines looked tired, but fine otherwise. Wynn nodded at me. "Welcome back. Debrief in an hour." Nothing but love.

Priscilla sat at the head of the table in the large ready room, surrounded by her Amazons. The Dag talked with Dorian and Nicky. Obi floated in a corner, meditating. Everyone but Obi had a drink, presumably from the cauldron. They all appeared quite solemn.

"Does anyone have a spare cup?" I asked. "I really could use that drink now." I threw Pandora's Box onto the table.

Solemnity broke out into raucousness. The Dag grabbed me into a huge bear hug. A couple of ribs almost gave way in his embrace. "Well done, boy. I haven't had that much fun in centuries. And everyone made it home."

Drea stormed over and slapped me almost as hard as Mairsile had, but I managed to stay on my feet. Barely. The table came in quite handy.

"I thought you were dead." Onyx broke out in nervous laughter that edged on tears.

Before I could answer, Drea stormed out of the room. *Yep, nothing but love in the room.*

Dorian slapped me on a shoulder that I didn't know hurt until then. "Not bad. Not bad for a first outing as a leader."

"I only did it because of all of you. My thanks to you all. Debrief in an hour."

I took the cup from The Dag and gulped down the potent brew. It tasted a little different from earlier. It numbed my aching body and washed away a few of the worst scenes from my mind.

Fortified, I found Drea in a small room down the hall. "Hi there."

"You planned to die," she said. "I saw it in your eyes when you raised that shield."

I shook my head. "Actually, I didn't. I didn't have a plan and really didn't know what I was doing when I raised the shield. I was just focused on making sure you were protected. I did my job, and you got home. All of you. And I'm here now. I'm fine."

She shook her head. "You're different somehow." She hugged me and walked back to the others. In that moment, I knew she'd seen much more than I ever had. How could I see what I had and not change? What was it she saw in me now?

I was not ready to deal with any more at that moment and decided to take a shower before the debrief started. The hot water felt fantastic. The cold was pulled from my bones, and my muscles loosened up. As the feeling returned to my body, everything started to hurt, but the pain meant I was still alive.

The shower could only wash so much away. After I was clean, I Pushed a fresh skinsuit to look like a kilt and my favorite shirt. The old suit was only fit to be burned, and I dared not think of what was permanently stained into it.

I finished off my drink and returned to the party. I refilled my cup and listened to a few war stories. A couple of people asked what happened, but I waved them off. I wasn't ready to reminisce about the deal I had made.

Shortly, we gathered in the ready room. Wynn and the team were already seated. Wynn ran through a post-action report. The Dag, the Amazons, and Obi all looked amused at bureaucracy at work. Dorian, Nicky, and I were used to the process.

My turn finally came around. "We still need to get Drake." I did not add what I intended to do with him. "I believe Claire and Abbie are still at risk." I excluded their full family history. I trusted Wynn to a point, but not necessarily the agency he worked for. They would dig deeply into Claire and Abbie's lives and the lives of those around them if they were exposed. The Underhills' anonymity was at enough risk.

Wynn and I agreed we would escort Abbie, Claire, and the other hostages back to their families. After a few moments on the phone with Mr. Underhill, we decided to use his house for the reunions. There was more space, and most of the families had been gathered there already for a couple of days. Obi agreed to take Mr. Xiang's daughters home.

Wynn and Raines sent the rest of his team home as well. Priscilla took her girls and The Dag back to the resort, and we agreed that we would all meet up later at Obi's. Dorian opted to go to the Underhill house with us. Nicky disappeared to wherever it was he went.

Wynn, Raines, Dorian, and I piled into one of the Suburbans and drove toward the Underhill estate. All of the former hostages had been loaded into a bus and would follow us with an escort team shortly.

By the time we arrived, dozens of cars were parked along the drive. The Underhill estate was decked out for the party. People gathered under a large tent. Underhill had arranged for refreshments for the families while they waited.

He greeted us as we got out of the car. He was obviously exhausted, but relieved. Anya and his daughters mingled with the other families under the tent. I took Mr. Underhill to the side. "We need to sit down and talk. Tomorrow is fine, but we have things to discuss."

Underhill seized my hand. "You have my greatest thanks. I am at your disposal."

The families gathered as the bus pulled up and everyone piled off. The Underhill family gathered around Claire and Abbie.

Anraoi leaned against a pole in the corner. He was obviously overjoyed but stayed out of the way. He smiled as I walked over. "I see you brought them all home. I am ever grateful."

I shook his hand. "She has the necklace. It brought her out of Drake's power, but we need to talk. Away from here. I think she remembers more."

Anraoi nodded. "I understand. You will return tomorrow?"

I nodded.

Anraoi grinned. "Until then." He faded out.

Wynn and I retreated toward the Suburban as Sonja's voice reverberated over the speaker system in the tent. "Your attention, please. Mr. Underhill wishes to still have the party planned for tomorrow. We invite all of you and your families to join us, as well as those who rescued our loved ones. We will celebrate their safe return."

"Did you know about this?" I asked Wynn.

He shook his head and frowned.

Mr. Underhill looked a bit surprised himself, but seemed to agree.

"Let's discuss this at Obi's," Wynn said.

WE ARRIVED LATE at The Gin House. On the drive over, Wynn and I discussed arrangements for the party at the Underhills'. Wynn agreed that a full but discreet contingent should be present inside and outside the grounds. He called one of his team commanders to coordinate the arrangements.

I knocked on the door, and Ichabod slid the panel aside. Wynn had stopped at a small sushi place up the street, and I'd picked up a couple of party platters. I waved the first one in front of the slit. Ichabod quickly opened the door and gave me a huge toothy grin. Wynn looked a bit nervous as he inched by Ichabod and his mass of tentacles.

I handed the trays to the bouncer. "I'm really sorry about the other day. When this is over, we'll hit the place up the street. Until then, this tray is yours."

Ichabod took the trays and gave me a wave of his tentacles, which I took to be a thumbs-up signal. Obi gently chuckled in the back corner.

Everyone else was gathered around The Dag's punchbowl. It was twice the size his drink cauldron had been in the ready room, but who was I to argue? Before I could reach the party, Drea walked over to me, carrying two cups. She handed me one and took a sip from hers.

221

I looked into her eyes as she stood very close to me. Her eyes always gave away a lot. After a moment, she looked down and sighed. Then she touched my hand and raised her head, looking deeply into my eyes. "What in Zeus' name did you do to my car?"

Yeah, she would be fine.

Drea laughed. "You've given Kizzy weeks of work. She'll be happy."

She firmly grasped my hand and led me to the rest of the group. Nothing more needed to be said between us.

The Dag was spinning some story about the last time he'd hit a Fomorian, saying they knew how to take a punch in the old days.

Drea rested against me for a few moments. I whispered to her that I would return then headed in Dorian's direction. He leaned against the bar, listening to the half-truths flying around.

"Where's Nicky?" I asked him.

"You know he hates that name," Dorian said.

I smirked. "I know, but he hates me too."

Dorian gave a small sideways nod. "You're growing on him, like a fungus. He's off doing his thing. You know how he loathes parties. And he's not that fond of people. I believe he's reviewing the treatise on the demarcation between the Fae Lands and Divine presences."

I nodded. "I'm in that much trouble over Melvin's toy?"

Dorian took a deep breath. "It won't help your case, I suspect. You can call Melvin as a character witness." There was a small gleam in his eye.

I rolled my eyes. "I'm a dead man."

Dorian grasped my arm. "You did amazingly well today, regardless." He patted my shoulder reassuringly then rejoined the party.

I realized how spent I was. I made my way back over to Drea. "I'll see you back at the suite," I told her.

Ichabod gave me a love tap on the back as I made my way out the door. One of Wynn's team drove me back to the suite.

A flying furball greeted me at the door. The concierge from the hotel who had played puppy sitter all day slipped quietly out the door.

I fell into bed, and the furball started to snore seconds before I did.

At some point in the night, I felt a presence and struggled to open my eyes. Drea knelt next to the bed, staring at me.

When she saw I was awake, she kissed me and then slid into bed next to me. Within moments, she was on top of me.

I didn't sleep much, but when I was finally allowed to, it was dreamless.

I AWOKE SLOWLY to bright sunlight streaming in through the windows. The surf roared through the open sliding doors. The small furball stretched and climbed onto my chest, apparently ready for a walk and breakfast. I was famished, so I threw on shorts and a shirt.

Onyx was spread out on the couch. "Drea headed over to Priscilla's. She said she'll meet you at the Underhill party later."

I waved. "Sounds good. Is there breakfast?"

She pointed to the several carts sitting in the kitchen. "Well, your highness, we expected you to rise before the mid-day. I'll order something hot."

I waved her off. I took a couple of cold sausage links and a piece of toast. "This'll do. Apparently I'm running late anyway."

I took the furball down to the beach for a quick walk. The Dag sat in a lounge chair with a walking stick in one hand and a Bloody Mary in the other. The sunglasses indicated he'd had a long night of celebration. He waved me over. "You missed a party, lad."

I laughed. "From the looks of it, death warmed you over."

"Bah. That bastard and I are old friends. But he did throw me in an oven this morning."

I remembered it was the solstice, and I noticed it was gearing up to be an unusually hot day, even for summer in LA. "Will I see you at the Underhill party later?" I asked.

The Dag nodded, leaned back in his chair, and began to snore.

The furball finished his business, and we walked back up to the suite. Onyx had dressed in her finest party wear, no doubt thanks to a Leviskin skinsuit. "Go get ready." She snapped her fingers at me as I walked through the door.

I slipped into a fresh skinsuit and added fresh magazines, blades, and other items into their appropriate slots. Wearing the skinsuits was starting to develop into a habit. I holstered my 1911 in a shoulder rig and slid my Sig into an ankle holster. After tossing a few extra items into my satchel, I Pushed my look into jeans, a T-shirt, and blazer.

As I stepped into the living room, Onyx laughed. "You aren't going out like that, are you?" My next few attempts didn't meet her approval, so I let her talk me into something she considered fashionable.

We walked through the lobby, and Onyx climbed into the driver's side of an Audi TT convertible. It looked like one of Kizzy's custom jobs. Onyx said there was no way I would be allowed to drive after what I'd done to Drea's car, and she directed me to the passenger side. She peeled out, and we headed for the Underhill estate. With the way she drove, the ride may have been the most life-threatening event I'd experienced in days. We cruised along with the top down and the radio blaring. After a few minutes, Onyx turned the music down. "So, you and Drea finally..." she blurted out.

I look at her and smiled. "None of your damn business."

Giddy as the teenager she was, she cranked the radio again. "About time," she yelled.

The neighborhood was packed with media vans, and paparazzi prowled like sharks. Despite the job Wynn and team had done locking down the media and exposure while the kids had been missing, the story of the rescue had spilled out quickly. We pulled up through a checkpoint composed of Underhill's private security and Wynn's detail. We were waved straight through. Cars were parked along the winding drive, but we pulled in next to Wynn's very active command center.

Onyx bounced off for the party, and I headed into the command center. Raines and Hicks were giving directions to security teams. Hicks nodded at me. He was moving stiffly where he was bandaged up. "The boss is out wandering around. Everything is quiet. Except for all of the kids." This celebration was light duty for both of them, but it was an all-hands event.

The party had been in full swing for several hours. From the monitors, I could see a live performance happening in the circus tent,

225

a band playing under another tent, and food being served in the larger tent. Tracers showed where all of the security details worked the perimeter and inside of the grounds.

Wynn could be seen on a monitor. He was talking to a team covering the area near the large food court. "See you later," I told Hicks.

Raines smiled and stuck a tracker on me. "We'll be seeing you sooner." She pointed to the array of monitors.

It took a few minutes for me to find Wynn. He nodded as he saw me walk up. "Nice to see you show up for your own detail." He led me on a walk around the inner perimeter and pointed out a few of his personal concerns. But overall, security looked tight.

Wynn left for his errands, and I wandered around. I stopped at the food tent. Most of the parents and older family were there. We engaged in small talk, and I noticed that strain still showed on their faces, but relief did as well. Maybe the celebration would help everyone recover.

Whatever performance was under the big tent had ended, and kids were dancing to some band. Underhill had booked a good band, but the latest teen heartthrob had decided to stage a surprise performance for the rescued hostages. Jake something-or-other. Apparently, he had good hair.

Drea slid up beside me and said something about it being quiet.

"What?"

She was back to being all professional. "Everything is quiet." The passion and vulnerability she'd shown the night before had left with the sunrise.

I smiled. "Good. The party will be over soon. We can go somewhere quiet."

I saw a slight smile. "Okay. Together." She had a slight lift in her step as she resumed her patrol. Maybe a little of the night before was still there.

I felt drawn to Underhill's garden. I rounded the corner and found Anraoi on a small bench, looking pensive. "What's up?" I asked.

Anraoi shook his head. "I'm unsure. Something feels... off."

"Can you be more specific?" I opened my Senses, but all I felt was a lot of energy. Between the variety of beings and all the teenagers, anyone I Sensed would feel off. I attributed it to residual energies from the Winter side and Drake's workings.

Anraoi stood. "It may just be all of the people." He shook my hand. "Thank you again for saving my Claire." He held a charm out to me. "A small token of my thanks." I recognized the fetish charm as belonging to the Woodland Fae. "You are welcome in any Woodland lands as a member of our people."

I proudly took it. "Thank you for the honor." I had never heard of non-Fae being taken in. "Have you seen Evan—I mean Aindrias—or Carlyn?"

"Not in several hours," Anraoi said. "But they've been socializing. Many of those taken belong to powerful families. And they are still unaware as to their true identities."

That made sense if they were trying to form bonds with some of the powerful families in the area. Maybe I was a little jaded.

"Shall we find them?" I asked. "Have you decided what to tell them?"

Even with the nod, Anraoi looked apprehensive.

The Underhills were not to be found amongst the guests, but we found Evan in his office. He was leaning over his desk, looking for something, when we walked in. "Hi," he said. "I'll be right back out.

I needed a few more cards. Many of the families wish to stay in touch."

We walked in, and I shut the door. "Mr. Underhill—"

He stopped me. "Evan. Please call me Evan."

"Evan, have you seen anything odd since Claire and Abbie returned home?" I asked.

He shook his head. "No. They seem to be doing remarkably well. I'm not sure how much they remember of the ordeal."

Claire burst in at that moment. "Daddy, can the band keep playing?" she asked.

She saw me and immediately ran over to hug me. "I don't even know your name, but I know you saved me. Us, all of us."

I smiled. "I'm Grey."

She looked at Anraoi beside me. "Hi, have we met?" she asked. I saw a glimmer of recognition in her face even though she had been an infant when she was taken away. She rubbed the thin necklace.

Sonja entered, looking at her tablet. "Mr. Underhill, do you wish to release…" She stopped midway into the room. From the look on her face when she saw the four of us, I knew something was wrong, even without opening my Sight.

She pursed her lips in thought. It triggered something in the back of my mind, but I couldn't grab a hold of it.

Evan looked up. "Yes, Sonja?"

She forced a smile. "It'll wait." She quickly began to back out the door.

Claire shook her head. "Wait, Sonja. You were… over… there. The prison."

228

Sonja's eyes clouded over as she debated with herself. Deny? Run? It was clear the moment she made the decision to fight. She stepped backward through the door with a Cheshire Cat grin and said something I didn't understand. The door slammed shut, and the room burst into flames.

Fire enveloped both doors quickly. I threw a table into the window. The table broke without leaving a scratch on the window. The fire had triggered the suppression system. The bookshelves and pedestals fell into fireproof housings inside the floor.

Underhill began to panic. "The window is bullet-resistant."

I summoned a wave of energy and threw it at the window. It flexed and rippled. The frame moved slightly. The fire spread to the ceiling.

I drew out the small dagger. I Pushed some Will into the blade and was able to cut around the edge of the window. A second energy ball blew the window out of the frame. I rushed everyone through the window and into the yard.

I opened my communicator system. "Wynn, grab Sonja, Underhill's assistant. Consider her dangerous. And get someone to hit the fire suppression in the entire house."

Anraoi rushed Evan and Claire for cover. A call came in from the side of the house. Rushed commands and cries blasted over the comm.

One of the catering staff was changing into a brown robe. The sigil of Erebus was emblazoned on the front. Before he could decide on a move, I launched into him and flipped the acolyte onto his back.

He appeared to be in his early twenties. Fury and darkness swam in his eyes. He was under the influence and was a true believer. "Prepare to bow before your new god," his thin voice said.

Nothing useful was going to come out of this one, so I knocked him out and secured him with riot cuffs.

Wynn shouted over the comm, "Sonja has run into the circus tent. There seems to be some sort of barrier now blocking it."

I radioed back, "We have the cult of Erebus on the grounds. I just took out a caterer changing into their robes. I think we have something big coming."

People were running everywhere as I reached the front of the house. At least a dozen people in Erebite acolyte robes carried weapons and herded people under the food tent.

A second barrier had been raised outside the grounds. It sealed most of the security detail outside on the perimeter.

"Wynn, Hicks, Drea, anyone out there?"

"I'm hiding in the circus tent," Drea whispered. "It's full of, well, I'm not sure."

"I have a team trapped in the food court," Wynn replied. "They seem to be blocked in the middle and can't get to the outside to help. I'm in the command center."

I ran to meet Wynn. He glared at the monitors. "How did all of the security details get pushed outside the boundary?"

He shook his head at me. "Including you, Hicks, Drea, Raines, and me, we have nine people inside the boundary. Four are trapped in with the hostages."

I counted at least thirty Erebites.

"We have to stop whatever they're trying to do. The one I took out said something about getting ready to meet the new god. I'm guessing it's Erebus."

We raided the weapons locker. I removed a grenade launcher, a belt of tear gas, and another belt of smoke bombs and tucked a belt of grenades into my satchel. Wynn and Raines checked their own weapons. We all took gas masks for ourselves, and each of us took a couple of spares. The comm system was filled with static and interference, rendering it almost useless.

Confusion rippled through the throng of people as the acolytes steered them under the food court tent. We threw a mix of smoke and tear gas grenades in that direction, which triggered panic and gave people some chance to run for cover. Wynn and Raines ran into the chaos. When both belts were empty, I tossed the grenade launcher over my shoulder, drew the 1911, and worked my way toward the circus tent.

An acolyte turned on me with a shotgun. My first shot caught his arm, and his blast went wide. My second round struck home in the center of his chest, and he dropped. Panicked people ran from the corner of the food tent in which the acolyte had been covering. With the opening, the Longbow team worked to the outside of the tent and started to herd people toward the command center.

One end of the Underhill home was blazing. Smoke rolled out and mixed with the tear gas. Visibility was fading fast. An acolyte had taken a full face of tear gas and was huddled on the ground. I lifted her by the throat. The blond girl couldn't have been more than twenty years old. She was hacking and crying.

"How do I get through the barrier?" I yelled through the gas mask.

The tear gas was interfering with the trance that had been placed on the cultists. She shook her head. Tears streamed down her face. I slipped a couple of riot cuffs onto her hands and dropped her to the ground.

The smoke and tear gas was dissipating. One of the older cultists had escaped the tear gas. He had barricaded himself behind the band stage and was taking random shots at anyone in range. He drew my attention when I took a shot in my left shoulder blade from behind. My vest took the impact, but it knocked me off balance.

I turned around. He was taking careful aim at me for his next shot. I emptied my 1911 into the stage near him and rolled for cover. After a moment, I reloaded and moved around the side of the stage. A lucky shot had caught him in the head, most of which was sprayed onto the speakers and the Underhills' patio.

Elsewhere, Erebite acolytes and Underhill's guests were on the ground, coughing, crying, and vomiting. Wynn and team were cleaning up the remaining acolytes. I tossed the gas mask to the ground and studied the energy barrier surrounding the circus tent. Through my Sight, I saw that the deep blue field had created a bubble over the outside of the entire circus tent. It stretched twenty feet past the tent walls into the yard.

"Drea, are you there?" I yelled into the comm.

I was met with static.

My attempt to summon an energy ball fizzled. Whatever energy I had gotten from the crystal was gone, and I was rewarded with a jolt for trying to summon a power bound from me. I found a rock and threw it toward the tent. The field splashed as if a pebble had been thrown into a lake, and then it evened out to look as smooth as glass. Voices shouted from the tent, but all of the openings were closed.

The tear gas had completely dissipated, but the black smoke from the house still fouled the air. Wynn's team was rounding up the last of the acolytes and directing everyone else to a safe area near the command center. The outer barrier stood strong.

Something was generating a massive energetic signature at the corner of the estate. I found three acolytes hidden in a copse behind a veil, meditating around a large blue crystal. The crystal was holding up the outer barrier. The acolytes were in such a deep state, they did not see or hear me approach. I fired an explosive round into the crystal.

The stored energy of the crystal was released at once, and it exploded, throwing shards of the crystal in all directions. The shock wave knocked me back ten feet and temporarily overwhelmed my senses. When I sat up, I had a splinter from the crystal sticking out of my side. It had not penetrated deeply, and there was little blood as I pulled it out. A few other nicks and scratches stung as the shock to my system wore off.

The three acolytes were not as lucky. One of them was clearly dead. A large chunk of crystal was buried deep in his chest. The other two were covered in lacerations and lay unconscious but still alive. The outer barrier had weakened and was starting to dissolve.

I stood at the front of the circus tent, at the edge of the smaller barrier. "Sonja!" I yelled.

After a moment, she walked out. The *real* Sonja. She was a dark elf and had changed into the cloak of a high priestess of Erebus. Her thin face was now light-blue, and white hair was braided down her back. A delicate tiara of white gold sat on her head. "Hello, wizard." Her words poured from her lips like an avalanche of hate.

I stared at Sonja. "It's over. It's just a matter of time. Go home."

She laughed like a catbird that had just swallowed a Yeti whole. "I think not."

Drake walked out, clad in an Erebite cloak as well. A large Fomorian carried a barely conscious Drea out of the tent. A small trail of blood ran down her temple. Looking past them into the circus tent, I saw an incredible sight. The tent looked as though it had been transformed into the cold side of hell.

Blue flames licked the tops of ice braziers, and a huge structure built of ice stood in the center ring, but I couldn't see high enough to know what was on top.

"A trade," Sonja said. "You come in, she comes out."

Drea stared at me, resolute. She struggled to mouth, "Don't do it."

The Fomorian put her down and forced her to her knees, placing a large sword at her neck.

Sonja beamed a malevolent grin. "Your choice. You may enter and join the festivities, or you may watch as hers is the first blood spilled at the dawning of the new age."

The rage built within me. "I very much would like to see your little ski lodge."

Drake lifted Drea by the back of her neck and forced her left hand to the barrier. "Place your hand on hers," he snipped.

My hand met hers on the barrier. The energy wall became gelatinous and allowed me to move through. Halfway in, we met, and she kissed me. I felt her stiffen, and then rough hands yanked me inside.

Drake held a bloodied dagger, and I saw red spreading from Drea's side. The dagger was a rough, black blade, but very sharp. The handle wrapped around a deep-purple amethyst at the hilt. Onyx, Raines, and The Dag ran to Drea. I glared at Drake. "You will die for that. Painfully." I did not care how much it hurt me in the process.

Drake cackled and walked back into the tent.

Drea's body lay on the ground. Onyx was crying. Priscilla stared at her granddaughter's body with fire in her eyes. The Dag held the end of his staff to Drea. He looked at me and shook his head.

With some prodding, I followed Sonja into the tent, and she closed the flaps. Some cold cultists were about to share Drea's experience as I resolved to find out how much power I really had.

I WAS SEIZED by large, calloused hands as I entered the tent. Two frost giants held me in place as I was expertly frisked and stripped of weapons. Sonja loomed in front of me with an all-knowing grin. She hit me with a spell that held me powerless. She seemed confident she had won the game and that I was still working on the rules.

The circus had become an ice temple. Rows of bleachers were coated with ice, and thirty or so spectator-sicles were frozen in their seats. Red lights provided a hellish effect. Circus performers had been frozen into symbolic positions around the center ring, which held a large, circular, thirty-foot platform. Ice steps circled it, leading to an altar at the top. A dozen dark elves and a few human cultists draped in Erebite cloaks stood around the base of the altar. Several ice giants stood watch.

"So, Mr. Forrester, we have worked quite hard to keep you alive despite your best efforts," Sonja said. "Drake even had to protect you on the beach from an angry Fomorian."

So Drake had been the archer. "And why is that?"

Sonja appraised me with a look. "You have in you a very rare gift. So rare, you may be the first in all of history. It seems you have chosen to ignore it though, if not repress it entirely."

"The gift of destruction, of bringing death to those closest to me, dragging chaos like my shadow?" I asked.

Sonja paced around me. "Those are just the unfortunate consequences of a lack of control over what resides in you. Your friend Dorian has been unable to help you. He fears you most of all, as he has an idea of your raw power. We can help you learn the control you need."

"Does this have anything to do with Winter Fae teaming up with the lord of one of the nastier realms of hell, Tartarus?"

Sonja leered at me with her sly grin. "Lord Erebus believes you can lead his armies. You will be his general. We will unite the realms of the Fae with the world of mortals to take all of life's birthright."

I stole a peek at Drake. He was seething in the background. "So, I am to be the agent of entropy."

Sonja jumped into my face. "No. The symbol of order, of discipline. Hope for Fae and humans alike. We will bring a lasting peace and order."

So Sonja was the true believer. She believed she could carry off the impossible task that madmen had tried for millennia.

I stared deeply into her eyes. "This is quite an offer."

She gasped with anticipation.

"But I will have to politely decline."

I was surprised to see her eyes brighten. "Excellent. We have a much more suitable host for your gifts."

Before I could form a snarky response, a blast of energy came from behind me. Dazed, I tried to focus as I was half-dragged, half-carried up to the altar. I had the sensation of being stripped and strapped onto a frigid block. Coldness crept around my body, and my life force slowly flowed out into the ice. Claire was strapped down and partly buried in ice next to me. She had paled and was turning a light-blue. Only the most meager of breaths raised a fog over her mouth. Robbie stood frozen in a block of ice over her. Her guardian was a seven-foot-tall werehamster, posed like a Kodiak bear.

Drake leaned in, inches from my face. I fought through the haze to look into his eyes. "I am so going to kill you," I said between chattering teeth.

His face was replaced by Abbie's. She gazed deeply into my eyes. Power circled in her eyes like a hurricane. For a moment, my mind fog cleared. I realized that Abbie, not Drake, controlled the puppets. "I think you will do nothing to my betrothed. Especially once I have your life and your power." She leaned over and whispered in my ear. "Had you have accepted the offer, you could have taken his place as my king."

The ice continued to grow and cover my body. Sonja called out commands. "We must start the ceremony. The time of the solstice approaches."

Hypothermia took my consciousness as something else tapped into my soul.

The keep buzzed with an unused power as the double doors strained and failed to contain it. Energy ribbons streamed across the floor as the bottoms of the doors were eaten away. Simple barricades were barely holding the doors closed. The energy hammered at the buttresses until they inched loose and crashed out of the way.

Even here, I was freezing. The cold was sapping my life away, but something more was happening as well. Something or someone was tapping directly into me. I was a life-source Popsicle. Outside, past the drawbridge, thin black tendrils were creeping in. Storm clouds built on the horizon. Rain and hail pelted the world outside. I pulled the drawbridge closed and raised a shield over the keep. The protection wouldn't last long, but maybe there was something there that would help me if I could buy enough time. Unfortunately, time was one thing I had overdrawn.

If someone was going to drain me dry, I was going to know what was behind those doors. It couldn't be any worse than what was outside, and maybe there was an escape. I might lose my body, but I had to safeguard whatever they wanted and keep it out of their hands. It seemed as if the beast behind those doors was the prize.

I remembered I had the key and drew it from around my neck. Slowly, carefully, I slid it in and turned the lock. The doors burst open as energy ribbons in all of the colors of the rainbow enveloped me. They sucked me deeper into the keep in a flood of power. The doors slammed shut and locked as I was drawn ever deeper into the keep.

I was unable to move. I was frozen solidly into the block of ice. The power inside of me took control. A warmth spread throughout my entire body, and the ice around me began to melt. The thinning ice began to crack as I strained, but straps held me in place.

Abbie stood over me. Despite the rage and the billowing clouds of fury in her eyes, I noticed they were otherwise pretty. She held a black dagger over me. She barked something in a long-dead language and plunged the dagger downwards at my chest.

Detached from the moment, my curiosity set in as the dark blade deflected away, inches from ripping into my body. Etheric armor of some sort had formed over me as Abbie moved to strike. *The skinsuit, maybe?* I thought I remembered it being stripped off of me. As she watched the dagger fly from her hands, her face turned from anger to confusion to fear. A golden glow lit up everything around me. I felt... warm. She backed away and edged to the stairs.

The straps securing me fell away, and my body floated straight up. I felt as though I was watching my body from outside. Claire was unmoving as I waved a flaming sword over the top of the ice. I briefly wondered where it had come from. I swung it past Robbie next. The ice around Claire and Robbie evaporated in a faint haze. I lifted Claire from the frozen altar and flew her carefully out of the tent, laying her body on the grass in the warming sun.

I flew back into the tent and to the top of the altar. Robbie had transformed back into his human self. He leaned against the ice, coughing and shivering. He was dazed and in shock as I carried him and placed him next to Claire.

Dozens of people stood at the edge of the energy field. Drea still lay on the ground. The Dag stared with wide eyes. Dorian had a look of amazement and waved.

I turned back to the tent. The flaps were open, so I raised a shield of my own so Abbie, Drake, and Sonja couldn't escape. Vengeance was warming my heart and shaking the chill from my body. The voice in the back of my mind cackled with shock and glee as frost giants melted under the blade of my flaming sword? From the looks on their faces, the four that I hit were just as surprised to find it out as well. The dark elves were blocked in their attempt to port out, and they were deflected back to the ground off of my shield.

Energy flickered from the ends of weapons as they waited for my attack. With no desire to chase them around, I unleashed a stream of fire from the sword and vaporized most of the dark elves. The last two were dispatched without their heads.

Human Erebite acolytes tried to block the staircase to the altar in an attempt to delay me. Abbie, Drake, and Sonja were ringed around the altar, performing a ritual. I walked through the stands and used the sword to thaw out all of the people frozen in their seats. I circled the performers who had been frozen into grotesque statues and released them from their icy sculptural cells. As they thawed, they stumbled like zombies out of the tent and into the sun.

The ritual was taking form. Icy winds blew and tore at me. Spears of ice vaporized as they struck me. Snow was threatening to bury me. It failed. Once the tent had cleared of innocents, my sword unleashed a jet of flames through the ice altar. I gave it a solid shove to speed its collapse. Abbie and Sonja fell and somewhat gracefully tucked and rolled to a stop. I leapt through the air and caught Drake by the throat—to help him land safely, of course. Then I decided to use him to cushion my fall.

While he struggled to regain his wind, I kept my grip as I rolled, and lobbed him across the ice into the shattered base of the altar.

The mixture of heat and cold returned me to my senses. The coppery smell of blood was diluted by an overwhelming stench of burned flesh and hair. I was standing naked on the ice, but I felt back in control of myself again. What the hell had just happened?

My skinsuit was shredded on the collapsed altar. My satchel and weapons that had been stripped from me were piled at the entrance. I ignored the cold and steeled myself for what I was about to do. I picked up my silver dagger and the 1911. The shoulder holster was cold against my flesh, but it wouldn't kill me. Mairsile might, however, for what I was going to do to her daughter.

Drake propped himself against the base of the tower. One of his arms was broken, and a shard of ice protruded from his side. Abbie and Sonja glanced at me and frantically dug into the ice with their bare hands. Drake was closer. Anger surged through me. He had killed Drea. I lifted Drake by his throat and hurled him toward Abbie. He curved a little and crashed into Sonja.

The impact knocked all of them over. All three of them were bleeding. Sonja shoved Drake out of the way with a kick, and his body slid across the ice. Drake pleaded with Abbie. "Help me," he said.

From across the room, I could easily see that his limbs were splayed at odd angles. He was severely broken.

Abbie looked at Drake with pity. "You were a means to an end. This is the end."

Sonja hurled a fireball my way. I really needed to find out why Winter liked fireballs so much.

I deflected it back, directly at Sonja. It glanced off of her shoulder and slammed directly into Drake.

Abbie's eyes flared. She took Sonja's non-burning arm in her hand, reached into the ground with her other hand, and they both vanished. Somehow they had ported out. Maybe Ailbhe had prepared a portal long in advance. It didn't matter how; she and Sonja were gone.

But I had Drake. I stood over his shattered and bleeding body. His legs were charred from the fireball, and much of his body was severely burned. His right eye had burst and was leaking. All of his hair was singed off. It still wasn't enough.

I knelt next to him. His one remaining eye stared straight at me. Charred skin was blistering and peeling. It had to be agony. "You get to live, for now," I said. He would have to live with the pain. And I would be able to keep on giving it to him.

"Coward," he croaked through a singed windpipe.

THE BARRIER DROPPED with a final Push of my Will. I walked out the front of the circus tent into the sun. Medical teams rushed past me. Robbie was protecting Claire with his body. The crumpled body of a dark elf lay next to the tent. It looked as though his chest had been crushed by a massive hamster claw. *Go, Robbie.*

Someone handed me a set of sweats and shoes.

Priscilla rushed to me. She was obviously shaken. "Her body lives."

"What do you mean?" I asked.

Priscilla took a deep breath. "The Dagda was able to save her body. It's as if her spirit is gone."

I opened my Sight and my Sense. I couldn't see her spirit or feel any of her essence. "Where… where is she?"

Priscilla handed me Drea's car keys. "She's being taken to a facility. We have a hospital for special cases. Give them some time, and you can see her. Onyx has gone with her."

I still had work here. I found a medic and one of Wynn's security detail. "You have one wounded in there. Keep him alive. I don't care if he's comfortable. In fact, I very much would prefer if he was not."

I went back into the tent and leaned over Drake's face. "What did you do to Drea?"

He laughed, ejecting a fine mist of blood. "I take it the lights are on, but no one is home." He continued to chuckle at his private joke.

I searched him for the knife but found nothing. My Sight exposed plenty of discarded weapons around the tent. The medics loaded Drake onto a stretcher as he let out low cackles, his one eye following me in my futile search around the remains of the circus tent. Drake's blade was not among the weapons.

I stopped the medic as he tried to roll Drake out. "Where's the blade? Your dagger."

Pain and madness had taken Drake. Abbie had severed her connection with him, and for the first time, possibly in a very long time, he was alone with himself.

Drake parroted to no one in particular, "Where's the blade? Where's the blade? Where's…"

I poured two vials of my healing potions onto his body before waving the medic on. He had to live long enough for me to find out what was happening.

Dorian entered the tent. He placed an arm on my shoulder. "I'm sorry, lad. It was not your fault."

I stared at the ground. "My operation. My responsibility. She is my responsibility."

Dorian nodded. "There's more to it, though. I see how she looks at you and how you look at her. She's not as stone cold as she would like everyone to believe."

I gave a little nervous laugh.

Dorian nodded in understanding. "There's more to it, then?"

243

"Yes."

He lifted my face. "She knew the risks much better than you. She has faced death countless times. In this life, we love, and sometimes we lose. Look at the lives you saved today, many of them for the second time in as many days."

I leaned back and took a deep breath. "I'm not done yet. No rest for the wicked."

Dorian raised an eyebrow. "Speaking of which, your new trick was quite impressive."

No one, not even Dorian, could be allowed to know I had not been in total control. "What did you see?"

A small smirk crossed his face. "That's a good question."

I left the tent for the warmth of the sun. The day was beginning to cool as the sun dipped toward the horizon. More than half of the Underhill mansion had burned before it was brought under control. Smoke billowed out of a few windows. Part of the roof had collapsed.

Claire sat on the back of an ambulance, being examined. Robbie refused to leave her side. Anya, Emma, and Fawn were being checked out nearby.

"How's Claire?" I asked as I joined Priscilla's conversation with Evan Underhill and Anraoi. Evan's arm was in a sling.

"They say she'll be fine," Priscilla said. "Anya and the girls have some smoke inhalation. They were tied up in the house. It looks like Sonja had this plan building for a while."

Priscilla put a hand on my shoulder. "They will be staying in the other suite on the floor next to you. I suggest we talk later tonight."

I nodded. "See you all then."

THE COMMAND CENTER was a flurry of activity. Wynn was barking orders while Rebecca, the team medic, tried to patch up a cut over his eye.

"How are things stacking up?" I asked.

Wynn waved me over. "Drea is being looked after, but you know that. I've got five of the team in the hospital, none too serious. Apparently, there was a fight outside as well, but it looks like it was meant to be a diversion. Seventy-two civilians are in or headed for hospitals, none life-threatening. Fifty or so more are being treated here on the grounds. Eight of the cultists are dead. The rest are on their way to a holding facility. We have not done a tally yet on the numbers you racked up inside the tent. Drake is also on his way to the medical wing of the holding facility. All in all, it could have been much worse."

The entirety of what the cultists had been trying to do settled on me.

Wynn grasped me firmly by the arm. "Grey, you did okay. Go get some rest. We can debrief on this tomorrow. It will take that long to pull everything together. Go check on your girl."

The back door to the command center opened. A beautiful, tall blonde sauntered in, wearing a power suit and high heels. "I assume you're Forrester, the one we can thank for this mess."

Wynn stepped in. "Grey, this is Selene LeGasse, public relations for the Longbow Initiative." His tone hinted that I should escape as quickly as possible.

I grabbed her hand in an unwelcome greeting. "Hi."

She sneered at the variety of dirt, fluids, and gore I left on her. I had not noticed how much of a mess I really was. She took a towel from Rebecca's bag and wiped herself off. "Charmed," she said with one last sneer.

Wynn nudged me. "You might want to grab a shower in the back before you hit the public."

LeGasse ignored me and gave Wynn an earful. "We pitched to the media that the extremist group that kidnapped the kids was striking back as retaliation for the rescue."

I interrupted. "What group?"

Without looking at me, LeGasse continued. "If it bleeds, it leads. We told them it is still under investigation. We can feed the press something later. So, Girard, what did the people on the grounds see?"

I took this as my dismissal and hit the shower. My humanity returned as the dirt and gore washed off of me and into the drain. But I was not sure I would ever truly feel clean again.

When the hot water ran cold, I decided to face reality again. A clean pair of gray sweats, a shirt, and a pair of running shoes had been set on the bench for me. I was half-dressed when Rebecca entered and shut the door. "You aren't leaving until I at least give you a cursory check."

Ten minutes and a few blood samples later, she cleared me to leave.

Wynn stopped me in the control room. "See you soon, Gerry."

"You too, Grey," he said.

I waved and walked out the door.

THE MEDICAL FACILITY was a nondescript six-story office building. A security guard at the desk made a call as I walked in. Onyx was waiting for me on the elevator as the doors opened and waved me on. We stopped on the third floor and stepped out into a state-of-the-art facility. She led me into a room. A bank of monitors beeped along with Drea's vitals. A tall woman stood over Drea. The woman had light-yellow skin, greenish hair, and was wearing a white gown. She passed a crystal over Drea's body.

Drea looked relaxed and asleep.

Onyx whispered in my ear. "The woman is a Woodland healer. Anraoi brought her in."

The healer made a note in what I assumed was Drea's medical chart. She smiled politely as she left.

Onyx delicately sat in a chair next to the bed as if she thought any loud sound would break Drea's tenuous hold on life. "They say her energy body, her soul, is gone."

My Sight showed she had a faint aura, but just a basic one. A very faint silver thread led off into the ether. I touched Onyx on the shoulder. "I don't see her in there, but she isn't dead. I can see a thread running to her."

Onyx got excited. "To where? Where is she?"

I shook my head. "I don't know. Not yet. But I will find her."

Onyx deflated slightly but now had hope. She fidgeted nervously while we sat and made small talk.

I gave Onyx a hug before I left. I leaned over and gave Drea a kiss on the forehead and took a few of her hairs. "I'm coming for you," I whispered into her ear.

My next stop was on the fourth floor in the secure wing.

Security greeted me at the door. This area looked more like a sterile prison than a hospital. One of Wynn's men stood guard outside of a room. I waved my credentials, and security buzzed me through the outer security doors. Agent Helms greeted me from where he stood guard. Drake was visible through the full glass door.

Tubes ran everywhere around Drake. What remained of his body was heavily bandaged.

Helms nodded to me. "He just came out of surgery. Be careful, sir. My understanding is he's still dangerous."

"He is," I said. "So am I. Who do you think put him in there?"

Helms's pupils dilated slightly. "Yes, sir."

Drake's lone eye followed me as I walked to his bed.

The small amount of his mouth I saw under the bandages stretched into a grin. His legs and left arm had been amputated. A strap secured his bandaged right arm to the rail.

His gaze was locked onto me. He was sedated, but not heavily. I opened my Sight. I stared directly into his soul. All that remained was a storm of madness and chaos. A thin trailing connection tied him to Ailbhe.

I sat in the chair and stared at him. He gurgled out a word that sounded like "Coward."

"Don't get up on my account. I'll be back soon enough. I made a promise, and I will keep it. But you will suffer until I find her." I dabbed a gauze pad into some of his oozing fluids and put it in an evidence bag. "You will have no peace until I do."

I had spent all of the time I could take in a hospital. More gurgling bubbled from Drake as I walked out of the room.

I KEPT CALM as I left the hospital for the parking lot and drove to the suite. The night air was soothing through the open windows.

I stopped not far from the resort and pulled into a small parking area off the beach. I was not quite ready to be around others. All of the stress of the last few days finally took its toll, and I began to shake. I stepped out of the car and walked into the ocean, stopping waist-high in the cool Pacific. A barbaric and terrified cry escaped me and flowed out with the tide.

Finally spent, I dripped my way back to the car. The moon hung high over the water.

Glowing red eyes appeared in the distance. Scar lounged on top of a dune, watching me. I sensed no other beings around, hellhound or not. I flipped him off. "Not in the mood." If a five-hundred-pound hellhound could smile, he did.

I waited for the inevitable attack, but the beast got up and walked into the night. A thought chilled me as I climbed into Drea's car. If hellhounds had the ability to turn normal dogs by tormenting them, attacking them, and carrying them to the edge of death, what would happen if they did the same to a person? What if that was what they were trying to do to me? What sort of beast would that unleash?

A sense of resolve passed over me. Let them try. I pulled out onto the Pacific Highway.

WITH MY FEELINGS buried deep inside, I walked into the suite. Priscilla, Dorian, Anraoi, Evan, Anya, and Claire sat around the table. I took a seat on the end. Claire was holding and petting the little black furball.

"I have lifted their blocks, so they know who they are," Priscilla said. "At least Carlyn and Aindrias remember."

Claire rubbed the wispy necklace I had given her, the gift from Anraoi.

"We cannot go back to the Summer Lands, not right now," Anraoi said. "And I think the Underhill life is a bit exposed."

Dorian looked at me and smiled. "We thought you might have an idea of a new home for them."

"You're recommending Phoenix Grove," I said. "It might be a little slow and quiet compared to what the girls have grown up with."

Anya/Carlyn spoke to me for the first time. I saw life and resilience that was not there before. Her voice was quite strong. "I expect that the quiet will help the girls' transition, as well as help them make a choice about the Fae life."

"Claire needs time to get to know her real father," Evan/Aindrias said.

Claire shifted a little nervously.

"We have raised you and loved you as our own," Evan/Aindrias said. "And now you get to know one of the ones who gave you life and has loved you from afar. Until now."

It would take time for them all to adjust.

I pulled Anraoi aside. "I'm sorry about Drake. He has…"

Sadness showed in Anraoi's face. "Another time. Tonight, I have regained my daughter. My son has been lost for a long while."

I debated telling Anraoi about Daire but decided I needed more information. It was entirely possible she was really his Summer queen, but it could just as likely be another game. Dorian agreed to negotiate for space in my home village for the displaced Fae.

"It will be better to distance yourselves from me while you settle in," I said to the gathered crowd.

Evan\Aindrias slammed a fist into the table. For the first time in a long time, the warrior surfaced. "Like hell. Not after what you have done for us."

That fight was for another time. I couldn't let them destroy their lives trying to save mine. My sentence was all but assured. After a few more minutes of small talk and planning, I excused myself.

I took another hot shower, trying to wash off the seawater and the memories of the last week. No matter how much I scrubbed, I still felt as if I was covered in blood and gore. When I stepped out, the suite was empty, and I was hungry.

I opted to go down to the bar.

The Dag sat alone in a small circle of chairs. I imagined a much larger group had been there earlier. He saw me exit the elevator and gave a friendly wave. A few other people sat scattered around the lounge.

I took one of the empty seats across from Dag. His walking stick leaned against his chair. "Can I buy you that drink now?"

"Shouldn't I be the one buying you the drinks?" I asked.

The Dag gave a hearty laugh. "Gods, no. Besides, you can't afford my tab."

Later, I vaguely remembered platters of food and pitchers of drinks landing on the table, and the two of us devouring all of it. There was plenty of laughing, crying, and mostly decompressing with The Dag.

At some point, with my world spinning, I crawled away to bed.

I HID AWAY most of the day, trying to recover from The Dag's therapy session. Late in the afternoon, I made a stop by the hospital to visit Drea. Onyx sat in a chair next to her. We exchanged a few pleasantries, then I drove over to see Priscilla.

She sat behind her desk. When she saw me enter, she sauntered over and hugged me. She looked like a sexy soccer mom in tight jeans, a silk shirt, black high-heeled boots, and a ponytail.

A tea set was delivered before we could sit down.

Priscilla grinned at me. "This will help. The Dagda came by earlier today to give his farewells. He said the two of you had quite a time of it." She poured a blue fluid into a juice glass and handed it to me. After two gulps, I started to feel human almost instantly.

"So, what are your plans?" she asked.

I shrugged. "I'm working on that. I'm starting to trace Abbie... Ailbhe. I think she has the key to helping Drea. I suspect I'll be hearing from the council on the happenings of the last few days, so I'm going to do as much as I can before they call."

Priscilla smiled sadly. "She's been in love with you for years. When I sent you away with Dorian, I thought it would fade. Normally, Amazons will select a mate to reproduce every few years and keep the people going. Amazons rarely mate for life. Drea has never taken a mate, and she has already had a very long life. Hopefully, she will have a lot longer. If anyone can restore her, I believe you will try."

I felt an emptiness in my chest. "Did you know what would happen?" I asked. "Is that why you sent for me?"

Priscilla smiled thinly and looked away. It was a rare moment of raw truth. "Anraoi asked me to find the one who could protect the realms and find his daughter. Sibylla told me it would be you. She couldn't see how or what would happen. I tried to find another way. I feared what you might unleash in the process."

"And what is that? What am I?"

Priscilla pursed her lips, deep in thought. "It's bad form for a deity to admit she's not omniscient," she finally said. "I do not know what you are. I do know who you are. I loved your parents, and I love you. You are a good man. I believe you're strong enough to rein in whatever powers you have in you. Based on what I saw with the Underhills, you have quite a lot of potential."

"And what did you see?" I asked in frustration.

She leaned back with a laugh. "I don't know. I have never seen anything like it in my long life. Sibylla has put all of her prophetic and visionary abilities into researching you. She reports a hurricane of possibilities, but they're snippets of visions, some grand and some horrific. I still wonder if I should end you now, for the sake of the future."

I was not sure what to hope for myself. "What have you decided?"

She sighed and smiled. "You will find a way to help my granddaughter, Drea. Besides, I have a lot invested in… you. A discussion for another time."

"Did you find out anything about the sigil on my chest?" I asked.

Priscilla leaned over and opened my shirt. The redness had faded to a thin red outline on my chest. "I see in it some familiar lines and symbols. Thus far, my resources have hit dead ends. We will keep searching."

She poured two cups of tea and handed one of them to me. "Maybe you will feel well enough for this now. As to the suite…"

I stopped her. "I'll be heading out in a day or two. I can stay down here or elsewhere."

Priscilla laughed again. "If that is what you prefer. I was going to suggest you keep it as your residence in LA. Drea is the only one who ever uses it. The top three floors in that building are suites I reserve anyway. What's the point in owning a resort if you can't keep family in it?"

Stunned, I managed a sad "Thank you."

Priscilla liked her little surprises.

We sat and talked for a while, and she gave me a few ideas about my own situation and how to try to help Drea. Dorian, Anraoi, Claire, and the family formerly known as Underhill had left midday to evaluate moving to Phoenix Grove. They had taken Robbie with them. Phoenix Grove was probably a good spot for Hamster Boy.

I stood to leave. Priscilla gave me a final hug. "You can use anything from the garage you wish, but I believe Kizzy has something special in store for you."

I couldn't wait. I wondered if it was a four-wheeler that would try to eat me.

"I will be there for the Inquest," Priscilla said as I walked out the door. "See you then. Hopefully sooner."

KIZZY GREETED ME as I wandered into the garage. She had already brought Drea's car in and started to do maintenance on it.

She peered over the hood at me. "Well, well, see who is looking for a ride. Join me." Kizzy hooked my arm with hers and led me to a back corner. She pulled a tarp off of my Indian. The Blue Bomb had gotten a makeover. "I gave her a tune-up. You really should care for this beauty more. Fire her up and listen to the engine purr."

I climbed onto the bike, put on my helmet, and a voice purred into my head. "You had better treat me better this time."

Oh no. "Special K?" I asked.

"In the real steel," I heard back.

Kizzy snickered. "We couldn't save the Softail, but Ktesippe likes you. We migrated her over into your Indian. She seems to be taking to it quite well, but she's becoming a little butch. The Indian and the rolling disaster area you're towing are also now fitted with the Leviskin material, so you can deck them out at will. There's also a new sidecar for your little friend."

I couldn't help but laugh as Kizzy rolled over a classic sidecar. On the seat of it sat a small leather jacket, a harness, and a small crash helmet and goggles.

I climbed off K2. "Thanks, Kizzy." She gave me a greasy but warm hug.

As I pulled out of the garage, she waved. "See you soon. Remember—maintenance!"

I hoped to see her soon as well. For many reasons.

Ktesippe droned into my ear as we cruised over to The Gin House.

Ichabod greeted me at the door. "Are you up for dinner?" I asked.

Obi waved from the bar and gave a nod. Ichabod smiled his huge toothy grin. We got a few looks in the sushi place, but they knew him there and gave us a dark corner booth. I wasn't sure which would have been cheaper, The Dag's bar tab for a day or sushi for Ichabod, but I knew which check I got.

THE FURBALL WOOFED as we took a walk on the beach. Girls ran over, wanting to pet the little stud. He finally tired out, and we returned to the suite.

I called Wynn at home. He told me that in the last few days, Erebite cults had gone active around the world. We discussed a plan, and I agreed to continue as a consultant. We had a lot of work to do, and I hoped something would help me find a cure for Drea. I had to find her before I was called home to resume the trial. Odds were, I wouldn't be able to help myself, much less anyone else, when it was over.

Whatever power had been locked away was no longer lying dormant. I had no control over it yet, but it was overpowering the bindings on my abilities. I would need to work to see what was being loosened and learn to restrain it quickly.

The furball and I climbed into bed. The suite was absolutely quiet. I scratched his small head. "Are you sure you really want to go with me? I'm sure we can find you a good home. Mel really likes you."

A small face looked up at me. He sniffed and gave a small "woof." I turned out the lights and felt him curl up at my side. I guess that was my answer.

I found myself lying on the floor in the hallway of the keep. The double doors to the outside were locked behind me. It was quiet outside.

I rose, and my footsteps echoed as I walked down the hall. I passed a small pantry and a kitchen. At the end of the hall, a set of stone stairs circled upward. I climbed past the second floor and heard muffled noises above me. The third and fourth floors fell behind me. I calculated that I was in the tower where the light and movement and shadows had been through the window.

A small wooden door opened into a huge library, much larger than the outside walls suggested could be contained inside. A beautiful young woman in a white robe with long golden hair sat at a table, playing chess on a crystal set. Her opponent was an older gentleman in a golden suit. He had long golden hair that was lightly frosted at the temples.

The woman smiled at me. "Welcome."

The man looked up with a slight scowl. "It's about damn time you got here. We have much to discuss."

Epilogue

Nora closed the book. This was not the person she had heard about all her life. Why did she have to see this?

She unfolded herself from the chair and placed the book on Miss Tee's desk. "Miss Tee?"

Miss Tee was delicately working to restore the bindings of a codex. "Yes, Nora?"

Nora debated how to ask and decided the direct way was best. "Miss Tee, I don't understand. How is this the same person we are taught—"

Miss Tee stopped her. "Nora, my child. The truth is never wrapped in a pretty bow. No one is ever absolutely good or evil. Even the Devil himself is still an angel. And journeys are not down a straight road."

Nora nodded even though she didn't comprehend what Miss Tee had just said. "So what do I do now?"

"This is for you and you alone," Miss Tee said. "It's not the time for this to be shared. Even your mother knows little of this." She looked up from her work. "Do you understand?"

Nora nodded. "Don't tell anyone."

"Exactly. In a little time, the next volume will be ready, and I will let your mother know."

"Thank you, Miss Tee."

"Take care, Nora, and I will see you soon."

Dismissed, Nora left the study. The eyes on the paintings seemed to follow her as she walked down the long hallway. She wanted to run but kept her nervousness in check. The large front door opened easily and closed gently as she left.

She looked closely at the house. Ivy climbed the walls and hid the scars from a great battle that had occurred not that long ago. Large stones held residual energy from protections that had been woven into the fabric of the building.

She now understood that the house carried the weight of the secrets it held inside. They would one day belong to her.

About the Author

Jim has a long-standing love for history, anthropology, the sciences, and literature, which have been run through the blender of his twisted mind to produce this work. When not trying to get the strange ideas that float around in his head out in text, Jim lives in the central Carolinas with his wife, three dogs, and the occasional fish. When not clicking away on a laptop, pretending to be a monkey writing Shakespeare, he is usually behind a different laptop adding to twenty-plus years on technology projects or playing with glass in fire.

To contact Jim with snarky comments, please visit

http://jim-mcdonald.net/ and sign up for the mailing list.

Or follow him on Facebook:
https://www.facebook.com/jimmacauth

Goodreads:
https://www.goodreads.com/author/show/8119076.James_McDonald

Twitter: @JimMacAuth

And Email: jim@jim-mcdonald.net

Thank you for reading, and please watch for the next installments, *Mistrials and Tribulations* and *Unbound and Determined*. Reviews are always appreciated—they let authors know what you think and what you loved so we can give you more of it.

Happy reading!

www.ingramcontent.com/pod-product-compliance
Lightning Source LLC
Chambersburg PA
CBHW031123210626
46816CB00016B/2012